Feb 2010

To Florence

Thank you for having faith in me. With my very best wishes

Juanita

COGSLEA
REVISITED

VIOLET OAKLEY
(1874 - 1961)
Artist famed for her murals in Pennsylvania's State Capitol, reflecting Penn's ideals of justice & peace. Also noted for her work in stained glass; book & magazine illustrations. One of three women artists who moved in 1906 to "Cogslea," she lived & worked here until 1961.

M. JUANITA TAYLOR

Library of Congress Control Number 2010920171

1. Red Rose Girls: Violet Oakley 1874-1961;
Jessie Willcox Smith 1863-1935;
Elizabeth Shippen Green 1871-1954—History
2. Women artists–Fiction 3. Philadelphia–History
4. African wild dogs–Fiction 5. Cogslea–History

ISBN 978-1449593261

Published in the United States of America by
WEARY DOG BOOKS
wearydog@gmail.com

First Edition

Main cover photograph used with permission of
The Library Company of Philadelphia

❀

For my family

❀

❁

Acknowledgements

I would like to thank the following for their help along the way.

My husband, Jack, for taking care of the design and the nuts and bolts of getting this book into print.

Friends and former owners of Cogslea, Marilyn and Louis Hill, for introducing me to "The Red Rose Girls."

Esther Cristol for her careful editing and honest critiques.

Author, David Delman, for pushing me in the right direction.

Gail Seygal, for "moving the story along."

Wordsmith Lionel Libson, early reader Arlene Martin, cheerleader Carolyn McCorriston Karcher.

The keepers of history at Augustus Lutheran Church in Trappe Pennsylvania, the Bryn Mawr College Library, Chestnut Hill Historical Society, The Free Library of Philadelphia, Germantown Historical Society, The Library Company of Philadelphia, and Historic RittenhouseTown.

Malindi, Katavi, Kalahari, Kenya, Mara, and Moremi; Khosi, Ncoma, and Phemba; Tut, Ptolemy, and Cleopatra. And all African wild dogs for dancing in the circle of life.

❁

CHAPTER ONE

S am did not want to pick up the hitchhiker.

"But, Sam, look how sad," Caitlin said, frowning.

"Mmm, she looks harmless enough. We're going in that direction anyway." Sam stopped the car and beckoned to a forlorn figure in baggy jeans and torn shirt standing on the off-ramp of the highway service station. She held a tatty makeshift sign that read, "Philadelphia." When she was settled in the car, Sam locked the door and pulled away.

"Thank you, Sam," Caitlin said, inching closer to her husband. "You're just an old softy after all." She put her hand on the back of his neck and stroked it lightly as she studied his craggy profile. Sam had fantastic features: high cheekbones and a hawk-like nose—like the Indian portraits by Joseph Henry Sharp she so admired. He was lean and trim like a panther with a disposition to match. Equable until provoked. A year ago she had cracked that stoic veneer; now she was confident that Sam would do almost anything for her.

Caitlin glanced back at their passenger. It was obvious that the sullen girl did not like sharing the back seat with their odd-looking dog. Malindi disregarded her as well and, separated by an invisible line down the center of the leather upholstery, the two stayed well within their own territory. Insulated from the buzz of highway traffic in their top-of-the-line Mercedes, silence permeated the air until Caitlin reached into a canvas tote bag at her feet and pulled out a crackly bag of potato chips.

"Chips?" Caitlin asked with a smile. The girl accepted the gift without comment, then hunkered down in her seat and turned to stare out the window.

"I could use some water, Caitlin," Sam said. "Maybe our guest could too."

As Caitlin leaned over to dig around in her bag, her long, honey colored hair came loose from the silver and turquoise barrette that Sam had bought her in New Mexico. She tried, without success, to secure the thick strands in the clasp.

"Leave it down, Caitlin," Sam said. "I like it down."

"Well, you're not helping," she said, laughing and pushing his free hand away as he ruffled her hair. Caitlin unscrewed the cap of bottled water for Sam. He took it, drank some and placed it in the cup holder. Caitlin held a bottle over the head rest and felt it snatched from her grasp.

"One usually says, 'thank you,'" Sam said, none too subtly.

If only to pass the time, Caitlin was determined to make polite conversation. Leaning around her seat, she said, "Malindi's an African wild dog. I adopted her when I was assisting a researcher in Botswana. Don't you just love her Mickey Mouse ears?" No answer. "Every dog has a different coat pattern, that's..."

"Calico cat."

Caitlin and Sam looked at each other in surprise. These were the first words the girl had uttered. And, as it turned out, they would be the last ones spoken in the car.

"Uh, yeah," Caitlin said. "Their coats are sort of like a calico cat. Ochre, black, and white."

The girl blew air through her lips and shrugged her thin shoulders.

Sam turned to Caitlin and grinned. Caitlin soldiered on. "African wild dogs are social pack animals. Like wolves. All care for the young." In that instant she observed Malindi stretch out her long legs and scratch the girl's arm with her toenails, breaking the skin.

"Are you okay? Do you want a Band-Aid?" Caitlin asked. She was rebuffed with a snort and a flip of a hand.

"Let it go," Sam said. "Malindi's got all her shots." Under his breath, he muttered, "Not sure if she does, though."

Caitlin pursed her lips and drummed her fingers on the seat. She wouldn't give up. Then she remembered the box of used tapes she had purchased for her niece at a flea market in Texas. She opened the glove compartment, took out the box of tapes and a head set. She moved to hand them to the girl but Sam held up a hand to stop her.

"Wait a minute, Caitlin," Sam said. "Before you do that, let's get a phone number and address of someone in Philadelphia where we can take this young lady."

"Good idea." Caitlin gave the girl a small spiral notebook with attached pen. After a moment, she got it back with a telephone number and the word "Mother" scribbled on it.

"Now, you might just find something in here you'd like," Caitlin said, passing the box of tapes to the girl. She guessed (correctly) that the girl's eyes were rolling upward behind her oversized sunglasses.

The girl tugged her cap further down over her bruised and battered face. As she pawed through the box, her lip curled in a sneer. Suddenly her jaw dropped; she popped a tape into the player, adjusted the head phones, leaned back and turned the volume up to its highest decibel. The screams and thumps of Kurt Cobain's "Smells Like Teen Spirit" throbbed through the car.

Sam said through his teeth, "Caitlin?"

Caitlin leaned around the front seat and patted the air with her hand. "Turn it down, way down." The girl complied.

"Maybe we should drop her off at the next State Police Station," Sam whispered to Caitlin. "She's been in some kind of trouble and we shouldn't get involved. Let them handle it."

Caitlin considered it. "I think she'd be better off at her mother's house, Sam."

Sam breathed deeply and after a tense moment, said, "Okay."

Later, with their passenger absorbed in Madonna's "Like a Virgin," Caitlin retrieved their cell phone from her purse and dialed the scribbled phone number. On the first ring, a woman answered in a breathless voice. "Yes?"

"I believe we have your daughter," Caitlin said. " She was hitchhiking on the turnpike. We can be in Philly in less than an hour."

The woman let out a shriek; Caitlin held the phone away from her ear. Between strangled sobs the woman gave Caitlin her address.

✿

They exited the Pennsylvania Turnpike in the northeast section of Philadelphia. At the toll booth, Sam rolled down his window. A blast of hot, humid air hit him in the face.

Caitlin laughed. "Welcome to Philly, Sam. It gets hotter than hell in the summer. And the humidity's just awful. Nothing like the dry high desert air of Arizona."

Easing onto Roosevelt Boulevard, Sam cursed a red convertible that cut in front of him. Speeders used this six lane divided street like a raceway. Sam wished he was in uniform so he could turn on a siren and ticket the "bastards."

"Follow that Camaro with the broken muffler and turn left, Sam."

Once the hub of industry for blue collar workers, crumbling red brick buildings with shattered windows loomed ahead like sunken ships at the bottom of the ocean. After several blocks they came to the graffiti zone — a canyon of narrow, treeless streets with shabby row homes, boarded up crack houses, and closed corner shops. Caitlin tried to explain the overlapping block letters that adorned the walls to Sam, unfamiliar as he was with graffiti.

"I guess you could say they're like modern hieroglyphics, Sam. Like the petroglyphs carved in the cliffs in Arizona,. Only this

4

is done with cans of spray paint."

Sam grunted and shook his head in disbelief.

"Ooh, scary one: 'Live like me, die like me,'" Caitlin said.

After a bit, the scenery changed for the better. They were now on a tidy, well-maintained street where, lining the sidewalk, bright plastic flowers spilled out of halved rubber tires with pinked edges. Religious statues and ceramic animals peered through lace curtained windows. Bent on the task of giving her front stoop its daily scrubbing, an elderly woman straightened to watch Sam squeeze their car onto the pavement. The trio disembarked; Malindi stayed to guard the car from a group of youths lolling on the corner, glaring at the expensive, shiny black Mercedes.

Heat rose from the cement sidewalk in palpable waves. Sam wiped his brow and knocked on the front door. Suddenly, they were sucked into a tiny house that stored hot air like an efficient brick oven. Several chattering women in flowered house dresses surrounded them, nudging Sam and Caitlin toward a sticky, plastic-covered sofa. Two burly men, cigarettes dangling from their lips, leaned against the furniture, eyeballing Sam.

"Tastykake?" asked a heavyset woman with pink curlers in her hair. She placed two boxes on the coffee table and said proudly, "We have two kinds—butterscotch and chocolate."

"Thank you," Caitlin said, separating one cake from its twin. "I love the butterscotch." She smiled and handed one of the Krimpets to a little girl who was peeking out from behind the woman's skirt. The child took it and did an odd little curtsy.

A thin, stooped shouldered woman rushed down the stairs wailing. She wore her Sunday go-to-meeting dress, shiny from ironing and with an uneven hem. Her hair was poofed and over-sprayed. The runaway's mother. She wept and hugged her passive daughter. Watching them, Caitlin's heart tightened. She looked away and her eyes fell on a sour-looking man watching a baseball game on television in the other room. The father. He looked like he just couldn't wait for a chance to whack his wayward child.

"Hot, ain't it?" asked one of the women, fanning herself with a magazine. Caitlin suppressed a gasp. It was a copy of *Glamour*.

5

Trite conversation was always painful for Sam, but Caitlin had no trouble conversing with the women on several subjects: the weather, the Phillies, hair styles, food. Finally, Sam whispered in Caitlin's ear, "Time to go. There's nothing more we can do here." He left and joined Malindi in the car.

Saying her goodbyes in the open doorway, Caitlin was pulled aside by the hitchhiker's mother. "It's awful to lose a child," the woman said. "When they're little, if they're out of sight—you panic. You do your best to keep them near but sometimes they just get away from you. I don't know if my daughter will ever tell us where she's been. And who knows what would have happened if another driver had picked her up instead of you..." Her voice drifted off and she shuddered.

A heavy cloak of self-doubt fell across Caitlin's shoulders. Could she ever handle the responsibility of motherhood? "It's all right," she said. "I can see the love in this house." Except for your husband, she wanted to say.

In the car, Caitlin turned back to look into the woman's troubled face. "It's awful to lose a child," she had said. It would be a long time before Caitlin could erase those tortured words from her memory.

❀

Sandwiched between affluent Chestnut Hill and middle-income Upper Germantown, West Mt. Airy is composed of a medley of small homes and big estates. It is a stew of racial diversity, mixed marriages, same sex couples, and a somewhat equal mix of liberals and conservatives.

"This is going to be a great summer," Caitlin said, as they paused at a four-way stop sign. "Just think, we'll be staying in the same house that three famous women artists—the "Red Rose Girls"—lived. They were called that because..."

"Now just a minute, buddy," Sam said, scowling at the driver in an on-coming car. "It's my turn. Sorry, Caitlin; the Rosy who?"

Caitlin laughed. "I'll explain later, Sam. Quick, turn now;

then make another left at the first street."

Entering a wide, tree-lined street, Caitlin told Sam where to park. Common access to Cogslea was gained through a rear driveway, but she wanted Sam to see the house from the front. She opened the passenger door. "Come on, Sam, Cogslea is way back there.

"Malindi's thirsty; let me give her a drink first." Sam poured water into Malindi's collapsible bowl while Caitlin waited in front of a padlocked gate.

At the end of a narrow slate path lined with a hedge of trimmed boxwoods, the sedate house with black shutters and trim sat well back from the street. Freshly painted, it had the look of burnished ivory. Her plain, flat face was broken only by a protruding rain roof over the front door and third-floor gabled windows that winked through branches of tall oak trees. Shrubbery hid a ground level, add-on living room and greenhouse on the left, a small potting shed on the right. To the curious viewing the house from this angle, Cogslea seemed far from complex, but Caitlin knew of its nooks and crannies, hidden staircases, unexpected doorways, and multiple split levels built to accommodate the sloping terrain.

Cogslea's atmospheric history had always captivated Caitlin. She imagined what it would have been like in the early twentieth century.

The landscape would be different. Instead of a formal garden there would be an expanse of emerald grass, the perfect setting for an afternoon tea party where guests played croquet and lawn tennis, or sat at small, lace covered tables nibbling on frosted cakes, drinking English tea poured from ornate silver tea sets.

The ladies wore dresses of airy, lightweight cotton in delicate sweet pea colors of sugar almond, dove gray, or plain white that fell in a fluid line from a lowered neckline to an ankle length hem, broken only by a pastel sash tied around the waist.

Gone were the shelf-like bustles and pads, the armored corsets of wire and bone, the swaths of cumbersome draped fabric, high collars and enormous puffy sleeves that created the hourglass image of the ideal woman as dictated by the Victorian male. These ladies were emancipated in lifestyle as well as dress, ready to accept the challenges of a male dominated society.

Conspicuously absent at this party were men.

Frolicking between swaying tea dresses, a St. Bernard dog with a stolen croquet ball tucked inside his mouth played hide and seek with a young girl wearing a floppy pink bow in her hair. A tug of war broke out. During the tussle, the girl's bow fell off and the dog quickly traded his ball for the satiny prize. Several women, jostling and laughing, joined in the chase to retrieve the bow. A woman with a wide-brimmed straw hat who had been painting the dog and young girl, now waited patiently for her models to return, meanwhile, working on a background of red roses and hollyhocks. Joyous, carefree laughter reached Caitlin and she longed to join them. She took a step forward.

Startled, she jumped. Because the instant Sam touched her shoulder the scene vanished. But not before the artist at her easel turned, smiled and waved to her.

CHAPTER TWO

"Impressive," Sam said, linking his arm through hers.

Caitlin leaned on Sam for support and murmured, her voice shaking, "Uh-huh. Let's go."

They got back in the car, Sam made a u-turn, jogged left and almost missed the hidden driveway that dipped down and curved into a flagstone courtyard. Sam got out of the car, placed the palms of his hands on the car roof and stretched out his calves. Cogslea and a stone carriage house were within sight; the air smelled of pine and wild roses; soothing gurgling sounds rose from a nearby brook. Occasionally, a car would rumble across McCallum Street Bridge above the brook.

The path to the front door of Cogslea lay behind a padlocked iron gate; Caitlin went into the potting shed and rang the service bell. Sam and Malindi joined her there. They heard a woman's voice calling from inside, "Lee, can you get that please?" Several minutes passed. "Lee?" Another minute ticked by, then locks and latches clicked and slid. Finally, the door opened and a flustered looking woman with a hairbrush in her hand stood in the doorway.

"I'm so sorry; I thought Lee was coming." Marny pulled them into a room that hummed with washer and dryer activity. "Let me look at you. Caitlin, you look wonderful." She kissed Caitlin on both cheeks then turned to Sam. "Sam," she said, standing back to study him. "I'm so happy to meet you." She nodded and smiled her approval. "I want to know what you two have been up to for the past year, but..." She waved her hairbrush in the direction of a thumping

9

noise above them.

"It's okay, Marny," Caitlin said. "We can catch up on things when you get back from France."

"I'll just go over the 'laundry list' with you though."

Caitlin, familiar with the running of Cogslea, listened patiently, for Sam's sake.

After a brief rundown of housesitting instructions, Marny lifted her chin toward the door. "As you can see, Lee killed all the plants in the potting shed." She pulled down her mouth. "And forget the greenhouse. If the garden gets out of hand, just call Robertson's and they'll come to weed and trim."

"I wouldn't mind doing that," Sam offered.

"That would be great, Sam," Marny said, smiling broadly. She had an easy smile that radiated good humor.

Caitlin smiled. "You may yet discover your green thumb, Sam."

Marny continued. "What else? Oh, yes. I've asked our neighbor, Ed McGregor, to look in on you once in a while. Ed's a retired professor from the University of Pennsylvania, a widower and real sweet. His twelve year old grandson, Toby, can dog-sit if you want to go out." Marny did a little pirouette. "Now, is my outfit okay?"

"You look terrific." Caitlin had always admired Marny's understated good taste. A silver starfish pin by local jewelry designer, Olaf Skoofors, was fastened high on the lapel of a dove gray pantsuit that skimmed her slender body.

"Ooh, let me say hello to Malindi. Sorry Malindi, my little doggies aren't here; they're staying at my daughter's." Marny bent down and scratched Malindi's head while Malindi leaned her muscular forty five pounds against Marny's legs, almost knocking her over.

"Whoa, I'm used to my little ones," Marny said, straightening up. "Oh, I almost forgot. Maggie will be in on Thursdays to clean. She's no bother really. If she talks too much, just tell her you're busy and she'll take the hint. Now, there's iced tea and sandwiches in the refrigerator; please make yourselves at home." Something crashed to the floor overhead. "Oh dear. I've got to see what Lee is up to."

They followed Marny as far as the kitchen where they loaded food and drinks on a tray and went out to the patio to relax in the shade under a black and white striped awning.

Directly ahead, down several wide stone steps, *koi* swam in a small circular fish pond. A wisteria-covered pergola lay to the right, backed by a stone wall with two flush lion fountains. In the middle of the wall an ornate iron gate opened on to a small formal garden.

The terraced grounds sloped gently downward, then met with a thickly wooded area where the land graduated into a steep hill that formed one side of a ravine. A small tributary called Cresheim Creek flowed at the bottom and continued another mile before joining the wider Wissahickon Creek, which ran for another eight miles before discharging into the Schuylkill River.

Malindi, who had set off to explore the yard, burst through the shrubbery when Sam called to her in a long, trilling whistle. Bounding toward them, she screeched to a halt when a flash of orange caught her eye. She sat down at the edge of the fish pond to wait for the strange water creature to reappear.

Marny popped her head out the door. "The cab should be here any minute. I think we're ready. Lee, come and say hello to Caitlin and Sam."

"I've been wanting to, but you keep sending me off to fetch something," Lee drawled.

Towering above his wife, the dignified, former state senator ambled out, again reminding Caitlin of Jimmy Stewart in *Mr. Smith Goes to Washington*. Lee acknowledged Caitlin with a shy hug, then shook Sam's hand. He began to question Sam about the Bureau of Indian Affairs.

"Tell me Sam. Is the government keeping its promises to the Navajo Nation regarding health care for uranium miners?"

Caitlin watched Sam's face. She knew it was an awkward moment for him: his father, a miner, had died of yellowcake poisoning.

"To some extent, sir, they are. Suppose I help bring your bags down?"

"While we wait for the cab, come inside and look at the pictures of our rented villa in Provence overlooking the Mediterranean," Marny told Caitlin.

Caitlin examined the 8" x 10" glossies. "It's beautiful," she said. "I'd love to paint in the south of France. Maybe one day Sam and I..." The cab honked its arrival; she slipped the photos back in the manilla envelope.

Marny fretted while Lee dawdled upstairs. "I just know he's got Sam cornered and is explaining in great detail the panic buttons," she told Caitlin. "Caitlin knows all about the buttons, Lee. Come on, please," she called up the steps. On the way out the door, Lee stopped to show Sam the alarm system, and Marny had to urge him along again. "I've written it all down, Lee." This time there was more than a hint of impatience in her tone.

They hugged, shook hands, bon-voyaged and waved. At last, the cab drove away only to come to a sudden halt. Marny jumped out and ran back into the house, mumbling, "Lee forgot his passport."

In the interval, Malindi climbed into the back seat of the cab. "*La*, Malindi," Caitlin told her, dragging her out. "We are not all going to the airport and to France."

Finally, the cab disappeared around the bend of driveway. "Phew, that was hectic wasn't it Sam?" Caitlin breathed.

He laughed and pulled her to him. "Would you like to go to Provence, Caitlin?"

"Mmm," she murmured, locked in his arms. "Provence sounds heavenly, an artist's paradise. The lovely blues, the lavenders, the pinks."

"Not as blue as your eyes, Caitlin. They're as blue as a cloudless Navajo sky."

She loved to hear him say that.

They fit their bodies into each other and kissed. "I'd go to Provence or anywhere you want, Caitlin. I don't care as long as we're together."

They could go to Provence, or anywhere, all she had to do was say the word. Money was not a problem. Sam had invested wisely and owned a profitable rental on Lake Powell in Arizona;

she had a lucrative career as an artist and had inherited a tidy sum from her aunt and another from a friend. In a year or two, they would buy a house and start a family; Sam, currently on a leave of absence, would go back into the park service or another form of law enforcement. The future looked wonderful. But then so did today.

"But Sam, we have our own private villa right here for six whole weeks." She nudged him forward. "Let us choose our bedroom in this charming villa."

He followed her upstairs and down the hall. "This is quite a house, Caitlin."

"There are two bedrooms on the third floor; four, plus a den on the second." Continuing down the hall—"Seven fireplaces, four and a half baths. Which room, Sam? I like this pretty blue one that looks out on the back yard. It's a lady's room, though."

His eye swept past the flowery blue chintz and white lace decor and landed on a high, cast iron bed. "As long as you're the lady in that bed."

"Were you expecting someone else? The ghost of Violet Oakley, maybe? Marny thinks the house is haunted, you know."

He dropped the suitcases and wrapped his arms around her. "Not a ghost of a chance."

"Oh, good grief, I married a comedian." She tweaked his nose and escaped to the hallway.

Eye level with a crystal chandelier hanging from a high, barrel-vaulted ceiling, an open balcony overlooked the living room. Plump leather chairs and matching sofas faced a small country-style fireplace. Paintings by renowned artists graced the walls and fine antiques settled in corners. "The architects were crazy about arches," Caitlin said, indicating the arched windows and recessed shelving that cast soft, rounded shadows on the white walls. "This room is huge; we're used to smaller living quarters." She was referring to their cottage in the woods in Arizona. "I'm sure we'll spend most of our time in the library."

"Or in the ladies room," Sam said, trying to pull her back into the bedroom.

"Later Sam," let's check out the kitchen."

13

Sam peered into the well-stocked refrigerator. "How about a tuna casserole and a salad for dinner?"

"Sounds good."

He lifted the casserole out of the freezer and squeezed the package in between a gallon of milk and a five pound can of coffee. When he turned, he found Caitlin chewing her bottom lip. "What are you thinking?" he asked.

"I'm thinking I should call my parents and let them know we arrived safely."

"Uh, huh," Sam said, and pinched his lips together.

Caitlin hunched her shoulders to brace for the ordeal. "If my mother gets out of hand, I'm going to give you a signal; I want you to call me, so I can hang up graciously."

"Make me your accomplice in this caper, Caitlin?"

"When you meet my mother and the rest of the family, Sam, you'll understand." She removed the receiver from the wall, sat down at the kitchen table and dialed her parent's home in Ronksville, New York.

"Hi, Dad. It's me. Yup, we're here. Yes, it was a nice trip, we did a lot of sightseeing. It's beautiful here, but hot. How's everything up there?"

Caitlin and her father exchanged a few more pleasantries and some inside jokes before her mother got on the phone.

"Hi, Mom. Yes, everything's fine." Caitlin listened for a few minutes, then held the phone out at arms length and made a face.

"Mom, I told you. Sam and I really are married. We had a lovely Navajo wedding in Arizona last year." She paused and listened. "I don't care what anyone thinks. Mom...Mom.. We've had this conversation a dozen times. I never wanted a big wedding." She tapped her fingers on the table and wiggled in her chair; she raised her eyebrows and held out her hand, palm up, pleading. Sam grinned and shook his head slowly.

"Hey, Mom, Sam is calling. I have to go. I'll talk to you later. Yes, uh, huh. We're coming up right after our stay at Cogslea. Cogslea—it's the name of this house. It's an acronym, Mother, I told you that. The initials of the four women who lived here.

14

C for Cozens—Henrietta Cozens. Who was she? She was their housekeeper, secretary, friend, uh, whatever. Never mind. *O* for Oakley, *G* for Green, *S* for Smith and *lea* for the meadow. Yes, mother, meadow." Caitlin bent her neck, rested her forehead on the table. Her muffled voice said, "Right. Well, say hi to everybody. See ya." She jumped up and slammed the phone into its cradle. It fell to the floor, Sam picked it up and replaced it on the wall. He put his arms around her.

"Calm down, Caitlin."

"*Grr*, why does she do that to me?"

"She'll fall in love with me and forget all about a big wedding, don't worry."

"Ha! Fat chance. You don't know how prejudiced my hometown is. With the exception of my brother, Ollie and his family, that is."

"Caitlin, I can handle prejudice, believe me."

"Sorry Sam. Of course. But I can't seem to convince them that you are an American Indian and not a Calcutta bandit or something. So, what shall we do now? Want to take a walk?"

Malindi, trying to retrieve a moldy piece of dog food from under the dryer, heard the magic word, "walk" and moved to the door to wait for Sam and Caitlin to put on their sneakers.

❀

Instead of going up the driveway to the street, they turned left and descended a short hill that brought them to Cresheim Creek.

"I'd like you to have a sense of where you are, Sam. It's more isolated here, since most hikers prefer Forbidden Drive—over by the Wissahickon Creek."

Before going under the bridge, she stopped and crept closer to the water's edge. The mucky ooze seemed to pull her in. Feeling uneasy, she backtracked a few steps.

She called back to Sam, "There's supposed to be the remains of an old grist mill here somewhere. I've always wanted to find it."

"What? Can't hear you Caitlin. Malindi has to pee."

"I said...Oh, there it is, on the other side of the creek." Covered with vines and thick vegetation, half hidden behind the cement bridge abutment, not just a crumbling foundation, but a solid, stone structure and a water wheel glinted in the shadows. "How can we cross though?" She continued on the path, looking for a shallow place with linking stones suitable for crossing.

Sam caught up with her. "What did you say, Caitlin?"

"I'd like to see that old mill on the other side, but we'll have to do it on the return trip. We can't get across here."

"It's nice and quiet here," Sam said. "Like a miniature green canyon."

They meandered for a mile through islands of woodland and meadow. The land flattened out, houses sprung up, the path ended and the creek disappeared into a culvert.

"This is Germantown Avenue, Sam." Caitlin pointed to an elaborate fountain across the street. "That used to be a watering place for horses; it marks the dividing line between Chestnut Hill to the north and historic Germantown to the south."

A helicopter whirred overhead, cars rattled on the loose Belgian block cobblestones, a green and cream-colored bus belched noxious fumes as it stopped at the corner to pick up passengers. Malindi leaned against Sam's legs; Sam put his hand on her head. Caitlin laughed. "Looks like you two are eager to get back to the peace and quiet of Cogslea," she said.

"So, where's this old mill, Caitlin?"

They had returned on the opposite side of the creek and were walking back and forth under the bridge and up the hill almost into people's back yards.

"Never mind, Sam." She jerked her head in the direction of Germantown Avenue. "It must be back there and I missed it somehow. It doesn't matter."

But it did matter. She had a sinking feeling in the pit of her stomach. Nevertheless, she preceded Sam at a sprightly gait up the

16

stone steps that led to the street. They crossed McCallum Bridge on a narrow pedestrian path and were soon at Cogslea's door. Caitlin was unusually quiet but her mind was racing. Dear God in heaven. I know I saw that mill. I know I did. She hurried inside and went straight to the powder room on the first floor.

"Are you all right, Caitlin?" Sam called after her.

"Have to go to the bathroom." She closed the door and leaned her back against it. Oh, dear God, please tell me I'm not hallucinating again."

❀

In an effort to hide her anxiety, Caitlin forced herself to act normal. They had a late dinner on the patio and watched the sky turn a deep hot orange. Birds twittered their last calls before retiring. Bats, readying for flight, yawned and stretched their wings.

Malindi stretched out beside the fish pond, watching fireflies twinkling in the lengthening shadows at the edge of the yard. In another time and place she might have tried to catch the luminescent creatures. Instead, she concentrated on distinguishing the lights from any paired amber ones that could be floating a few feet above the ground. Waiting. The smoke/lions that came in search of caitlin/dog/ mama in Ah-free-kah; in the den of her brother; and in the red dirt place where Sam/dog/baba lived. They were not here. She turned and looked at Sam. He would not let them come. sam/dog/baba would not let them come. sam/dog/baba would not let anything hurt caitlin/dog/mama.

CHAPTER THREE

Sam made cheese omelets, he toasted English muffins, sliced a cantaloupe and placed it all on a large silver tray.

"You're spoiling me, Sam," Caitlin said from her lounge chair on the patio.

"It's the least I can do for the woman I love." He poured her a cup of coffee.

Caitlin worried that Sam would get bored in Philadelphia. She had plenty of things to do herself: paint, prepare for an exhibit at the Art Alliance, get in touch with her friends, reconvene her painting group. She expressed her concern aloud.

Sam took a sip of coffee and observed his wife over the rim of his cup. "Don't worry about me, I couldn't be happier. I'll find something to do." He gestured with his hand toward the garden. "Lee has started to undercoat the lattice; I wouldn't mind working on that. I could try my hand at gardening. Between using the exercise equipment in the basement and walking in the park, Malindi and I should be in great shape." He thumped Malindi's side. "Want to run on the treadmill, girl?" Apparently not, Malindi chased a squirrel up a tree and sat down to enjoy its angry chatter.

Caitlin stood, leaned over Sam, took his cup and put it on the cast iron table beside his chair. "I think you're in great shape," she said, poking his stomach with her index finger.

He pulled her down on his lap and nibbled her ear. "Mmm, so are you Caitlin. I can think of plenty of things we can do for the next six weeks."

She leaned back. "Seriously, Sam, I should get my stuff out of Carolyn's apartment. Remember? I told you she took over the lease when I went to Africa? There's not much — mostly my paintings and books and odds and ends—which I could put in storage or in my brother's barn with the rest of my things. Since we don't know where we'll be living after Cogslea."

The doorbell's outdoor extension buzzed. Malindi raced through the house and sat by the door while Caitlin and Sam followed at a slower pace. Sam squinted through the fisheye, then undid the complicated locking paraphernalia and opened the door.

"Hello, I'm Ed McGregor, your neighbor and this is my grandson, Toby. Just wanted to see how you folks are doing."

Marny had said that Ed was in his mid-seventies, but this fit and weathered looking gentleman appeared much younger. He was dressed in boat mocs, a faded blue polo shirt and khaki shorts. Caitlin could have sworn she'd seen his picture in *Outside* magazine.

They gathered in the kitchen. Caitlin poured Toby a glass of orange juice and a cup of coffee for Ed. Ed helped himself to artificial sweetener and low-fat creamer. The subject of fishing came up.

"Come on, Toby, Caitlin said. "Let's leave these men to their fish stories and go outside."

Malindi engaged Toby in a game of frisbee until the disc arced low and splashed into the fish pond.

Leaning over the pond, Toby brushed his unruly sandy colored hair away from his eyes and hooked it behind his ears. "Oh, look," he cried. "Come see, Caitlin, there's a humongous frog in here."

She left her chair and sat cross-legged at the pond's edge, smiling at his exaggeration. Like a lion tamer training his beast to sit on a box, Toby tapped a broad lily pad with a stick. Half a dozen frightened goldfish huddled on the bottom. Malindi watched, fascinated.

"Do you go to school around here, Toby?"

Toby straightened, pushed his rimless glasses higher on his nose. "No, I live in Chester County with my parents and Wendy, my kid sister, but I'm staying with Granddad for the summer. I'm going to soccer camp and taking a few courses at Chestnut Hill Academy. Last summer I attended tennis camp at CHA and Granddad and I took bell ringing lessons at St. Martins in the Field. We're building a canoe in his garage. He volunteers at the Germantown Historical Society, and I'm helping him catalog colonial dinnerware. We're going surf fishing at Cape May. Maybe you and Sam could come with us?"

"That would be nice, Toby. Thank you. Sounds like you're pretty busy."

"I am, but I can sit with Malindi if you want. Just let me know." He scooped up the frog and held it gently in his cupped hands. The frog expanded a bright yellow throat and bulged out his eyes. "He's a big guy. Isn't he beautiful?" Toby let the frog slide back into the water. He picked up his stick and threw it to Malindi to fetch. "Malindi looks like *Lycaon pictus*."

Caitlin was surprised that Toby recognized the species, let alone knew its latin name. Most people didn't. This was one smart kid. Sort of like her favorite nephew. Same age too.

"Where did you get her, Caitlin?"

"I was working at a research station in Botswana when a hand-reared African wild dog gave birth to a litter of pups that were sired by a wild-caught male. I was lucky enough to get special permission from the authorities to keep Malindi. Something unheard of before."

"So you're half wild, are you, Malindi? Let's see how you play stick toss," Toby said.

As Caitlin watched them play, she noticed that Toby kept his eyes on her a lot. Uh, oh, I feel a love triangle coming on. From Toby's looks, I think he likes me and Malindi sure is smitten with Toby.

"C'mon Toby—don't want to hold these folks up any longer," Ed called from the patio steps. "Nice to meet you, Caitlin. Hope you don't mind if I borrow Sam to help build our canoe." He put his arm around Toby's shoulders as they walked to the door. "Sam built an entire thirty-two foot cabin cruiser all by himself. How about that?"

"Wow! Can he go fishing with us?"

"Yup, we have it all planned."

Sam closed the door and Caitlin said, "Well, it looks like you're going to be pretty busy after all, Sam."

❀

After lunch, Caitlin sipped her iced coffee and sighed with contentment. "As my Aunt Jane used to say, 'Life is good.'"

"Life is good," Sam repeated.

"What now, Sam. It's such a lazy summer day; I find it hard to muster any energy."

"Me too, Caitlin, but I thought I'd paint the rose trellis in the garden that Lee started."

"I'd offer to help, Sam, but if there's one thing I hate to do it's paint lattice. I painted miles of it in my grandparents' yard once and swore I'd never paint another piece of lattice again." She raised a celery stalk and declared, "As God is my witness, I'll never paint lattice again."

She did, however, join him in the garden to do a watercolor. First, she strolled up and down the narrow brick paths bordered with vibrant pink and red impatience, held back by a tapestry of colorful summer blooms.

"The garden is so lovely; I don't know where to begin." She positioned her fingers in a square, squinted and looked through the opening. "Should I do the blue hollyhocks lining the wall? The pink heritage roses covering the picket fence? These yellow day lilies and purple phlox?" She opened her folding easel and put her supplies on a matching folding table. "This is as good as any. I like the burnt orange and deep purple of the pansies and the little cherub statue. Besides, I can see lovely old you from here, Sam."

Each time Sam finished a section of lattice, he stood back to look at Caitlin.

She felt his eyes on her. "What, Sam?"

"You look like a kid," he said. "Not thirty-four."

"Yes, well, you don't look forty-four either."

"Ouch, thanks for reminding me."

"I'll keep you young Sam. I'll soon have you wearing goofy

logo shirts like mine." She pointed to the green Philly Fanatic cavorting across her chest.

"It's not the shirts that will keep me young, sweetheart, it's those skimpy shorts that are creeping up your thighs."

"Well, let's hurry up and finish our work so we can do something about that," she told him in a saucy voice.

She deepened the center of a bright orange pansy then put down her brush. Already thinking about her next painting, she tipped back her signature wide-brimmed straw hat trimmed with black grosgrain ribbon that shaded her face and studied the house. Cogslea had an ambiance that inspired. Three renowned artists may have painted on the very same spot where she now sat. Independent women. Well, she was independent too, even though she was married. It was a good relationship and Sam was keeping his promise to give her her space.

A cloud moved across the sun. She must paint every day. Six weeks could go by very fast.

Malindi moved from where she had been sleeping and plopped herself down beside Caitlin to continue her afternoon nap. "Hey, Malindi," Caitlin said. "I wonder what you dream about. Skeptics say that dogs don't dream, but we know better, don't we girl?"

Malindi flew above the clouds with *Popo*, the bat, held gingerly in her mouth. *Popo* spread her wings. Her small darting eyes were alert. Her open mouth emitted high-pitched beeps that bounced off intercepted surfaces with radar-like precision. When the desired object was located, Malindi bent her head down and to the side. She flipped her head upward and tossed *Popo* through the air like a frisbee into Toby's open arms.

Toby had agreed to model for Caitlin and her friend, Gina. This morning, Gina's hair was as bright as a pumpkin; yesterday it had been dandelion yellow. With blue spandex stretched over her trim athletic body, she looked ready to compete in a gymnastics tournament.

"I'd love to paint Sam in the nude," she told Caitlin, with a sly smile.

Caitlin laughed. "No chance." Caitlin didn't feel at all threatened by Gina. Her friend was intensely interested in anatomy. She had studied Shiatsu massage therapy in Japan and had assisted in autopsies for a medical examiner—learning anatomy the old-fashioned way like DaVinci and Michaelangelo.

Caitlin watched diminutive Gina lay out two dozen twenty-four ounce jars of liquid pigment and a pile of four to six inch painter's brushes on a long folding aluminum table. "I see you still work big," she said.

"I'm experimenting with acrylics."

Caitlin respected Gina's energy and initiative to try new mediums and techniques. Her massive triptychs were displayed in her large Mt. Airy home; her tribe of ten-foot sculptured Zulu warriors in authentic dress were exhibited in the African American Museum. She was currently designing a giant tiled mural for a new movie theater in the suburbs.

Gina opened a wooden studio easel and lifted her five foot canvas onto it. "Seems like old times," she said, smiling.

"Yes." Caitlin knew she was talking about the painting group they had formed when they met in life drawing classes at Fleisher. "Too bad Marny never joined us, but she likes continuing the tradition of an art colony at Cogslea. More of the old gang will be coming next week and, if it's not too hot, Sam will pose as a mountie from *Little Mary Sunshine*.

Gina's daughter was stage manager at the Society Playhouse and had access to the wardrobe department. Caitlin was hoping that Ed would pose as Julius Caesar.

Caitlin finished setting up her supplies. "I'm going to get the drinks, be right back."

In the kitchen, she took three frosted glasses out of the freezer, a pitcher of freshly squeezed lemonade from the refrigerator and put them on an aluminum tray. On the way down the hall, she looked back at the powder room and saw Toby, in his costume, preening in front of the mirror. Amused by his actions, she stood still and watched him.

The dashing Pirate King from *The Pirates of Penzance* wore high leather boots and black pantaloons tied at the waist with a blood red sash. Toby pretended to twist a charcoal-drawn mustache on his upper lip. He opened the top buttons of his white linen shirt, revealing a scrawny, adolescent chest. He made a face and re-buttoned quickly. He sheathed his sword, plopped an oversized plumed hat on his head, took one last look at his image and swaggered down the hall.

Ahead of him, Caitlin descended the patio steps balancing the oversized tray. A beam of bright sunlight bounced off the crystal pitcher and she was momentarily blinded. In that instant she saw that Gina had changed into a white, ankle-length muslin dress and a blue artist's smock. Her wild hair was smoothed back and gathered in a knot on top of her head. What fun. The old painting group often dressed up like turn-of-the-century artists.

Caitlin blinked and caught her breath. Gina was suddenly back in spandex and pop-star metallic hair. She gasped and faltered on the steps.

"Are you okay, Caitlin? Do you need help?" Gina asked.

"I'm fine." Caitlin placed the tray on a garden table and sat down. "The sun was in my eyes."

Maybe the heat's getting to me, she thought. Get over it. I'm fine. I'm fine. I'm fine.

Toby bounded down the steps slicing the air with his sword and singing: "For I am a Pirate King, and it is, it is a glorious thing, to be a Pirate King. For I am a Pirate King."

"Hurrah for the Pirate King!" Gina sang.

"Hurrah for the Pirate King!" Caitlin said.

Toby bowed and then positioned himself under the pergola.

"Remember to put your weight evenly on both feet, Toby, so you don't tire one leg," Caitlin told him.

Toby swished his sword a few times before taking his stance.

He leaned one outstretched arm on his weapon, the other hand he placed on his hip. "The Pirate King knows how to stand, wench, so be careful or I'll make you walk the plank."

Caitlin and Gina laughed, then got to work.

By the first break Caitlin had the full figure sketched in and had worked up several light washes. The next step—contouring the figure with color—would bring this pirate to life.

Toby pulled audio buds from his ears and let them hang around his neck. He wiped his forehead with his pirate handkerchief.

"How's Farley Mowat's, *Never Cry Wolf?* Caitlin asked, still working on her painting.

"Awesome." Toby did a few jumping jacks and knee bends and declared that he was ready to pose again. At the next break, he asked Caitlin, "Can I see your painting?"

"Sure, come look."

"Wow! Is that me?"

"That's the Pirate King." She had created a dashing, handsome Toby, as he might look a few years in the future. "Like it?"

Toby gulped and seemed at a loss for words. "Uh, huh."

They worked for almost another hour. Even though Toby was willing to continue, the temperature had climbed to ninety degrees and Caitlin decided it best to stop the session.

Gina packed her supplies into a huge canvas carpenter's bag and folded her easel into a compact rectangle. "Sure you don't want to try Raku, Caitlin?"

"No, thank you very much." Anything that involved goggles, gloves, a mask, a propane burner, an 1800F degree kiln and combustible materials left Caitlin disenchanted. She'd stick with safe, reliable watercolor.

"Okay, see ya." Gina dashed off in a cloud of dust to get to her workshop in Media.

Toby, once again an ordinary twentieth century citizen, rolled on the ground with Malindi.

"Want to stay for lunch?" Caitlin asked.

"Can't, but thanks Caitlin. I have a French lesson this afternoon."

"Okay. Would you mind telling Sam to come home for lunch? Thanks." Sam was spending the morning at Ed's working on the canoe.

Malindi watched Caitlin pack hummus, grated carrots and tomato slices into pita pockets until her saucer-like ears picked up the sound of Sam's footsteps crossing the courtyard.

"Ed's invited us to dinner at Valley Green Inn tonight," Sam said, coming in. "He said that it's one of the last operating roadside inns in the area."

"I know Sam, I've been there. The food isn't always that great, but it does have atmosphere."

Sam reached around Caitlin for a carrot chunk and let it fall into Malindi's mouth. "Toby says he knows the way blindfolded."

Caitlin laughed. "I don't doubt it. And I'm sure he'll tell us plenty about the history of the Wissahickon. Especially the ghosts."

CHAPTER FOUR

E d carried his hand-carved walking stick—a gnarled oak staff with an eagle's head. Malindi had her eye on it and Toby was trying to distract her.

"*La*, Malindi. No. Get this stick. What's the word for stick?" Caitlin had taught him a few Swahili words.

"*Banzi*."

"*Banzi*, Malindi." Toby tossed a stick and Malindi raced after it.

"*Nzuri*, Malindi We're going for a walk now. *Twende*. Let's go."

Caitlin was growing quite fond of the boy. She knew that Sam was too. Toby had questioned Sam about the Navajo and in turn gave them a brief history of the Lenni Lenape Indians—the original inhabitants of the area.

They took the path along Cresheim Creek to where it joined the Wissahickon Creek. There, they crossed the smaller of the two streams at low water, stepping across three well-placed stones. Caitlin noticed Sam's subtle smile when Toby gallantly offered his hand to help her cross. They followed Toby up a steep hill and at the top looked down into a clear, deep pool.

Toby lowered his voice and said, "Devil's Pool is bottomless. It's a popular diving spot for—young boys." His eyes widened to dramatize his next words. "Unfortunately several have died in the attempt."

"How awful." Caitlin wondered if that was really true. When the others moved on, she hung back and stared down into the depths of the pool, searching for the bottom. She'd heard of people who felt compelled to jump from heights like the Empire State Building or from bridges. There was no railing or fence here and she began to feel a little dizzy. At first, she thought the sounds she heard came from hikers, but as she inclined her head toward the pool, she definitely recognized a kind of chanting. Like Hari Krishnas or Tibetan monks.

How weird. And what is that lovely smell. Oh, yes, mint.

"Come on, Caitlin," Sam called.

She rejoined the group and debated whether or not to tell the others what she heard, but Toby appeared to be very excited about something. On the path, he leaned down, picked up a small shiny thing and held it out to her.

"Look, Caitlin. Mica. A piece flaked off a chunk of Wissahickon Schischt." He pointed to boulders of muted tones of gray, brown, and blue. "In the nineteenth and early twentieth century, many houses around here were built from Wissahickon sch.." — he ran his tongue over metal-braced teeth — "rock. Granddad's house is made out of Wissahickon sch...the rock."

Caitlin held the nickle-sized piece in the palm of her hand and admired it. "It's beautiful."

Toby beamed. "You can have it Caitlin."

"Thank you, Toby. I'll treasure it always." She tucked it away in her shirt pocket. Over her heart.

Sam reined in Malindi when they reached the Valley Green Bridge, a graceful stone structure that arched over the creek with its reflection completing a perfect oval. Several children were leaning over the creek's retaining wall, tossing bread to the geese and ducks that gathered in noisy flocks below.

"I used to save stale bread and do that too," Toby said. He straightened his shoulders and walked faster. "But, I'm too old for that now."

Valley Green Inn, a whitewashed colonial-style building with forest green gabled roof and shutters, had an open columned front porch, perfect for alfresco dining. Scarlet geraniums in window boxes circled the porch and brightened windows upstairs and down.

"A table on the porch will be ready shortly," the hostess told them.

Caitlin tugged on Sam's sleeve. "I'd like you to see the inside dining rooms, Sam."

Sam ignored the glass and dinnerware but showed interest in the Early American tools displayed in oak cabinets. He gravitated to a painting on the wall, one among many of local artists' renditions of the inn and the Wissahickon area. It was a watercolor scene of a small cottage beside a mill titled, "RittenhouseTown."

"Hmm, the artist's name is Caitlin Gilbert. I wonder who she is."

Caitlin leaned into him. "I hear she's a witch. Or maybe a sorceress who gobbles up handsome men."

"I'd like to meet her," he said, returning her smile.

"Hmm, let's talk about that in bed tonight. I think our table's ready now."

Malindi reclined on the ground below their table and watched the passing parade of dogs exercising their owners.

Caitlin studied the menu. "Free-ranging pheasant and wild boar tenderloin were not on the menu when I used to come here. It was more like meatloaf and mashed potatoes or macaroni and cheese."

Toby expressed a strong opinion of what they should order and slapped his menu on the table. "Catfish and waffles for all of us," he told the waitress. "I'll have syrup with mine."

"It really has changed since my college days," Caitlin said. "I used to ride my bike in from town and hardly ever see another person. Now the paths are packed, especially on weekends."

"Fairmount Park is the largest, continuous city park in the country," Toby said proudly. "Eighteen hundred acres, with tennis courts, baseball fields, statuary, a Japanese tea house, a building from the Bicentennial Exhibition, historic houses, et cetera, et cetera, et cetera. But the best part is right here in the Wissahickon valley."

"You're an authority on the park," Sam said. "Where do you get all your information?"

Toby smiled and looked at his grandfather. "From Granddad."

Ed settled back and looked past the diners, past the human traffic on the drive. He seemed to be reacquainting himself with every tree within his range of vision. Finally, he said, "Most Philadelphians cherish the Wissahickon. I do too, but I have a personal interest in this place. At the present time, the inn is owned by the city and operates under private management, but in the 1940's my aunt and uncle ran the inn. They lived upstairs. They did the cooking and all the work. There were fewer people using the park in those days. Park guards often wandered into the kitchen to prepare their own meals. Hay rides and sleigh parties ended up here for dinner. Local equestrians were regular customers."

"Tell 'em about you, Granddad."

"I will, Toby. I was born in Scotland but came over to attend the University of Pennsylvania. During the summers I lived and worked here, helping my aunt and uncle with chores and such. I love this place. I've walked all over these woods, on and off the trails."

Toby started to rock back and forth. "Tell them about the monks. Tell'em." He rolled his eyes toward Caitlin and a wide grin spread across his face.

"Why don't you tell them about Kelpius first."

Toby took a deep breath. "In 1694, a mystic named Johannes Kelpius and his Pietist followers left Germany to escape religious persecution. They settled along the ridge in Roxborough and devoted themselves to farming, worship, astronomy, astrology, mathematics, and alchemy. They weren't dumb, you see, 'cept Kelpius lived in a cave and became known as the 'hermit on the ridge.' This is the best part; members of the sect watched from the roof of their tabernacle for the 'Woman of the Wilderness' to appear. She represented the pure spirit of christianity and her coming would signal the end of the world." Toby sat back and folded his arms across his chest.

Ed took a sip of ice water and continued the story. "Legend has it that the monks' spirits walk the Wissahickon at night. There

30

are several credible accounts of people seeing them on Forbidden Drive." Ed winked at Toby. "I often took midnight walks when I stayed here. One night I'd gone about half a mile when I saw movement coming from the opposite direction. I got off the path and hid behind the trunk of a tree. I could just make out a group of dark figures floating up the road, and I heard a humming sound or chanting in a low-toned mantra. They passed within a few yards from where I was hiding; so close, I could feel their breath as they passed. And I swear I smelled mint."

"They were ghosts of Johannes Kelpius's cult." Toby raised his voice and the diners at the next table turned in time to see Toby raise his quivering hands. He squealed in a high-pitched tone, "*Eeeeh*! Ghosts!"

"Settle down, Toby," Ed said, patting his arm.

Caitlin felt as if all the blood had drained from her face. At Devil's Pool—the chanting, the mint. An ordinary person would probably toss it off and say, "Wow, I witnessed that too." But she couldn't do that. It would open up old wounds. Fortunately, Sam hadn't noticed, he was making room on the table for the arrival of their dinner.

She forced herself to move on. She would think about it later and pretended to be interested in the food on her plate: crispy, deep fried, breaded catfish atop golden brown waffles. She watched Toby lavish maple syrup over the top of his and cut his food into portions the size of his open mouth.

Caitlin used the syrup sparingly; Ed and Sam spooned hot tartar sauce over theirs.

"This *is* good," Caitlin said. "I like the combination—sort of like salty pretzels and vanilla ice cream."

Toby nodded. He would have answered, but his mouth bulged.

"What are some other Philadelphia specialties?" Sam asked.

"Chicken with waffles was a favorite dish in the eighteenth century," Ed said. "Shad from the Delaware died off because of pollution—although they've been cleaning up the river and fish are coming back now. Pepper pot, a spicy soup thickened with small dumplings was a colonial favorite."

"The broth is made with the lining of a cow's stomach. Yuk." Toby made a face.

Ed held Toby's eyes and continued. "Then there's scrapple."

The corners of Toby's mouth turned down. He swallowed a piece of waffle and burst out, "Double yuk. Made from the liquid of a boiled pig's head. How about shoofly pie; it's made with flies."

A dignified "hiller" at the next table arched her eyebrows and said, "Young man, please."

"Sorry." Toby slid down in his chair.

Ed chuckled. "Now, Toby, you know that's not true."

"What about Philadelphia sticky buns," Caitlin said, feeling sorry for Toby. "I'll make them for you and Sam."

Toby brightened, sat up and speared his last piece of waffle.

"We mustn't forget Tastykakes and Breyers ice cream," Caitlin said.

"And Oreo cookies," Toby added.

The waitress came up to the table and cleared their plates. "I bet you want Indian pudding again," she said to Toby.

"Oh, yes, please. Caitlin you should get that too."

"Okay, Toby. Sam and I will share one."

"Well, I don't know, Caitlin; I might want my own. After all it is *Indian* pudding," Sam said.

When they finished their dessert they lingered over coffee and watched people heading home.

✿

"Wish I didn't eat so much," Caitlin said, climbing a small hill.

Toby stopped suddenly and made Malindi sit. He put his fingers to his lips and pointed to a bare limb midway up a tall hemlock tree. Outlined by the full moon behind it, a great horned owl blinked down at them. It hooted twice, raised its wings and flew silently over their heads to the other side of the creek.

32

Shards of silver moonlight danced on ripples of moving water, tree frogs peeped, and pine needles fell softly to the earth.

"Oh, how wonderful." Caitlin put her head on Sam's shoulder to share the moment with him. Now if only those damn monks would appear and we'd all see or hear them, I couldn't ask for more, she mused.

They turned and headed home, following Ed's small flashlight in the dark.

❀

Malindi lay with the frisbee between her paws. She watched a bat fly over the pool and scoop up a mouthful of water.

"I think I have a rival," Sam whispered in Caitlin's ear.

Caitlin traced his nose and lips with her finger. She knew full well the answer but asked anyway, "Do you mean Ed?"

He caught her fingers and kissed them. "Ed's still a good looking guy; I'm surprised he never remarried." He pressed her closer to him and said, "But then, I guess he wasn't as lucky as I was—finding you."

"Toby then. Are you sure?"

"You know that tree we passed with all the initials and hearts carved on it?"

"Yes, the soft gray bark of a beech tree is the perfect canvas to dig into with penknives. Toby didn't...?"

"No, Toby would never be that destructive, but I saw him trace with his finger a heart and T M loves C G."

"Oh, dear."

"Be careful with that young kid's heart, Caitlin. He's crazy about you. And I know how that feels. Now, let's go to bed."

CHAPTER FIVE

Toby and Sam headed out for a walk with Malindi. Caitlin waved to them from the doorway, hoping that the adage "out of sight, out of mind" would apply to her in Toby's mind. The young were resilient. She stared after them for a few minutes before going back inside.

She removed a train schedule tacked on a cork board over the dryer, scanned the schedule and decided that the 11:15 would get her in town in time for her appointment at the Art Alliance. But first she'd have to decide on what to wear. It was going to be a very hot day. Again.

Several outfits landed on the bed before she decided on a rectangular cloth in a bold blue and black pattern. She'd grown accustomed to wearing the wraparound *kangas* in Africa; they were cool and comfortable. She selected a necklace of blue ceramic beads from her jewelry box, put on a pale blue T-shirt, slipped into Clarks sandals and gave a quick brush to her hair.

Plenty of time for another cup of coffee; she refilled her cup, added cream and took it into the library where she settled in a comfortable Eames chair with a stack of biographies, bodies of work, and first editions of Cogslea's earlier residents beside her.

Caitlin studied photographs of Violet Oakley's Art Nouveau paintings. She'd always admired the artist's mastery of the fluid, graceful line, whiplash curve, and freeform shape based on motifs taken from nature. But her murals of massive allegorical females could only be appreciated on site in the capitol building in Harrisburg. She and Sam should take a trip up there one day.

She leafed through copies of women's magazines such as *Harpers*, *Colliers*, and *Ladies Home Journal*, already flagged for illustrations by the "Red Rose Girls." She smiled at Elizabeth Shippen Green's romantic portrayal of a woman's home-life early in the twentieth century: the contented wife and mother gardening, sewing, reading, having tea with a friend. In contrast, her storied illustrations of ethereal women caught in gothic situations were surely designed to satisfy those same bored homemakers. What would Caitlin have been like if she had lived then? She chuckled. Not the mousy housewife. Never. She would prefer to be the woman in the gothic stories. Who wouldn't?

Of the three, Jessie Willcox Smith was Caitlin's favorite. She adored *The Water Babies*, *Child's Garden of Verses*, and *The Little Mother Goose* books. Set in friendly, fairy tale scenes, where everything was pristine and beautiful, Smith's children were enchanting, rosy faced and chubby, hair perfectly coifed, clothes tidy, shoes shined. Never a dirty face or scraped knee among them.

Caitlin lay the book in her lap and daydreamed about her own happy childhood hours when Aunt Jane read to her. Her mother read to her too, but she didn't put the magic in it like her aunt did.

She jumped when the antique French clock on the mantle struck the half hour. Whoa! Where did the time go? She quickly replaced the books on the shelves.

As she turned, something white scurried out the library door and around the corner. A white cat? Alice's tardy white rabbit reminding her that she was late? She looked into the foyer and in all the rooms on the first floor. No cat. There couldn't be a cat, Marny did not own a cat. Must be her imagination. Or too much coffee.

On the way out, she grabbed her brief case and pocketbook, set the alarm and closed the door.

❀

Caitlin retraced the steps of Violet, Jessie, and Elizabeth, who often took the train into town to attend parties, lectures, and concerts. She walked briskly past the playing fields of Allens Lane Art Center and turned the corner. In a few blocks she came to a red brick, Victorian station house where she purchased an off-peak, round-trip ticket. To get to the southbound platform, she had to climb a rickety wooden staircase, cross a pedestrian bridge that spanned the tracks, then go down another flight of stairs. The train chugged up the track and Caitlin boarded with a bunch of sleepy students bowed under heavy backpacks, bound for the University of Pennsylvania or Drexel University.

Caitlin enjoyed viewing the scenery from a train window, even though at times it was not pretty. For a short distance, trash, socks, the odd broken chair littered the banks. The saving grace here was a lone gardener toiling among rows of vegetables in one of the city's converted vacant lots.

Crossing the Schuylkill River, she could see wheeled and footed exercise taking place along the river drives. A few scullers skimmed the water, the Art Museum and tall office buildings serving as their backdrop.

On the west side of the river, summer visitors walked toward the Victorian gatehouse of the Philadelphia Zoo in droves. Before the train dipped into a tunnel, she leaned her forehead against the window to search for a familiar face in the service driveway that skirted the grounds. Yes, there was the keeper who cared for Malindi when she was quarantined after they arrived in the states.

Caitlin got off at Suburban station, climbed to the street and checked the time on the City Hall tower clock before crossing Market Street. She glanced toward Wanamaker's Department Store. Freshman year. She was a stock girl there for all of three hours. A wreck by lunchtime, she got on the down escalator, walked past the bronze eagle, out the revolving doors onto Chestnut Street and didn't go back.

She walked down Broad Street, heading for Utrecht Art Supplies. There she picked up several tubes of paint and a couple packs of conte crayons. Two students were ahead of her in line, posturing, trying to look cool. They were from the art school across the street.

Now the University of the Arts, it was called the Philadelphia College of Art when she attended. And before that something else; and before that...She tapped her fingers on her briefcase. Were these kids ahead of her ever going to stop talking to the cashier about last night's party?

Her mind drifted to the past.

At eighteen, full scholarship in hand, provincial hometown far behind, Caitlin enjoyed every minute of her new freedom. What would she have been like if she had stayed in Ronksville? Would she have turned into the perfect housewife in a ticky-tacky house with a boring husband and two well trained, unimaginative children like her sister? Not likely.

She never quite fit in with her peers. While her friends played Barbies, she played with stuffed animals. When her girlfriends dated, she played softball with the boys. The girls in high school planned dances, she organized Earth Day celebrations. If they were at the mall on Saturday, she was listening to the Metropolitan opera on the radio. They went to dances, she went to museum lectures in New York City. As much as she loved her hometown and her family, she was quite happy with the lifestyle she found after leaving.

"NEXT!" the purple-haired cashier with multi-piercings and a black mouth barked, bringing her back to the present. He processed her credit card, crammed her items into a tiny plastic bag and looked past her when she thanked him.

It's the Philly way, don't let it get to you.

Traffic inched along Locust Street. The stereo in a convertible thumped like a berserk heartbeat. Women wore power suits and conducted business conferences on cell phones pressed to their ears. She had worn jeans and escaped to galleries or the park on her lunch hour. After two years in Africa and a year in Arizona—where time was measured in sunrise and sunset and not luncheon dates, work commitments or hairdresser appointments—downtown Philly was overwhelming.

By the time she reached 19th Street, she was eager to enter the quiet, green oasis of Rittenhouse Square. She looked around. The park seemed to be peopled with ghosts from her past. The wizened old men playing chess under the maple tree. The sad young boy playing a violin. The young woman lying on the grass sunbathing. The lovers behind an azalea bush reminded her of herself and Tom, her first true love. But that was another story.

So that no opposing sitter had to face another, benches were strategically staggered. Caitlin found a seat and watched a woman dressed in purple from head to toe toss chunks of bread to the pigeons swarming around her feet. Up the path, a toddler tried to climb the bronze goat sculpture, worn shiny by countless caresses.

An elderly woman sat down beside her. "That was Leopold Stowkowski's favorite," she said. "When he was old and living in Europe, he told a friend, 'Pet the goat in Rittenhouse Square for me.'"

"That's a nice story," Caitlin remarked. The sky, cloudless when she left home, began to darken. She and the woman exchanged comments on the weather.

After a brief silence, the woman talked about how difficult it was to fill up the days since her husband passed away. A sister in California had invited her to visit. "I don't know if I could go; I've never flown before. Have you ever been on a airplane?"

"Yes, many times. It's exciting." The woman frowned. "I know what you mean though. A lot of people have qualms about flying. Have you considered taking the train?"

The woman wrinkled her brow. "No, I haven't. My sister didn't mention the train."

Caitlin gave her a few tips on train travel, then checked her watch. "Goodness, I have to go. I have an appointment at the Art Alliance." She gathered her belongings, said goodbye and crossed the square to the street.

The Art Alliance, a palatial, stone-blocked building and once a private home, was designed by the same architectural firm that had designed Cogslea. All the exterior and interior arches simply shouted Day and Klauder. She walked alongside the cement balustrade, skipped up several flat steps and entered the building. A quick nod to the guard, she crossed the lobby and went upstairs to the curator's office. She tapped lightly on an opened door.

A woman stood in front of a velvet draped window that offered a spectacular view of the square. Caitlin pictured her whipping off her horn-rimmed glasses, unbuttoning the top buttons of her pink and green Lily Pulitzer dress, shaking out her sun-bleached hair, then, like the drab heroine in a movie, she would be transformed into a sexy, stunning beauty. That, of course, would never happen. Not to a member of an aristocratic Philadelphia family with very old money.

"Caitlin, it's good to see you. It's been...what two years?"

"Three." Caitlin smiled. She liked and respected Anne. They would never be best friends, but they had always worked well together. "I've ordered lunch. Caesar salad, beer bread, and iced tea." Anne raised her arm and checked the time on her slim, gold Tiffany watch. "It should be here any minute." Instantly, a young man dressed in black pants and crisp white shirt arrived bearing a silver tray. He placed their lunch on the library table, pulled out matching oak chairs, and disappeared without a word.

Over lunch, the conversation centered mainly around happenings in the art world. Caitlin gave Anne a brief summary of her past three years, ending with her marriage to Sam.

"That's wonderful, I'm very happy for you Caitlin. Are you coming back to Philadelphia to live?"

"We haven't decided yet. There's no hurry."

"I'm engaged myself. We've set the date for June 12th of next year."

Caitlin extended her best wishes. She noticed the expensive diamond ring sparkling on Anne's finger. Not a huge stone, but a perfect one. And Anne didn't wave it about like some engaged women she knew. Caitlin had a nontraditional wedding ring with a blue turquoise stone surrounded by creme pearls that Sam bought for her in an antique shop in Santa Fe.

Caitlin visualized Anne's wedding. It would be a huge affair, well documented in the society pages. Her dress — silk faille with touches of antique Italian lace and tiny seed pearls; the veil — miles of French tulle. For her own wedding, Caitlin wore a vintage blue linen outfit purchased in a thrift store. Sam, looking ever so handsome, wore the traditional Navajo headband and blue velvet shirt. Their wedding took place beneath cottonwood trees alongside a stream in a red-rock canyon and was attended by a few friends.

It was beautiful and there was no way it could get any better than that.

As if on cue, their luncheon tray was whisked away. They moved to a buttery soft leather sofa and Anne looked through Caitlin's updated resume.

"Here are copies of my reviews from last year's Santa Fe Art Museum exhibit," Caitlin said.

Anne read the favorable reviews of Caitlin's exhibit of paintings of the southwest and of Africa.

Many painters attempt the fusion of reality and dreaminess but few actually achieve it. Caitlin Gilbert's mastery of her subjects, her use of translucent and glowing light, the simplicity of line, reveal an artist at ease with her medium. The forms in her landscapes are slightly askew but that touch adds interest and depth to an often overblown, mundane subject.

Anne looked up and smiled. "Admirable, Caitlin. Now let's see the slides." Caitlin pulled several plastic sleeves from her briefcase; Anne spread them on a light table on her desk and flicked the switch. "I love your ability to tell a story, Caitlin. These paintings underscore the similarities of poverty in Africa, the Tex/Mex border, and the Navajo Reservation. The shaded faces and huts are actually interchangeable and equally deplorable. This works well with our theme for the fall." She opened a thick accordion folder with Caitlin's name on the label. "My copies?" Caitlin nodded and Anne slipped the slides into the folder. "Looks like we're all set then. I'll send you a draft of the fall schedule."

"That would be good, Anne. Thank you."

"We'll be in touch. Have you looked at our current exhibits?"

"I'm going to. Goodbye, Anne."

Caitlin breezed through the upstairs galleries and barely looked at the work of emerging artists. She thought the ornate rooms in themselves were far more interesting than the artwork they displayed. The exhibits downstairs were interesting but the air was stuffy. She was beginning to feel claustrophobic and left the building in a hurry.

The instant her foot touched the sidewalk, a streak of lightning split the sky over West Philadelphia. Black thunderclouds moved in fast, covering the last fragments of blue sky. "Just enough blue to patch a dutchman's pants," her Aunt Jane used to say. As she cut through Rittenhouse Square, light spritzes of rain cooled her flushed face. She saw the "train woman" bent in conversation with another gray-haired lady, apparently sharing their sorrowful tales. There were a lot of lonely women in the world. She took a deep breath and sighed.

She checked her watch. Not enough time to make the next train at Suburban; she might as well walk over to 30th Street station.

Standing on the Market Street Bridge, she took a moment to look down at one of her favorite Philadelphia scenes, one she'd painted many times: the Waterworks; a cluster of neoclassical buildings hugging the banks of the Schuylkill, mimicking their lofty Grecian temple neighbor, The Philadelphia Museum of Art.

She steered herself toward the grandiose 30th Street Station. In the main concourse she slid into a phone booth to call Sam.

"Sorry, I'm going to be late, Sam; I missed my train. Shall I pick up something in the Food Court for dinner?"

"Not necessary, Caitlin. I've defrosted a vegetable lasagna and I'll make a salad."

"I can pick up a loaf of bread at the bakery here. See you soon."

She bought an Italian loaf, tucked the package under her arm. Since it was past off-peak time, she would have to purchase another ticket. Standing in line, she listened to a conversation taking place behind her.

"Thank you very much for lunch, Mrs. Stevenson," said a young voice.

"You're quite welcome, Laura," said an older woman. "Need I remind you again, my dear, of your responsibilities to your parents?

You are obligated to write to them regularly."

"No, m'am. Yes, m'am."

"And you will remind the ladies of my *soireé* Saturday evening?"

"Yes, m'am."

"Then I will expect to see you Friday night at the Academy of Natural Sciences for Dr. Griswold's lecture on the giant clams of the Sargasso Sea?"

"Yes, m'am."

"Good day, Laura."

"Good day, Mrs. Stevenson." In a lowered voice, Laura said, "Old biddy, I'm planning on having a bloody awful headache next Friday and miss old Dr. Griswold's boring lecture."

Caitlin couldn't help but laugh out loud. As soon as she got her change and her ticket, she turned to see what the spirited Laura looked like. But she was gone. Only a group of impatient looking young men were behind her.

She went upstairs to wait on the open platform. Out of curiosity, she tried to pick out Laura, but no one seemed to fit the bill. When the train arrived, people poured on and she was happy to get a seat on the zoo side again. She saw Dulary, the Asian elephant, throwing hay at a group of visitors. Once, Dulary had snorted and slimed her. She loved the experience, but her friends thought she was crazy.

She settled back in her seat and looked out the window. The day had been a success. She would tell Sam about Anne, the old lady in the park and the students in Utrecht's. Sam was a good listener.

It was raining hard now. Rivulets of water shimmied down the window, obscuring her view, taking her to another time and place. Last year—Arizona. She'd gone out to visit a friend and to paint. Her friend hadn't a clue that she'd just come through a really bad patch. She was good at hiding her problems, her instability, her fear of commitment. Until she met Sam. She gave him a hard time but he was so persistent. Dearest Sam. I don't ever want to put you through that again.

When the train slowed for Allens Lane station, the sky

opened up, drenching the unprepared. Now she wished that she had picked up a cheap umbrella from one of the enterprising vendors on Chestnut Street.

As she stepped off the train, she immediately collided with someone. Someone caught her arm. Someone dressed in white cotton. In a heartbeat, their faces almost touched. The young woman had intense emerald green eyes and she smelled of roses. The woman smiled, then was swallowed up by a group of carefree Masterman students. Caitlin ran—or tried to run—after the woman. The group of students broke apart and Caitlin caught a glimpse of the retreating figure. She wore a long skirt and fitted blouse with puffy sleeves; her hair was piled on top of her head, Victorian style.

In her confusion and haste to catch up, Caitlin bumped into an elderly man, knocking the newspaper out of his hands.

"Goodness," he exclaimed.

"I'm so sorry." Before stooping to pick up the loose pages soaking up rainwater, she checked the direction the woman was taking. She shoved the wet papers into the man's hands. "So sorry."

'Well, I say."

She raced to the bottom of the overpass and looked up. Mingled with various footwear, black laced boots and the hem of a white dress ascended the stairs. Caitlin cut and pushed around people, ignoring their startled protests. Up, across, and down again. On the platform, she looked both ways but saw only mushrooming black umbrellas. There was a shortcut—an alleyway adjacent to the tracks. She raced toward it, but no woman in white walked with train travelers. Nor was she anywhere to be seen up on the street. Unless the woman was a speed racer, she had vanished into thin air.

Caitlin pressed her back against the iron fence on the bridge. Water ran down her face, her clothes stuck to her like a second skin. She was splashed by passing cars but took no notice.

Maybe she's an actress like the woman who plays Betsy Ross, or one of those other Colonial performers at Independence Hall. Maybe there's a Victorian dress-up party somewhere. Or is someone playing a trick on me? Gina? Gina was capricious but not freaky enough to go this far. What really unnerved her was the thought that she could be hallucinating again. One thing was clear though—the white cat in the library was not a cat at all. It was the hem of a long white dress.

Red tail lights, blinking and fuzzy in the rain made her look up. "Caitlin," Sam said, putting his arm around her. He covered her with an umbrella and half carried her into the car. Malindi licked her face.

"Caitlin are you all right?" Sam took her hands in his. "Your hands are cold. It was raining so hard I decided to meet your train."

She covered an inner trembling with a broad smile. "I'm glad you did Sam. Sorry I didn't see you; I had something in my eye."

Sam insisted she take a hot shower and put on dry clothes while he fixed dinner.

"The bread—it's probably ruined," Caitlin said, handing him the soggy package. Sam pulled out the loaf, turned it over and declared that he could salvage half of it.

His eyes shot to the wet shirt clinging to the curves of her breasts. "Now get out of here before I scrap dinner all together."

Passing the library, she averted her eyes. For sure she would not be telling Sam anything about these weird episodes. She had worried him enough last year.

CHAPTER SIX

Pellets of rain drummed against the bedroom window, harmonizing with the dripping spout. Half asleep, Caitlin trudged downstairs, set two cups on the counter, stared out the kitchen window and waited for the coffee to brew.

Malindi had balked at going outside until Sam donned a rain slicker and joined her. "Phew, it's pouring," he said, shaking out his rain gear. "How about french toast?" He ruffled Caitlin's hair. "Sleepyhead. Sit down, I'll get it, if you don't mind frozen."

She nodded her approval. Sam was almost too good to be true.

❀

Sam was engrossed in the *New York Times* crossword puzzle and Caitlin was frowning at the editorials when the phone shattered the comfortable silence. Toby's voice came over the speaker.

"Hi. Since it's raining and we can't go for our walk, how about if I bring over some board games? Hello?"

Over the top of her paper, Caitlin mouthed the words, "I forgot." Sam raised his eyebrows with a look that said, "Better do it." She grabbed the receiver off the kitchen wall.

"Hi Toby. I was just wondering what to do. Sure, come on over."

Caitlin ran upstairs to dress. Minutes later, she greeted Toby at the door. He was dripping wet and holding a trash bag filled with games. Wearing an oversized black hooded rain jacket; he looked like a trash bag himself.

"It's raining cats and dogs," he said. He removed his jacket and tossed it on the dryer. Malindi grabbed a sleeve, pulled it down and dragged it across the floor.

"Malindi. What's got into you?" Caitlin picked up the jacket

45

and hung it on a coat hook. "Shall we play in the library?" She still felt a little uneasy about that room, but hell, she'd have to get over it sooner or later. "Sam are you playing?" Sam disliked games.

"If you don't mind, I'll do my crossword puzzle." Sam settled on the Eames chair and propped his feet up on the matching ottoman. Caitlin sat on the sofa and Toby pulled up a straight-backed chair. Malindi lay across Toby's feet with her frisbee between her paws.

"Scrabble, Trivial Pursuit, Monopoly, Jinga, Clue, Cribbage, playing cards, and a one thousand piece picture puzzle," Toby said. He spread the game boxes on the coffee table. "What shall we play first Caitlin?"

Caitlin picked up a box. "Jinga? I don't remember this. *Jinga* means 'to build' in Swahili. I'd like to play Jinga."

Toby arranged small wooden blocks into a tower. "There are fifty-four pieces. We take turns and remove one block and put it on top of the stack. If the tower falls, you lose. It's fun."

As play progressed, the tower grew more unstable. Toby calculated his next move but Malindi intervened. She touched her nose to the bottom piece. The situation worsened but the tower stayed intact. Toby's eyes widened and he held his breath.

"Your turn," Caitlin said.

"Okay, I can do this." Toby carefully removed one block. The tower swayed but didn't fall. "Your turn, he said, rotating his shoulders."

Caitlin attempted to remove a piece, but the blocks tumbled down with a crash and scattered across the table.

"Nice try," Toby said. "Want to play again?" Caitlin won the second game. They each won a game of Monopoly. Toby was cackling over winning Clue by declaring that Mrs. Peacock did it with a candlestick in the living room when Ed telephoned. It was time for Toby to go home as they were scheduled to volunteer at the historical society.

"Would you like me to leave the puzzle?" Toby asked.

"I would, thanks. See ya later. Say hi to Ed." She waved goodbye and watched Toby as he deliberately splashed through every single puddle in the courtyard. He reminded her of her brother's son. She and Sam wanted children; maybe they shouldn't wait another year as planned. But would she make a good mother that little inchworm of doubt asked her. Could she handle it?

Sam came from behind and pulled her close. She turned her head as far as his tender grip would allow. "That was fun. I like having Toby around."

"More than me?" His mouth grazed her neck.

"Sam, I should do the laundry, detail a few paintings. And I really need to call my friends and let them know..." her voice trailed off. He picked her up and carried her upstairs. The moment for any serious discussion about children had passed.

❦

Most of her friends were at work; she left messages on their answering machines at home. But she reached Carolyn at her desk at the University of Pennsylvania.

"Carolyn? It's Caitlin. Do you have a minute?"

"Sure, for you I always have time. I was wondering when I'd hear from you. What's up? I'm dying to meet Sam."

"I know. I want you to meet him too. How about dinner tomorrow night? Our treat."

"Sounds good. We can have coffee and dessert at my apartment."

"We'll pick you up at seven. Where shall we eat? Let's go some place quiet where we can talk. I take it you still don't have a car?"

"No, can't afford it. South Street's too noisy. How about that restaurant near the Italian Market we used to go to?"

"Good idea. How's the novel coming?"

"Slowly, but at least I can do the research here at the university on my time off. Caitlin, I'm so glad I took this step. Uh, oh, gotta go. I'll see you tomorrow."

Sam was having a cup of coffee at the kitchen table. Caitlin sat down and filled him in on Carolyn's circumstances.

"Carolyn's husband had an affair, the divorce was messy, and his extravagant lifestyle left her with a settlement that really stinks. Now she has a part-time job so she can pursue a writing career that she gave up to support him."

Sam nodded and poured her a cup of coffee. She added cream.

"We met at a party. She was a senior at the Philadelphia High School for Performing Arts, majoring in Creative Writing. When I heard that she was goofing off and cutting classes, I encouraged her to finish high school; then I got her a job in the writing department of the advertising firm where I worked."

"That's typical of you, Caitlin. Wanting to help others."

She looked surprised. "Of course, why not? Anyhow, later, when she married and moved to the suburbs, we drifted apart."

"I thought you lived together."

"We did after her divorce. She took over my lease when I went to Africa." Caitlin drained her coffee, put down the cup and covered his hand with hers. "I'm happy you and my best friend will finally get to meet each other, Sam."

❀

"*Humpf*," Caitlin said, pulling on her seat belt. "So much for our faithful dog; she latched on to Toby and didn't even say goodbye to us."

"Just like a woman," Sam said. "Where do I go, Caitlin?"

"Go over Allens Lane, down Wissahickon Avenue to Lincoln Drive. You'll see RittenhouseTown on your right. It's the site of the country's first paper mill. The mill's not there anymore; it vanished over a century ago." They covered the distance to RittenhouseTown in several minutes. Caitlin pointed to the old homestead on their right: a quaint stone cottage under the willows beside a stream. "I painted that scene lots of times."

Sam leaned forward and looked past her. "I know, Caitlin. I saw your print in the Valley Green Inn, remember?"

While they waited for the light to change, Caitlin rolled down her window. A faint odor of rotten eggs and wet rancid laundry drifted up her nose. She considered asking Sam if he noticed it too, but she was suddenly overcome by a sense of confusion, disorientation. The sounds of moving traffic and idling motors faded away, replaced by water splashing, wheels creaking and a dull, rhythmic pounding noise. She trembled.

"What is it? Sam asked.

"*Brrr*. I don't know, Sam. Funny feeling. Like someone just walked across my grave, as they say." She patted his arm to assure him that she was okay. "I'm fine, Sam, really."

I'm fine. She knew that Sam hated that ubiquitous answer. It could mean a number of things, often as not it meant that she wasn't fine at all. He was looking at her hard. "Really," she said, trying to sound perky and convincing, but she was sitting on her clenched fists. Sam white-knuckled the steering wheel and screeched through a yellow caution light.

"This is an old carriage road and wasn't built for speed, Sam. Lot's of careless drivers end up in the creek." She tilted her head to the right.

"Thanks for the warning."

Where the Wissahickon Creek spilled into the Schuylkill River, Caitlin said, "We're on Kelly Drive now, Sam. It's named for millionaire bricklayer, John B. Kelly, Sr.? You know—Grace Kelly's father? Princess Grace of Monaco?"

Sam made noises that he did not know who Princess Grace was.

She clucked her tongue.

"What?"

"I'm just trying—for the one hundredth time—to find something to admire in that statue by Jacques Lipchitz. The piece still does not speak to me." She pointed to a grotesque statue of a lumpy man holding a struggling eagle by its feet.

"Can't look now Caitlin."

Was she talking too much? Was Sam mad at her?

Sam eased the car onto Benjamin Franklin Parkway—a wide diagonal boulevard that cut across the grain of William Penn's original grid plan.

Not a man of many words, Sam said, "Very pretty."

"I think all visitors should see this view of the city first. Run up the museum steps like Rocky, stand at the top and look down the parkway lined with flags of all nations, toward City Hall, over the fountains and monuments, the golden dome of St. Peter and Paul. It's like the Champs des Elysees in Paris." She surveyed the changing Philadelphia skyline. "At one time, no other building could be higher than Billy Penn's hat, but that's all changed."

Sam said nothing. He was dealing with getting in the correct lane at Logan Circle. Windblown spray from the Calder fountain spotted their windshield; he cleared it with a few swipes of the wipers. Ankle deep in the fountain's pool, children darted under streams of water pouring from mermaids' pitchers and the mouths of large bronze frogs.

"Oh, look at the kids, Sam." Sam smiled at her and she felt vindicated.

Within a few blocks from the Parkway they pulled up in front of a four-story corner brownstone where Carolyn waited for them in the vestibule. She came out and slid into the rear seat of the car.

"Well, a Mercedes. I wasn't expecting that."

Sam would have opened the door for her, but impatient drivers were honking behind him. He pulled away and acknowledged Carolyn with a nod to the rear view mirror.

Caitlin assessed her friend's new look. At one time, having lost all self confidence, Carolyn had completely ignored her appearance. But now she was a woman of style and taste. Golden streaks highlighted an expensive, precision haircut.

"I like your new hairdo."

" Margarita." Carolyn said.

"Good for you girl, you deserve it. Eye shadow too."

"Is it too much?"

"No. It's perfect for your blue eyes."

Sam dropped them off in front of the restaurant in South Philly while he circled the streets for a parking place.

"He's a winner. Great rugged face. A good man, I can tell," Carolyn said.

"He is. And to think I almost turned him down last year."

They chatted on the sidewalk while waiting for Sam. Caitlin wore a white halter sun dress with an embroidered antique white silk shawl draped around her shoulders. Carolyn wore a classic black dress. A yellow Thunderbird roared up the narrow street and screeched to a stop; the driver rolled down a smoked window and leered at them. He maneuvered a cigar to the side of his lips and called out, "Yo, black and white. Hop in. We'll go for drinks."

"Buzz off, creep. Not interested," Carolyn said.

"Watch your attytood, north philly." The yellow monster drove away in a cloud of noxious black fumes.

"Now here comes someone to ride off into the sunset with," Carolyn said. Sam was dressed in faded jeans, black T-shirt and jacket. "Definitely cool, Caitlin."

"I know." Caitlin linked her arm through his.

"What do you know?" Sam asked.

"That you are the best looking guy around and I've got you."

Sam opened the restaurant door and a warm smell of cigarette smoke, roasted garlic, and rich sauce wafted out, along with the soundtrack from *The Great Caruso*.

The head waiter led them to a corner booth. When they were seated, he nodded toward an old upright piano in the front of the room where a young boy was playing chopsticks. "Everyone is encouraged to sing an Italian love song or operatic aria tonight," the waiter said.

They laughed and said that they would probably pass on that.

Sam noticed the autographed photos on the wall. "Who was Mario Lanza?" he asked.

"A romantic tenor from South Philadelphia who made it big in Hollywood in the fifties," Caitlin told him.

"Is that him singing?" Sam asked when another scratchy RCA vinyl record dropped on the turntable.

"Yes. He's idolized in South Philly. A legend. Too bad he died at the height of his career."

They ordered appetizers and a house wine. Carolyn asked Sam if he was a full-blooded Navajo.

"As far as I know," Sam answered.

"Well, you really are the best looking Indian around," Carolyn said.

Sam laughed and said that he was probably the *only* Indian around. "But thank you, anyway. What is the Indian population in Philadelphia; do you know?"

"Not very high," Carolyn said, rearranging her dinnerware to make room for a basket of warm bread slices. She swallowed a steamed clam and sucked up another. "You two are the only white and Native American combination that I know of. There are, however, plenty of other biracial couples." She sopped up clam juice with a crust of bread and her mouth twisted in a curious half smile. "But, who's counting. Mmm, garlic. I love garlic."

Pompous bastard husband, Caitlin wanted to say. Narrow-minded and prejudiced, always ridiculing Carolyn's unbiased beliefs. Then he turned around and married a black woman. Carolyn's views did not change, she just pitied the poor woman for marrying such a jerk.

Carolyn pushed back her plate and raised her wine glass. "Anyway, I'm happy for you both. I think you're a perfect match. Here's to you."

"Here's to us and to you," Caitlin said. She took a sip of house chianti and stared into the glass. Her candid friend would probably bring up the subject sooner or later.

"Sam and I agreed to have some quality time together before starting a family." She turned to Sam. "But you can imagine what beautiful babies we'll have. Half Navajo, half Irish. I wonder what they'll look like."

"I hope they look like you," Sam said and squeezed her arm.

Sam's first wife, after several abnormal pregnancies, died of an ectopic pregnancy. She knew that Sam worried that she might have a complicated pregnancy. "Don't worry Sam," Caitlin said. "I'm strong as an ox. I won't have a problem."

Their waiter bore a remarkable resemblance to Frank Sinatra and sang as he served them, "I Did It My Way." He brought extra plates so that Sam and Caitlin could split their pan fried brook trout and eggplant parmesan dinners.

"Still a vegetarian?" Carolyn asked.

Caitlin nodded. "I eat fish though. It's not a problem for us. Sam often cooks a steak or roast for himself."

"We get along just fine," Sam said. He refilled their wine glasses.

Caitlin leaned back. "So, tell us about your book, Carolyn."

Carolyn wiped red sauce from the corners of her mouth. "It's nearly finished. I just have to tie up some loose ends. A friend of mine is going to critique the manuscript before I start looking for a publisher."

"What's it about?" Sam asked.

Carolyn put down her fork, smiled and said, "It's a subject I know a lot about—lousy husbands and good wives."

Caitlin raised her glass. "Here, here." She snuggled up to Sam and kissed his cheek. "We don't mean you Sam."

Carolyn toasted and continued. "My novel follows the matriarchal line of a Philadelphia family over a period of two centuries. It covers the changing trends in husband and wife relationships and the way women's choices have altered and expanded over the years." She paused to sip her wine. "Sometimes it takes two or three days of research just to come up with a few lines."

"Despite all obstacles, you're on the right track," Caitlin said. "At last."

"I owe a lot to you, dear friend." Carolyn's eyes glistened with tears.

At that moment, a barrel-chested youth took possession of the microphone and belted out, "Be My Love," from Lanza's movie, *The Toast of New Orleans*. Diners stopped talking to listen to the novice tenor.

A woman at the next table, bursting with obvious pride and too much pasta, turned and said, "My son. He's a student at Curtis Institute."

Caitlin nodded. "He's very good."

The waiter arrived rolling a two-tiered cart of tempting desserts. Caitlin yearned for Italian rum cake, but declined since they were going to Carolyn's for dessert. "Just coffee," she said.

Sam excused himself to go to the men's room. As soon as he was out of sight, Carolyn fixed her blue eyes on Caitlin. "Okay, my friend. What happened in Africa? You never told me that you were even going there, you know."

Caitlin's shoulders slumped. "I'm sorry, Carolyn; I should have called you, but I thought I'd be back after I went home to be with my Aunt Jane." She sniffed and wiped away a tear. "She was diagnosed with cancer. Then when she died, I didn't know what to do with myself. One of the keepers at the zoo, who I had worked with on a behavioral study of their African wild dogs, contacted me to tell me there was an opening in Botswana for a researcher's assistant. I jumped at the chance to go."

"Okay." Carolyn leaned in a little closer. "But what happened to you over there?"

Caitlin sighed deeply. "A friend and I took a vacation to the Mountain Gorilla Sanctuary in Rwanda. While we were there that awful three month period of genocide broke out." She shivered and took a sip of wine. "It was all a blur to me but I ended up in a hospital in Nairobi. I was really messed up for a while."

"And?"

"I had a terrible reaction; nightmares, hallucinations."

"Then what happened?"

"I returned to the research station. I knew that I needed professional help. As soon as Malindi..."

"Malindi?"

"She's my African wild dog. She was born at the station. When she was old enough, I obtained official papers for her and brought her back to the states with me. I stayed at my brother's house in Ronksville while she was in the required quarantine at the Philadelphia Zoo for a month." She bit her lip. "I saw a psychiatrist for post-traumatic stress disorder."

They saw Sam coming back. "Good enough," Carolyn said

before he sat down.

An old man stepped up to the piano. He slicked back his hair with the palm of his hand and gave his listeners a shaky rendition of "La Donna e Mobile." The audience whistled and stood up to cheer.

They drained their cappuccinos, Sam paid the bill and they walked to the parking lot.

※

The apartment, a third floor walkup in a four-story building had a pullman kitchen and a bedroom not much bigger than a closet. A front room with wraparound windows and northern exposure had served Caitlin well as her studio.

While Carolyn made coffee, Sam and Caitlin stacked her french easel, drawing table, leather portfolio, a file box of reference photos, and two cartons of books by the steps.

An eclectic assortment of thrift store furniture competed for space in the living room. "Sam, don't sit down too hard on that end of the sofa," Caitlin warned. "Those springs still out of whack, Carolyn?"

"Yup, but I propped up the cushion with books underneath."

Sam moved to the middle cushion.

"*Ta da*." With fanfare, Carolyn placed a white bakery box on the coffee table in front of Caitlin.

"Omigod," Caitlin whispered. "Is it? Did you?" She opened the lid. Half a dozen tube-like pastries nestled beneath waxed paper. "Canollis! How many times did we stuff our faces with these? Sam, have you ever had a canolli?" He shook his head. She lifted each one to check the fillings. "Chocolate chip, lemon...oh thank goodness-- almond. If there's only one, Carolyn, I'll have to kill you for it."

"Like I didn't know you'd want almond, Caitlin? There are three. I'm on a diet, so eat what you want and take the rest home."

Caitlin licked the filling from one end and powdered her upper lip with confectionary sugar. "Nobody makes these better. Canollis would be a good reason to stay in Philadelphia, Sam."

Carolyn cut a chocolate one in half and ate it in two bites. "What the hell," she said and ate the other half. She sighed and sank back into an overstuffed, squeaky chair. Caitlin was in a state of delirium, so she directed her question to Sam. "Where do you think you'll settle? When Caitlin called me from Arizona, it didn't sound like it would be in Philly."

Sam put the remaining half of his almond canolli on Caitlin's plate. "I really don't care where we live. The southwest and west coast are probably out. So is Ronksville." He smiled when Caitlin snorted. "We'll go there after Cogslea so I can meet the family. Or visa versa." Caitlin snorted again and puffed out powdered sugar. "Then we'll take a trip up the east coast and into Canada." He put a hand on Caitlin's knee. "Where we live is entirely up to my lovely wife."

"My eyes were bigger than my stomach." Caitlin put the uneaten piece of pastry back in the box. She wiped her mouth and hands with a napkin. "We'll see; there's no hurry. But right now we should go home. I don't want to keep Toby out late."

They carried Caitlin's things to the street. While Sam went to get the car, Carolyn reiterated how much she liked him. Caitlin took the opportunity to ask her friend about her love life.

"Any prospects?"

"It's taken a long time to get over my animosity toward men, but I'm finding that there actually are some nice guys out there. We shall see."

"I know what you mean. Right out of high school, away from home for the first time, I jumped into a relationship with a stupid, self-centered jerk." Caitlin closed her eyes and shook her head in disgust.

"He was awful," Carolyn said. "Tom was sweet though. I'll never understand why you broke off with him."

"Too possessive," Caitlin said. "Sam knows he can't hold me down."

"Yeah, well, don't hurt him, Caitlin. We both know you had men keeling over with broken hearts in the past."

Caitlin looked inward. "Yes, but I wasn't committed. And I

felt that if I never married, didn't have children, then so be it. I was content. I treasured my independence. Sam lets me do what I want without hovering over me." She watched Sam get out of the car and felt her love for him well up inside. "Besides, I couldn't bear to see him hurt," she whispered.

Once Caitlin's things were stashed in the roomy trunk of their car, Carolyn thanked them again for dinner; they hugged and promised to get together soon.

❀

In the flickering glow from the television set, Toby sat transfixed, watching Tim Curry, in the role of an outrageously kinky transvestite, prance around in lady's underwear.

For their amusement, in an over-the-top performance, Toby mimicked Tim Curry's walk all the way down the street to his door.

CHAPTER SEVEN

An annoying mosquito drilled in Caitlin's ear. She whined, she swatted, she rolled over, but the pesky, persistent monster bug moved to the kitchen and droned into a megaphone. She threw off her coverlet, tiptoed into the hallway and hung over the balcony railing. The buzz continued, interrupted solely by an occasional grunt from Sam. She returned to the bedroom, donned a pair of shorts and T-shirt and padded downstairs.

Sam's face was void of expression as he leaned against the kitchen counter with his arms folded across his chest. The mosquito turned out to be a woman, fortiesh, with short salt and pepper hair.

"Hi, I'm Maggie," the woman said, reaching out her hand for Caitlin to shake.

"Hello." Maggie was the cleaning woman, Caitlin remembered as she poured herself a cup of coffee.

"I was just telling your husband that the temperature will be in the high nineties today, but in San Jose, Costa Rica it's only seventy five degrees. Costa Rica is the oldest democracy in the Americas, ya know."

Caitlin took a big gulp of coffee. Her head throbbed. Too much wine last night.

Maggie patted Malindi and began a dissertation on the merits of greyhound adoption. Sam excused himself and escaped to the garden to pull some weeds.

"According to cave drawings and artifacts, the greyhound's

lineage can be traced back eight thousand years," said Maggie.

The caffeine kicked in, Caitlin sorted out what she knew about Maggie. She was a high school dropout, self-educated, an avid reader with an insatiable thirst for knowledge.

At last, Maggie picked up her bucket of cleaning supplies and headed for upstairs. In the dining room, she called over her shoulder, "I'll be 'eddin' upstairs with me things now, m'am, if yourself don't mind. Let me know if there's anythin' in par-tic-u-lar you'll be wantin' done." Maggie laughed, a sound not unlike a mechanized amusement park clown. "That's my 'Upstairs Downstairs' impression."

Caitlin, a fan of the *Masterpiece Theater* series, chuckled at Maggie's accent. "Very good," she called out.

Sam cracked the patio door before entering the house, then he joined Caitlin at the table while she ate a bowl of granola. He whispered to her that in three minutes he had learned how to get rid of slugs, the benefits of ibuprofen over aspirin, and the weather report for the entire coast of Costa Rica.

"I forgot she was coming," Caitlin whispered back. "There's really not a whole lot for her to do, but..." she shrugged her shoulders.

"If you don't mind, I'm going to help Ed with his canoe this morning," Sam said, putting away the milk and cereal. "What are you going to do?"

Caitlin put her bowl in the dishwasher and gazed out the window over the sink. "I'm going to paint the remnants of that old apple orchard in the side yard." She turned and smiled, teasing him. "Maybe I'll paint in Van Gogh's style when he was committed to the asylum in France. A whirlpool of color and action; a swirling golden sky and crazy purple trees."

"Don't even think about it," Sam pulled her to him and pressed her tight against his chest.

"Now Sam. I'll let you know if I go off the deep end again." Sam still worried about her. With good reason. "Is Toby home?" she asked.

"No, he has soccer practice today. Miss him?"

"Mmm, terribly," she said, twisting a button on his shirt.

"Leave Malindi here, okay? Ed's yard isn't fenced and I'm afraid you men will be so busy you won't notice if she sneaks out. See you at lunch?"

Sam nodded, kissed her and left for Ed's house down the street.

❀

Caitlin found a spot in the side yard where the sun wouldn't hit her until about noon. She set her materials on a small iron table and unfolded her chair. Before putting brush to paper, she studied the twisted, gnarly shapes of the wasted trees, deciding to limit her palette to blues and browns.

Time passed; she leaned back in her chair and looked at her work. Spindly trees of dismal gray quivered beneath a sky of flat muddy ochre. Despite her intent to do a cheerful painting—except for a few bright patches of forget-me-nots in the foreground, it was a forlorn scene that spoke of abandonment and loss.

The blue flowers were the saving grace. Squinting, her eyes traveled from painted flowers to real. Were they more cobalt blue than pthalo? One of the flowers moved and fluttered upward. She gasped, then giggled. Silly, this flying forget-me-not is a butterfly. Pale blue, smaller than the common, invasive white cabbage butterfly.

The insect circled a few times in front of her. Then, skimming the ground, it sailed into the orchard where it joined another. The pair danced: rising, falling, twirling. Curious and eager to get a closer look, Caitlin advanced into the shadows. She leaned over the butterflies to watch their mating ritual.

Soft footsteps fell behind her, but so entranced by the dancers was she that she did not turn around. Suddenly, the impact of hard fists on her shoulders knocked her to the ground. She sprawled there, unhurt but angry. Half rising, she twisted her head, intending to admonish the ignorant jokester, attacker, or whoever would do such a stupid thing.

There was no one there.

Puzzled, she looked in all directions. Nothing. Nobody. She

got up and brushed bits of debris from her knees and clothes. She called to Malindi who was racing back and forth along an invisible path at the edge of the orchard. Malindi stopped, raised her head and emitted the high pitched bell-like, *hoo* cry of the African wild dog: the mournful call of a dog separated from its pack; a sound that could carry for three miles.

"Come on Malindi. Come here, I'm all right." Malindi sat down and would not budge, so Caitlin went to her. She peered back into the depths of the orchard, now brightening with fingers of sunlight. "Guess I tripped, Malindi. Don't worry about it, girl.

No longer in a mood to paint, she packed her things, stored them in the laundry room and cleaned her brushes in the sink. Malindi never left her side.

❈

Later, deeply immersed in an Agatha Christie mystery in the library, Caitlin was vaguely aware of the vacuum cleaner grumbling across the wall to wall carpeting upstairs. At some point, the vacuum stopped and a murmuring sound took its place. It sounded like women talking. She held still and strained her ears. No, just one voice. Must be the radio. She turned her attention back to Agatha until the library mantle clock and the grandfather clock in the living room chimed simultaneously. Sam would be home soon and she should be thinking about lunch.

❈

Caitlin shuffled items from shelf to shelf in the packed refrigerator. Maggie came in carrying a basket of dirty linens. She deposited the basket in the laundry room and returned, fanning the air with a menu.

"In a few minutes I'm gonna go over to the deli and pick up a sandwich for lunch. Can I get you and Sam anything?"

Caitlin sighed, closed the refrigerator door and perused the menu. She wrote down "two tuna hoagies" on a memo pad, found the appropriate amount of money in her handbag and gave it to Maggie.

Maggie stuffed the money and note in her fanny pack. "Before I go," she said, "I have to get an envelope from Lee's office to mail at the post office. Have you been down cellar yet?"

"Sam's been down there but I haven't."

Maggie screwed up her face and let out a long whistle. "You really have to see it. Come on, I'll show you. Watch your step on the split levels," she said, marching down the hall. Halfway, she stopped and pulled open the outer door of an old-fashioned iron-caged elevator. "Look at this, would you. An elevator that goes from the basement to the second floor. The Hillmans don't use it anymore, but it still works. Scary." She shivered and closed the door.

She swung open an adjacent door revealing a narrow, wooden staircase that led to the basement. "The lights are here," Maggie said, and switched on the middle button. A handwritten card over the panel read: "Hallway, Front Cellar, Back Room. Remember to turn off appropriate switch!" "Lee likes to label things." Maggie chuckled. "Bottom step is loose," a card taped to the last step said. Maggie and Caitlin held on to the railing and skipped the bottom step.

The cellar, a split level, accommodated the hilly terrain. A sign over the steps to the gym reminded one to, "Step up. Watch your head." Maggie laughed. "This one's meant for Lee. Only six footers need to duck here."

An entertainment center and full-length art deco mahogany bar filled half of the upper level, work-out machines the other half. Notes were taped to each piece of exercise equipment: the stationary bike—"Remember to reset to zero;" treadmill—"Remember to return to flat;" Nautilus—"work up to thirty repetitions;" rowing—"Mon., Wed., Fri.;" Nordic track—"Tu., Thurs., Sat."

"Lee's what you might call anal retentive," Maggie said. "Come down here to the lower level, Caitlin, this is interesting." Under the open stairwell, hidden behind the furnace and hot water boiler, there was a door to another room. Maggie tapped on the dividing wall. "This wall and the exterior corner walls are all that remain of an early nineteenth century farmhouse that was destroyed by fire."

They stepped inside. The room was white and austere and empty. A cold draft blew over Caitlin, draining her enthusiasm. "Let's get out of here," she said, shivering.

Lee's office, a pleasant room at ground level with windows looking out on the garden was as cluttered as his den on the second floor. Stacks of manila folders, bulging binders, books, and other ephemera covered every flat surface. Walking was confined to a few narrow paths trailing through a maze of paper.

"I'll wait in the doorway," Caitlin said.

Square in the middle of the desk, written on a pink postem, Lee had informed Maggie to, "please mail next week." Strategically placed, an Indian arrowhead pointed to a legal sized envelope addressed to the governor. With the important envelope tucked under her arm, Maggie headed for the stairs. She hesitated in front of the open, gated elevator. "I've always wanted to go up in this old crate? Whatd'ya say?"

"Sure, why not?" Despite her fear and trembling, Caitlin moved her feet into the elevator. Oh, sure, you sound brave, she told herself, but whenever you're in an elevator you just know it's going to drop to the basement. Ferris wheels—they'll tip over and you'll fall to your death. Roller coasters—forget about it.

"Come on, Malindi," Caitlin said.

Malindi had balked at going down the rickety wooden steps and she was not about to get into this box. She ran up the steps and waited in the hallway.

Together, Maggie and Caitlin slid the heavy accordion iron door open and shut. Maggie took a deep breath, held it and pushed the red button. They clutched each other as the elevator creaked and strained into motion. The crate shook; it rattled; it finally lifted. For once, Maggie was quiet. She looked at Caitlin as if to say, "What were we thinking?" Finally, the gears stopped grinding; they pulled open the inner door, the door onto the hallway, and escaped.

"I've always wanted to do that," Maggie said. "Piece of cake."

"I'll take the stairs from now on," Caitlin answered. She swore to herself that she'd never get in that death trap again.

❀

Maggie departed on her errands as Sam came walking down the hill. He met Caitlin in the kitchen. "I thought I heard Malindi *hooing* a while ago," he said.

"Really? Must have been an ambulance or a police or fire siren—Philly's white noise." She told him about the elevator. She did not tell him about her strange experience in the orchard. No need to worry him.

❀

When Maggie returned, Caitlin invited her to join them on the patio for lunch. Sam, a fast eater, finished his sandwich before Maggie finished her story of the Red Rose Girls. He excused himself to get the mail.

"At the turn of the century, Oakley, Smith, Green, and Jessie's companion, Henrietta Cozens, who was their housekeeper, gardener and bookkeeper, shared a rented house in Villanova called The Red Rose Inn. In 1906 the owner had other plans for the property and served the women an eviction notice. It wasn't easy for women to find accommodations in those days; most lived with their parents.

"Elizabeth Shippen Green's family was well connected in Philadelphia and—well, to make a long story short—her parents contacted their friend, philanthropist, Dr. George Woodward. He was in the process of building and renovating houses in suburban Chestnut Hill and then renting them to persons endowed with creative skills. The Red Rose Girls fit the bill all right, and so they moved into their new home, Cogslea." Maggie twisted her head to the side. "That building next door—on the other side of the fence—that was Ms. Oakley's studio. Now it's rented out to artists-in-residence.

Caitlin swirled her glass of iced tea and said, "You know a lot about this house and its occupants, don't you Maggie?" She did as well, but she let Maggie talk.

"Oh, yes, this old house, the land and its history fascinate me. And those women were so talented. I don't care what people say about them. Their sex life was nobody's business." Maggie smiled. "They used to call that kind of situation a 'Boston marriage.'"

A flash of iridescent green zipped past. The hummingbird paused in midair before landing on a red plastic feeder hanging from the grape arbor in the pergola. It was instantly displaced by another little hummer.

"Those little buggers sure are territorial, aren't they? Well, gotta get back to work." Maggie crushed her sandwich paper and left to do the bathrooms.

Caitlin had a bad feeling about her orchard painting. She didn't feel like starting a new one, so she accompanied Sam to Ed's house.

❀

Homes on St. George's Road were big, few and far between. Midway up the block on the opposite side, Ed's Queen Anne house was hidden behind a row of thick boxwoods. The rear of the house abutted the grounds of Allens Lane Art Center, separated by a thorny osage orange hedge and closely knit hemlock trees. The Center, spread out over seven acres and open to the public, had four tennis courts, a basketball court, playground, and playing field. Classes, workshops and related events for the performing and visual arts were held in a refurbished carriage house.

Ed sat on a wooden rocker in his garage admiring the framework of his canoe. "Well, Caitlin, glad you finally made it here," he said, rising. "Toby will be disappointed that he wasn't here to see you."

Caitlin ran her fingers over the finely sanded ribs of the canoe. "It's a beauty, Ed."

"We can start thinking about the color soon. Toby and I have narrowed it down to red or forest green. What do you think Caitlin?"

Until she was eighteen, Caitlin spent entire summers at the family's lake house in New York. "I had a canoe once that was painted Chinese red. I loved that canoe."

"Chinese red it is then. That's the color Toby favors. Come on Caitlin, let me show you the house."

They followed Ed to the porch and through a double dutch door into an entry room bright with the filtered, colored light from a stained glass window over the stair landing.

The interior was exactly how Caitlin expected it to be. Signs of a retired academic were everywhere: discarded clothing draped on chairs, empty cups and plates left beside opened reference books. But all of that could be overlooked in the golden glow of original oak woodwork and the patina of authentic early American furniture.

Caitlin and Sam seated themselves at a round oak kitchen table while Ed made instant coffee.

"Where's Malindi?" Sam said, suddenly worried. The leash was in Caitlin's lap, but she had no memory of removing it from Malindi's collar.

"*Malindi. Malindi,*" Sam called. "I know she came in the house with us, because I saw her rooting through Toby's backpack by the front door."

Ed hurried upstairs to look there while Sam and Caitlin called and searched downstairs. Ed returned quickly. "She's not up there. I wonder if she went out the screen door in the pantry. She might have pushed it open."

They hastened through the pantry and went outside. They called repeatedly but got no response. Caitlin had a sinking feeling in the pit of her stomach. This is what the hitchhiker's mother meant— the feeling you have when you don't know where your child is.

"Don't worry Caitlin, she has to be around here somewhere," Sam said. "Maybe she went home or down to the creek. Call Maggie, see if Malindi's there; I'll go down to the creek."

"I'm so sorry," Ed said. "I should have remembered the screen door. I'll take a look over at the art center; there's bound to be a bunch of kids playing ball; maybe she joined them."

The phone rang; Ed grabbed it off the cradle, knocking over

the desk lamp in his haste. He listened, chewed his lower lip. Caitlin watched. He hung up, ran to the front door and called to Sam.

"That was Maggie. Malindi's at Allens Lane ball field. Someone checked her dog tag and called Cogslea.

They slipped through the hedge and ran across the field toward a ring of young ball players in center field. In the middle of the group, Malindi lay prone across a flattened tree stump, her head between her paws. She didn't move.

"Oh dear God, no," Caitlin cried.

"She's alive Miss," a chubby adolescent said, shading his eyes with his baseball mitt. "She ran on the field right to this spot and lay down and we can't get her up. I was kinda glad when she did," he said with an impish grin. "Since I missed the ball and they scored two runs. Maybe they'll call interference."

"Huh, fat chance," an opposition player said. "You missed it by two miles."

"Did not."

"Did too."

"Yuh, unh."

"Yuh, huh."

Gently, Sam pushed the players aside and knelt down beside Malindi. Satisfied that she was not injured, he coaxed her up, attached her leash and led her away. Caitlin and Ed followed.

❧

Back in Ed's kitchen, they sipped their cooled coffee and pondered over the reasons for Malindi's strange behavior.

Caitlin sighed. "That was really weird. She never does anything like that. She never runs away."

Sam said, "Surrounded by kids and not playing with them? That's really unusual."

Ed refreshed their cups. "I can't figure it out. But, I will definitely fix that latch on the screen door."

Malindi's ears swiveled; she jumped up and ran to the front door as Toby pedaled up the path on his bike.

"Hey, Malindi, what's up? Is Caitlin here?" Toby asked. He added quickly, "Uh, and Sam?"

"Don't forget to put your soccer equipment away," Ed called from the kitchen.

"I did." Toby burst into the kitchen, his face flushed from his bike ride. (Or from emotion.) He stuck his head in the refrigerator, removed a bottle of orange drink and chugged it down. Ed related the events to him of Malindi's escape.

"Malindi, you shouldn't do that. Don't ever do that again." Toby bent down and hugged Malindi. She licked his face and wiggled with delight.

"I'm free tomorrow," Toby said, looking at Caitlin. "Can we do something together?"

"Sam and I were thinking about going surf fishing at Cape May tomorrow," Ed said.

"What about it, Caitlin? Would you like to go?" Sam asked.

She hesitated before answering. "I love Cape May, but I think Malindi and I will stay home. Next time, okay?"

Toby looked downcast but then his face brightened. "Deal. But only if Caitlin promises to spend time with me this weekend."

What's the harm? she asked herself. "Deal," she said.

Maggie's vintage turquoise studebaker was still parked in the courtyard. Sam retreated to the patio with Malindi while Caitlin started dinner. She was standing at the sink by the open window rinsing tomatoes when she caught a whiff of old-fashioned laundry soap. The washing machine wasn't running. Maggie's cleaning products did not have that particular scent. A clean, antiseptic smell. Familiar, but she couldn't place it.

Was she hearing things now? She tilted her head. Two voices upstairs. Radio, silly. Just the radio. She rinsed a tomato and debated whether or not to add another clove of garlic to the gazpacho.

Maggie's brogue cut into her mundane thoughts. "If you do not mind, I'll be takin' leave now, m'am. Miss Oakley says she's glad you occupy the blue room. That was her room and pleased she is to let you have it. It's the grandest one in the house, she says." Maggie held her bottle of spray cleaner like a weapon.

Caitlin stared at her. "Uh, Miss Oakley?"

"Sure, and it be her that I talk to. A great lady. Way ahead of her time, yes." Maggie stashed her cleaning items in the closet and turned to sniff the air. "Ah, garlic. Can't use too much garlic. Keeps the werewolves away."

Caitlin was at a loss for words. She watched Maggie grab her belongings and head for the door.

Maggie turned and said, "See you next Thursday. Say goodbye to Sam for me. I'm glad Malindi's okay. Have a good week." She jangled the locks and slammed the door.

Caitlin fell back against the refrigerator. Her muddled mind searched for the meaning of Maggie's words. Marny had mentioned Maggie's peculiarities but not that she talked to ghosts. What a strange day. She held her hand to her forehead. Thank goodness Sam is here or I'd think I was losing it.

The odd events of the day kept spinning through Caitlin's mind like horses on a merry-go-round. This was Violet Oakley's room was her last thought when she slipped into Sam's arms and let him sweep the clutter from her mind.

In her dream, Malindi pictured an orchard dense with sweet white apple blossoms. Birds filled the air with cheery song and butterflies tickled her ears with delicate wings. The sun was on her back, comforting and warm. She felt carefree and happy and stretched her long legs in luxurious contentment.

But slowly, ominous black clouds crept across the sun on inky feet, pitching the orchard into darkness. Malindi cringed. Anger rose in her throat like bile. She raised her head, rounded her mouth, and from the back of her throat came a long, high-pitched "*hoo*" sound. Her call was answered by another.

Obeying ancient instincts to retrieve a lost member of the pack, Malindi bounded toward the sound, but obstacles blocked her path. Hedges with clawing thorns tore at her skin. Giant boxes with windows for eyes sprang from the ground as fast as she could dart around them. Fences with curved iron teeth challenged her. She snapped a gate in two with her powerful jaws and gleaming teeth and tossed it aside. Entering a meadow, she raced toward the call.

Beneath the earth where a sapling hemlock grew came a chittering, birdlike sound: the bonding ritual of African wild dogs; the social greeting of a lost pack member.

CHAPTER EIGHT

Ignored the first time, the harping alarm raised its voice and beeped even louder. Malindi rolled her eyes toward Sam but stayed on her dog bed. Sam dressed in the dark and tiptoed downstairs with the aid of a flashlight. The timer on Mr. Coffee had worked perfectly; he filled a thermos and retrieved the lunch Caitlin had packed for him the night before. He slipped out the door and went to meet Ed and Toby for their Cape May fishing trip.

Over the past year, Sam and Caitlin were rarely, if ever, apart. It was good to be loved, good to be sitting in a lovely yard drinking coffee. "Life is good, isn't it Malindi?" Malindi bumped her head on Caitlin's knee in agreement.

The scent of laundry soap drifted by. She jogged her memory again. Of course; it's like the handmade soap Grandmother kept stored in a box in the attic, along with other World War II memorabilia. But where was the smell coming from?

Well, she couldn't sit around all day trying to figure that out; she had an idea for a painting and was eager to start. Laundry draped on a clothesline,: geometric shapes shaded with soft tints of blue and pink. She stood and Malindi scarfed up fallen granola bar crumbs.

Yesterday, before leaving, Maggie had run off a wash, but Caitlin had forgotten to put it in the dryer. She retrieved the still damp sheets and towels and hung them on a rope strung between the slim trunks of two birch trees in the back yard. Then she went back to the laundry room to get her painting supplies.

Ugh! She'd forgotten to dispose of the ugly orchard painting. Holding it out at arm's length, she made a face. Surely this was the work of a mad artist. Intent on throwing it out, she paused over the trash can. Hmm. She went to the laundry sink, took a small pointed brush, dipped it in water and a dab of blue pigment and added to the foreground two blue butterflies dancing in a shaft of sunlight. Ah, much better.

When a scene contained no sign of life, Caitlin would create one: a bird in the distance, a mouse under a blade of grass. Or simply a footprint on the ground. She left the enhanced painting on the laundry sorting table to dry and returned to the yard.

Determined to do a cheerful picture today, Caitlin worked steadily for over an hour laying in a background of trees and hollyhocks. The laundry line was shaping up, she put down her brush and sat back. Not bad, but it needed something. If only she had a model. A child would be perfect, but children were tough; they couldn't stay still. Years of croquis classes had trained her to do figures from memory. Only as a last resort would she use a photograph.

Her fair skin began to prickle. She moved her chair into the shade and drank some gatorade. The air was still, the laundry hung limp and unruffled on the line, but a teasing breeze whipped the loose ends of her hair, lifted the hem of her skirt. This was the kind of summer day that stirred up happy childhood memories.

A manual lawnmower with a stone caught in its throat coughed. Far away a dog barked, a hammer pounded dully on wood. Children chanted: "A, my name is Alice, B, my name is Betty." She closed her eyes and dozed off. Someone was baking bread and somewhere a baby cried.

❀

When Caitlin woke she felt disoriented, dizzy. Malindi snoozed beside her making little wheezing noises. The sun, having traveled to its late afternoon position behind the tree tops, was in the process of coloring the sky sherbet shades of apricot, peach, and strawberry.

How pretty, if I could just capture those lovely colors, but they change so fast. She could, however, do a quick wash. Her eyes fixed on the colorful sky, she reached for her small watercolor pad on the table, tipping over the easel in the process. Her painting fell to the ground.

A barefoot toddler stared up at her. She wore a blue pinafore and a dress of crude beige material She was tugging on a sheet, two middle fingers of her other hand were crammed into her sweet rosebud mouth. Her ebony eyes sparkled with animated mischief. She had blue black hair that shone like a beetle's wing, her skin was nut brown. A calico cat rubbed against her chubby legs.

Caitlin's head buzzed like a swarm of bees. "Omigod." Had she been so engrossed in her work that she didn't know what she was doing? Or did someone add the figure? She snapped her head around to look over her shoulder. Of course there was no one else around.

She studied the painting again. Her portraits tended to capture the celtic features of her family's fair skin and strawberry blonde hair, but this was definitely her own work, her style. She smiled. Perhaps this is what our child will look like. The thought lightened her mood.

She worked on, deepening the shadows with ultramarine blue, changed her brush and added details. Satisfied, she closed her paint box, gathered her supplies and called to Malindi who was taking a long drink from the fishpond.

Her stomach growled, gently reminding her that she had skipped lunch. She wanted to wait and have dinner with Sam, so maybe just a piece of fruit would tide her over until then. In the kitchen, she selected a ripe mango from the fruit bowl on the counter, peeled it and leaned over the sink to catch the juice that dripped down her chin. She dabbed at her face with a wet paper towel and felt the sting of sunburn. Her arms and knees were tinged with pink as well. Should have used sunscreen, she scolded herself.

The medicine cabinet in the powder room contained several

bottles and tubes of various soothing lotions and creams; she chose one and spread it on her face, enjoying the minty cool sensation. She applied some to the exposed areas on her arms and legs. When she put the tube back in the cabinet, a prescription bottle toppled and fell, landing in the sink, label side up. Caitlin recoiled as if the object were a venomous snake.

The bold letters jumped, swam, and jiggled before settling into a six-letter word. "LURIAM." Anger and fear surged up from the depths of her being like forgotten demons. This innocent looking pill, this common anti-malarial drug was the root of her past problems.

She held the bottle under the mirror's overhead light and read the fine print. *Ha!* Sure, only one in a thousand suffer side affects and I had to be that unlucky one.

For over a month, while in a Nairobi hospital, she was mistakenly administered mega doses of this powerful drug. As a result she suffered numerous unpleasant symptoms including horrific nightmares and hallucinations. The lingering effects lasted a year. She studied her reflection in the mirror. But I'm over that now. Right?

She shook the bottle as if to make it disappear. Why in the world would anyone have this stuff in the house? Then she remembered that Marny and Lee were in Kenya recently. An obstreperous wart hog objected that Lee and his camera were too close to her piglets and Lee tripped and broke his leg. Picturing the incident, Caitlin laughed and put the leftover prophylactic back on the shelf.

※

Later, while struggling to fold a cranky fitted sheet that was testing her patience, Caitlin remembered something. Calico cat. The only words the hitchhiker spoke. But the girl was commenting on Malindi's pelt, wasn't she? Is the calico cat in the painting some kind of message? Okay, calm down, it's just coincidence, word association or something.

Malindi was trying to entice a small rodent out of its hidey hole, but quickly abandoned the game when Sam appeared on the patio. She ran to greet him.

Caitlin threw the unruly sheet into the laundry basket and rushed to meet him too. "I missed you," she said.

He held her at arm's length. "I missed you too, Caitlin, but I'm afraid I smell fishy. I need to take a shower. We caught several bluefish; Ed's going to marinate them and tomorrow he'll grill them for us. He's got a great sauce recipe." He pulled her a little closer. "Mmm, you smell good."

"Moisturizing lotion." Caitlin touched Sam's chiseled features, ran her fingers down his cheek. The sun never affected his complexion. It was always the nut brown color of the toddler in the painting. "I don't mind catching your fishy smell," she said, "Gives us an excuse to take a shower together. Come on."

Sam, right behind her, stepped over her discarded clothing on the way upstairs.

CHAPTER NINE

Situated across from the silky tennis courts of the Philadelphia Cricket Club, the fields and buildings of Chestnut Hill Academy were surrounded by massive beech, oak, pine, sycamore, and chestnut trees planted a century earlier by railroad tycoon, Henry Houston. Now a private school for boys, in the late nineteenth century the U-shaped, three story building served as a three hundred room resort hotel for people seeking to escape the oppressive heat of the city.

As promised, Caitlin would devote Saturday to Toby. She, Sam, and Malindi had walked the short distance from Cogslea to the Academy. At the edge of the playing field, they met up with Ed as the game was about to start.

Toby played brilliantly and scored the two winning goals for his team. When the final whistle blew, he broke away from his circle of teammates and stood in front of Caitlin tossing the soccer ball up and down, beaming as she congratulated him. But he ignored Malindi desperately vying for his attention. Finally, she nosed the ball out of his hands.

His coach had to call twice before Toby responded. "Hey, Toby, let's have the ball." Embarrassed, Toby tossed the ball, bent down and buried his head under Malindi's chin.

Sam poked Caitlin in the side with his elbow; she dug her fingernails into his arm. "What would you like to do now, Toby? It's your day," she said.

Toby lowered his dark eyes and studied the laces on his sneakers. Faced with limitless possibilities, he couldn't think of a single thing to do.

"Let's go up to Harper's Meadow and have lunch at that little cafe on Germantown Avenue," Ed suggested.

Toby agreed. "We could go for a walk in the Wissahickon after, then go home and play croquet, take a swim in our neighbor's pool—they said we could use it while they're away, then go to the Inn for dinner and a movie after."

"Whoa, whoa, whoa." Ed laughed and pulled at the peak of his blue Academy of Natural Sciences cap. "That's a bit ambitious Toby. These folks might have something else planned. Besides, I'm grilling bluefish tonight."

Toby's face slid into dejection.

"I promised," Caitlin said. "Actually, the pool sounds wonderful. The bluefish for dinner and a movie afterward, okay?"

Toby brightened. "There's a new *Star Trek* movie playing at Plymouth Meeting."

Caitlin was a *Star Trek* fan herself. "Deal." She looked at Sam and raised her eyebrows. "But Sam doesn't like science fiction," she said.

Sam winked at her. "Tell you what, why don't you two go to the movie and I'll stay home with Malindi."

"Malindi could pass for a trekkie with her ears: I bet we could get her in the movie," Toby said, chuckling.

Sam grinned. "I don't think so, Toby.

"Can we trust these two youngsters out on the town alone?" Ed asked.

Toby blushed and headed for the car.

※

The pool idea may have been a mistake. Caitlin in a wet, black nylon tank suit was a boy's dream come true. She poised on the deep end of the blue-tiled pool and sliced neatly into the water. After a few laps, she tried to coax Malindi into the pool but her dog was having none of it.

"Isn't anyone else coming in? The water's great."

Sam had a swim earlier and Ed was busy grilling. Toby removed his glasses and did a perfect jackknife off the diving board.

"You're good," Caitlin told him when he surfaced.

"Race ya. Ten laps. Starting now."

Caitlin sputtered that it wasn't fair, he had a head start. She caught up with him and they swam neck in neck for a few laps. Toby finally pulled ahead. She'd probably never hear the end of this.

At the shallow end, Caitlin climbed the steps and bent to squeeze the water out of her hair. Sam grabbed a towel and wrapped it around her. Pointing to her nipples with his eyes, he whispered, "You're just too sexy sweetheart." Toby looked away and tossed a stick to Malindi.

"Dinners ready, folks," Ed called over the fence.

Caitlin slipped a terry cloth dress over her suit and they joined Ed at the picnic table in his yard. Caitlin served her salad of tomatoes immersed in olive oil, balsamic vinegar, and garden fresh basil. The bluefish was delicious, Ed's tangy yogurt sauce a perfect match for the bland fish.

"This has been a great day so far, don't you think Toby?"

Toby, finishing off a second helping of fish, smacked his lips. "Great Granddad. What's for dessert?"

"We have blueberries and pound cake with whipped cream. Would you bring it out? And take some dishes in with you, please."

Toby rose from his chair. "Sure. Want to help me, Caitlin? Sam? I want to show you Timothy, my turtle."

After they cleared the picnic table, Ed reached in his pocket, pulled out and stuck an unfilled, unlit cherry pipe in his mouth. Old habits died hard.

Their "date" may have been another mistake. Toby arrived smelling of something spicy. His hair was slicked down but a stubborn cowlick stuck up in back.

Before Caitlin got behind the wheel of the car, Sam pulled her aside. "No kisses on the first date, okay, my love?" he whispered in her ear.

Caitlin reassured him with a full kiss on his smiling mouth, then whispered back, "I don't know, Sam, he's awfully cute. Don't wait up."

Toby was unusually quiet for the first few minutes but warmed up when Caitlin asked him about his home life.

"What's your dog's name, Toby?"

"His name's Landseer. I named him after that English artist who painted animals. I call him Lance for short."

"Landseer was one of the first artists to paint animal portraits," Caitlin said. "In college, I earned money by painting people's pets, but often had to do it from a photograph. I wonder how he got them to sit still."

"Maybe they listened to audio tapes like I did when I modeled for you," Toby said, grinning.

"Yeah. I bet his models would like *Never Cry Wolf*, huh?" She asked him about his sister.

"Her name's Wendy and she's seven. In a couple of years she'll be able to spend summers with me at Granddad's.

Caitlin wondered why Toby stayed with his grandfather in the summer instead of at home. "What does your father do, Toby?"

"Dad's an airline pilot for United. "My Mom's a nurse. They have odd schedules, so it's just easier for me to spend the summer at Granddad's. Wendy stays with my aunt while Mom's at work.

Not such a mystery after all, she decided.

※

Afterward, on the way home, Toby, still wired with excitement over the final scene, analyzed *Star Trek: First Contact*.

"That was the best, wasn't it Caitlin? Aren't the Borg the scariest things you've ever seen?" She agreed. "What a nightmare for Picard. But I knew he'd find a way out, right Caitlin?" She nodded. "Wasn't it something when the Queen Borg's head came down and settled on her shoulders? Creepy!"

"Definitely creepy. Don't you think the Queen Borg was pretty though? Take away all that creepy stuff on her, I think she's a pretty woman."

"Mmm, maybe." Toby looked out the side window.

"Do you have a girlfriend, Toby?"

"No." He studied the houses on Willow Grove Avenue.

"I'm surprised girls aren't lining up for you."

"Nope. Girls don't like me."

"Toby, I don't believe that. You're great looking, fun, and interesting. Besides, I saw a lot of girls watching you at the soccer game."

"Really?" He turned to look out the front window.

"Yes, Toby. Really."

Caitlin pulled into Ed's driveway. "I had a great time today, Toby, I hope you did too." She waited for him to get out, but he leaned over and gave her an awkward, misdirected kiss on her ear. Then he scooted out the door and scampered up the path.

Taken aback, Caitlin barely remembered to wave to Ed, standing in his doorway

"Uh, oh. I am in trouble." What to do? Back off? Talk to him? Sam will know the tactful thing to do.

She parked in Cogslea's courtyard. Getting out of the car, a flash of light made her turn toward the carriage house. What was that? She strained her eyes through the moonless dark of night. A light from a candle or lantern filled a second floor window. She blinked, it was gone but reappeared a few seconds later in a different window.

A hand landed on her shoulder and made her jump

"Caitlin, aren't you coming in?"

"Oh, Sam, I didn't hear you. I think I saw a light in the carriage house."

"Can't be; it's not rented right now." He looked up at the darkened windows.

She followed his gaze. "Uh, huh. I guess it was reflected light from a passing car on the bridge."

Sam studied the windows for several minutes before leading her away. "You stay inside. I'm going to get the key and make sure the house is empty."

Caitlin waited in the potting shed with Malindi while Sam retrieved the key from the pantry. Nervously, she willed herself to peer through the distorted leaded glass and saw, framed in the second floor window, the golden glow of a candle illuminating a woman's smiling face. She gripped the edge of the plant table to steady herself. It was the woman from the train station. But the moment Sam stepped outside she vanished in darkness. Caitlin was not surprised that Sam found the carriage house unoccupied.

CHAPTER TEN

Stop reading about disasters; there's nothing you can do about it, Caitlin's psychiatrist had advised her. That meant skipping most of the articles in the front section and the op/ed pages of the *New York Times*. She searched for articles on the environment, but they were as bleak, if not bleaker. The world was just a mess.

Sam put down his *Times* crossword puzzle, lowered the back of his lounge chair a few notches and rolled his head toward Caitlin.

She grimmaced, she bit her lower lip, she shook her folded paper. "What? What?" she asked, catching him grinning at her.

"I'm thinking how much I love you. How happy I am."

"I know, Sam, me too. You're not getting bored are you?"

"Not a chance."

"What would you like to do this week?" She picked up the weekend section of the *Philadelphia Inquirer* and flipped through the entertainment section. "We could go to the zoo. The Philadelphia Museum of Art is a definite must. So is the Academy of Fine Arts. How about the Academy of Natural Sciences?"

"Sounds good."

"Run up to Harrisburg and see Violet Oakley's murals in the capitol building? And we could go to a Phillies game. Maybe Toby and Ed would like to go with us."

"Sweetheart, don't worry about me, I'm just happy to be

near you."

She discarded her newspaper, lowered the back of her chair and looked up at the cerulean blue sky to watch the wooly white clouds as they pulled apart, drifting on as they changed shape.

"Sam, when you were a kid, did you look for animals or faces in the clouds?"

Sam raised his eyes to the sky. "Yes, I did. When I tended sheep on the Rez, I used to lie on the ground and search for clouds that resembled sheep. I counted them, and if I found more than five, I believed that something good would happen to me."

"And did it?" Caitlin asked.

"No, it didn't."

She reached her hand over to his, he grasped and kissed her open palm. "But, I have an abundance of perfect sheep now," he said.

"Let's look for sheep, Sam." Try as they might, they could not identify a single figure or face. "Just clouds," Caitlin concluded. "Maybe you have to be a kid."

"Maybe."

Malindi bounded up the patio steps and planted herself in front of them.

"I think she wants to go for a walk," Sam said. "She doesn't believe in taking Sundays off."

Caitlin gathered the newspapers. "Well, let's go then. Is T.o.b.y. home?" She spelled out his name so that Malindi wouldn't get excited. "He might like to go with us."

"T.o.b.y. is visiting his family today, so you'll have to struggle along without your boyfriend."

She pulled a long face. "I guess I'll have to do with you then." He encircled her in an embrace and the newspapers scattered.

"Mmm. Maybe we should go back to bed," he said.

She disentangled herself and held him at arm's length. "Later, Sam. Look at Malindi, we can't disappoint her. Come on, we need to get out of here for a while. We need the exercise."

"I can think of..."

She cut him off. "Another kind of exercise, my love. We can

take the upper paths and then have brunch at the inn. What do you say?"

"I'd say life is good."

"Life is good."

That evening, as Sam was deeply absorbed in the *Times* crossword puzzle, frowning at a three letter word that had him stumped; and Caitlin was searching for the last piece of border on the rain forest puzzle, the phone rang. Caitlin looked up at the clock. "Late for anyone to call, isn't it?"

Without taking his eyes off the puzzle grid, Sam reached for the receiver.

"Hello." His eyebrows knotted into a straight line. His eyes flicked toward Caitlin, rested there for a second before darting downward.

Caitlin froze. Something was terribly wrong.

Finally, Sam looked into her eyes and whispered, "It's Mary. Her husband, Howard, was killed in a helicopter crash."

Caitlin sucked in he breath, experiencing both relief and guilt. Not anyone in her family. But it was Sam's brother-in-law.

"I'll make a plane reservation for Sacramento right away," Sam told his sister.

Caitlin had never met Mary nor her husband, a pilot in the Air Force. Now he was dead. Hot tears spilled down her cheeks.

"I know, Mary, but you must stay strong for the girls. There will be a lot to do. I'll call back as soon as I know my arrival time." Sam replaced the receiver.

"Oh, Sam, how awful, I'm so sorry." Caitlin moved onto his lap and pressed her face against his where their tears mixed in sorrow.

"I haven't seen Mary for five years. The girl's were six and eight. That was in Seattle right before Howard was sent to Guam. I should have gotten to know him better. I feel terrible that we didn't stay in touch."

"Sam, you must not feel guilty. Things happen, time passes. Now, you'll be there for Mary when she really needs you."

"Except for a few elderly aunts and uncles on the Rez, I'm the only one, Caitlin. My parents are dead; my older brother ran away when I was a kid and we never heard from him again."

"Do you want me to go with you?"

"Tempting but complicated. I'll only be gone a day or two. Let me see what the situation is out there first. What would we do with Malindi on such short notice? And what about the house?"

"Carolyn or Maggie could stay here; maybe Ed and Toby could take Malindi. We could work it out."

"That's true, but I want to leave early in the morning." He held her closer. "I hate to leave you alone."

This would be their first real separation. Something unclear and unsettling nibbled at the edges of her mind, but she pushed it aside.

"Sam, I'll be fine. Remember, I've been independent half my life. It's you I'm worried about. Now go, make your plane reservation."

"I have to get my credit card."

Before he stood, he brushed his lips across her cheek and she felt the cold empty space he left in passing. Her eyes darted to the door frame and rested on the floor where she had seen the hem of a white dress. She trembled as fear and reality washed over her. Why did she see things? Was she hallucinating? Then it hit her. She only saw things when Sam wasn't around.

❈

Sam placed a small carry-on bag containing toiletries and a few changes of clothing by the door. He looked so sad and her heart ached for him. She took his face between her hands and said, "Sam, I'll be fine, don't worry. You have to do this."

"I know, Caitlin, but I'll miss you."

"I'll miss you too, but you'll be back in a few days." She checked her watch. Five a.m. "We have to go, Sam."

❦

During the drive to the airport, they sat as close to each other as seat belts would allow.

"I'll call you every night around six o'clock," Sam said. He had just said the same thing a moment before. "Of course, California is three hours behind us. I think they're on daylight saving time. If for some reason I can't get to the phone, I'll call you at noon your time." He glanced at her. "Okay?"

"Yes, Sam."

"I'll call you on my layover in Chicago." His eyes moved to the dashboard clock. "It should be..."

She smiled and squeezed his arm. "Sam, mountain time, daylight saving, standard time — it gives me a headache. Just call me anytime. The middle of the night if you have to. I can be on a plane in an hour if you want."

The airport came into view, Sam took the lane for Departures. On the curb of U.S. Airways, he shooed away an airline porter and retrieved his small bag from the trunk. He leaned into the car and gave Malindi a reassuring pat on the head. Caitlin got out and they embraced until the cars behind began to pile up in the lane, honking.

"I love you, Sam."

"I love you, Caitlin." Sam spun on his heel and disappeared through the revolving door.

Caitlin climbed into the driver's seat fighting back tears. "Okay, Malindi, we are not going to get all mopey, you hear? It's only for two days at the most."

Malindi stared out the back window. Then she made a little coughing sound and lay down on the seat.

Caitlin focused on finding the airport exit that would get her on the Platt Bridge. Okay, the Philadelphia skyline was dead ahead, she was going in the right direction. Luckily, there were no overturned tractor trailers or jam-ups on the Schuylkill Expressway. Before the 30th Street exit she made a snap decision.

"We need a distraction, Malindi. How would you like to drive by the zoo?"

Malindi sat up and looked out the side window.

"Remember? You were quarantined there for a month when we came from Ah-free-kah?"

Malindi turned her head toward Caitlin.

"We won't be able to go in and see our friends today, but you can soak up some good smells and sounds, all right?"

❀

Caitlin drove into the empty 34th Street parking lot and pulled alongside the zoo's chain-link fence and stopped at the llama exhibit.

Malindi and the llamas scrutinized each other. "You mustn't sneer at those 'not from Ah-free-kah' animals, Malindi," Caitlin said. "They look like they might spit at you." After a while, she said, "Had enough animal enrichment? I have another idea. Let's be bad."

Apparently, Malindi knew what Caitlin had in mind because she trembled with excitement. Caitlin eased the car into the early morning crush of traffic and turned onto Zoological Drive: a one-way road traversing the perimeter of zoo grounds. Halfway around, she stopped and parked next to a high wooden fence.

"Stay in the car, Malindi," Caitlin said closing the door. "Let me see if the coast is clear." She peered through a gap between two chipped slats and saw three juvenile African wild dogs snorting and chuffing and pressing their noses through the slim space at the bottom.

"*Eeeh, eeh, eeh,*" they chittered. Caitlin chittered back. She scanned the rocky slope of the dog's exhibit and surveyed the public path below. The only sign of life was Shaba, the cheetah, sitting on a boulder in the adjoining yard, straining to get a better view of this exciting event.

Caitlin released Malindi, allowing her to communicate with her own kind. The dogs touched noses, crouched and chittered.

They clawed at the dirt. One of the dogs retrieved a large bone with fragments of flesh clinging to it and dropped it on the ground by the fence. This prompted another to engage in a tug of war over the bone with his den mate. The third dog raced around the yard, found a boomer ball and pushed it up against the fence. Malindi rolled on her side and twisted her head in a submissive posture.

All too soon, Caitlin coaxed Malindi away. "Sorry girl, we should go. The keeper will be here soon, and I have the painting group this morning."

Mournful hooing cries followed them as they drove away. Caitlin wondered if the visit had done Malindi and the dogs more harm than good.

CHAPTER ELEVEN

Estrelita sat in a chair by the fish pond waiting for the group to assemble.

Gina sported lime green and neon pink this morning. Her copper mop sprouted several twisted braids of purple. Her mother-in-law, Birdie, wore a modest, stone-washed blue denim dress from Talbot's, Chestnut Hill. Her gray hair was, as always, neatly combed and parted.

"Hello, I'm here." Joy arrived, transporting her supplies in an upright shopping cart. Due to debilitating arthritis, she moved slowly.

The phone in the living room rang; Caitlin dashed up the steps to answer it.

"Don't tell me; you're lost," she said. As many times as Laurel had made the trip from Havertown to Mount Airy, Laurel got lost. Caitlin gave directions and several minutes later, Laurel pulled up flustered and apologetic.

"I hear LaDonna coming," Gina said, grinning. "Sounds like she still has her red Vespa.

From scarlet hair to the tips of pointy red boots, there was nothing understated about LaDonna. "Hi guys," she said, waving red tipped fingers. Jerry Lee Lewis's "Balls of Fire" suddenly burst from her cell phone. "Sorry, just let me take this one call from Sweetie then I'll turn it off."

No outside interruptions was a standing rule. In the beginning, LaDonna tended to be a disruption, but Caitlin finally impressed upon her the importance of silence while they were working. Fortunately, Sam had telephoned earlier from Chicago.

"Okay," we're all here and ready to paint," Caitlin said. The model removed her robe and did several quick poses for their warm ups. For the long pose, she stood beside the fishpond pretending to pour water into it from a white enamel pitcher.

"I love this," Laurel said. "It reminds me of a Maxwell Parrish. I shall keep my palette filled with delicate colors."

Caitlin set the timer for half an hour. When it beeped, she marked the flagstones around the model's feet with masking tape, enabling Estrelita to take up the correct position again after the break. The painters milled around, checking each other's work, offering gentle critiques and encouragement.

"I don't know," Birdie said. "My work looks so childish."

"No, no," Caitlin responded. "You have bright, clear colors and your abstract figures remind me of Matisse and Chagall. Don't be so hard on yourself."

You are a remarkable woman, Caitlin thought. After teaching fifth grade at Springside School for Girls for fifty years, you pick up a paint brush for the first time? That's wonderful.

"I hear you're going to Italy next year to study with Giorgio Zafarelli," Caitlin said to Laurel

"Yes, I'm terribly excited. Come visit me, Caitlin."

"Thank you, Laurel. We'll see."

Joy leaned on a cane for support and circled the easels, expressing her envy and desire to draw a straight line.

"Joy, don't worry about a shaky line," Caitlin told her. "Whether or not it's your intention, your work is painterly. Some people try all their lives to get that effect." Joy laughed.

LaDonna snorted. "Yeah, just look at mine; I can't seem to control myself." Her canvas, splattered with blobs and streaks of paint, resembled an upside-down (or maybe sideways) Jackson Pollack. Caitlin believed that LaDonna had real talent but didn't take herself seriously. Instead, her artistic interests lay in the theater where she'd tried for years for a break through but hadn't gotten any further than working as a murder victim on a mystery-theme cruise ship. Rumors flew around town that the anonymous "Sweetie," was not only a married man but a high-ranking politician.

The group gathered around Caitlin's painting murmuring their approval. She had emphasized the roundness of Estrelita's breasts and hips, lightened the color of her hair as it fell over her shoulders and defined her reflection in the pool. The gleaming white of the pitcher appropriately drew the eye back to the center of the painting.

The timer beeped and they painted for another half an hour. At that time, Estrelita had to leave for a doctor's appointment but agreed to make up the time on a later date. Under these circumstances, usually one of the group posed for the remaining time. Birdie volunteered.

"Feel like dressing up, Birdie?" Caitlin asked. "I have one of Gina's costumes here. A beautiful tea dress from the musical *No, No, Nanette*."

"Sure." Birdie followed Caitlin into the house to where the dress hung in a first floor closet. Several minutes later, Birdie came down the steps wearing a deep rose colored dress of filmy chiffon. She held a white rose to her chin and positioned herself in front of a column under the pergola. "I feel like Ruby Keeler," she said.

Caitlin had forgotten to set the timer and they inadvertently worked well past the half hour. Birdie's slim, delicate figure was taking shape on Caitlin's paper when the model mildly protested that she needed a break.

"Oh, I'm sorry," Caitlin said. "I forgot. Somebody remind me next time, please."

They refilled their iced tea glasses and mingled. Birdie stretched and walked around before assuming her pose again. A half hour passed, the timer buzzed but Caitlin continued to work while the others gathered silently around her.

"Thank you, Caitlin," Birdie's voice finally registered in her brain. "You certainly have flattered me."

Caitlin stood back, did several head rolls to stretch the muscles in her neck. She opened her eyes and regarded her friends' expressions. Slowly, she turned toward her painting and felt her stomach lurch.

A young woman with lips curling in a charming smile stared back at her through emerald eyes. She wore a pure white dress and a red rose was tucked over her ear. A calico cat rubbed against her ankles.

"It's lovely Caitlin. You have great imagination," Laurel said. "Nothing personal, Birdie," she added.

"I understand," Birdie said. "Caitlin is a true artist."

Caitlin felt her knees give way and she slumped into a chair. She told her friends that it was just the heat. Everyone agreed that since it was so hot it was best to call it a day. They bustled about, packed their things, discussed future schedules and possible models. As if in a trance, Caitlin went through the motions of saying goodbye.

Gina stayed behind. "Are you okay, Caitlin? You seem a little off. Are you missing Sam?"

"Yes, I miss him, but I don't know. The painting...I surprised myself, I guess."

Gina put a hand on her hip and pouted. "Listen, Caitlin. If there's anything goofy going on in that genius artist's brain of yours, let me know will you? Can't have you going off the deep end because of a painting. Cutting off your ear or running off to Madagascar or something, you know?"

Caitlin assured her that she was fine. After watching her leave, she returned to the yard and stood in front of her painting.

It was not unusual for her to block out her surroundings when she worked. Or to add a cat. But a calico cat? And what of this woman? Her eyes locked on the spirited green orbs. This was definitely the woman she had seen at the train station and in the carriage house window. Familiar feelings were taking hold: a sense of detachment, a sense of looking down on herself from above.

Maybe she was still hallucinating. Maybe she would for the rest of her life. At least these events were friendly. If they turned into the nightmare hallucinations of before — like being attacked by lions and wild beasts — only then would she tell Sam.

❀

Best to keep busy. Throughout the afternoon, Caitlin kept moving: she took a long walk with Malindi; she went to the Farmers Market for fresh fruits and vegetables; she stopped at the library to pick up a few books.

As she was watching a TV dinner rotate in the microwave the phone rang. Sam?

"Sorry I didn't call earlier but my plane was late. I miss you, Caitlin."

"I miss you too, Sam. Should I come out there?"

"I don't think that will be necessary. I'll be back before you know it. Mary and the girls are exhausted."

"Sam, how will they manage now?"

"They're putting up a brave front, and they've told me a hundred times how happy they are that I'm here. There's a service tomorrow at Beale Air Force Base, then a private burial in Seattle where Howard's parents live. His father's terminally ill; there are no brothers or sisters."

"So, you'll be going to Seattle next?"

"Yes. The military will take care of all the arrangements and expense. Mary is closing the house in Yuma City; they don't want to live here anymore."

"Where will they move to? Seattle?"

"Not sure yet."

"Oh, Sam, how sad. Is there anything I can do?"

"Not right now, Caitlin. I love you."

"Love you Sam."

They chatted a little longer, hanging on the air between them, dreading the silence to come.

Ten minutes later the phone rang again.

It was Toby. "Hi, Caitlin. Granddad told me about Sam's brother-in-law. I'm so sorry. Would you like to come over for dinner and watch television or something?"

"I had an early dinner, Toby, and I'm going to bed early. Thanks anyway." She didn't feel like company.

"Okay. Granddad wants to talk to you. Hang on."

"How are you doing, Caitlin?" Ed asked.

"I'll be okay, Ed."

There was a pause in the conversation; then Ed said, "Sam asked me to keep in touch with you while he's away. Maggie's coming Thursday, right?"

"Right." Sam really was worried about her. She assured Ed that she was fine and hung up.

She went into the library and surfed through hundreds of channels on the television but found nothing of interest. She slid a double disc, "Gypsy Kings," in the CD player and worked on the puzzle until it was half done. Some time later, pressing the leg of a golden lion tamarin in place, she told the hyacinth macaw, harpy eagle, and three toed sloth floating in the thick foliage of a subtropical tree, "Tomorrow. Tomorrow."

She took her cup into the kitchen and put it in the sink. "Where did all these dirty dishes come from?" She covered the dinnerware with water. "Tomorrow," she said. "Tomorrow." Malindi waited by the patio door for their evening ritual. "Okay, okay, I'm coming."

The night air felt cool and fresh on her face. Below, the creek gurgled unevenly. A breeze, moving in and out of the bushes, whispered past.

"Malindi, where are you?" Caitlin skipped down the steps in time to see something white dart toward the open garden gate. Like pieces in her puzzle, white joined ochre and black and formed the shape of Malindi.

Intoxicated by the sweet heavy fragrance of honeysuckle and roses, Caitlin entered the garden. Malindi was a dark shape against the luminescent columns of the carriage house but her nose pointed upward. Caitlin followed that gaze to an upstairs window.

The woman held a thick candle beneath her chin, the soft glow highlighted her cheekbones and soft curve of her upper lip. Her green eyes glinted in the candlelight and her smile broadened.

She nodded to Caitlin.

"What do you want?" Caitlin's voice was wispy in the night air. "What do you want? What can I do for you?"

Caitlin tried to read a message in the breeze, in the scent of flowers, in the rustle of leaves, in the space between them. But there was nothing. Nothing. The image in the window faded.

She strained her eyes and ears in the dark, feeling an eternity slip away. Deflated, she went inside, double checked the locks, went upstairs and climbed into her empty bed.

I'm not afraid, just puzzled, she told herself. Tomorrow I'll call Maggie and ask her to go into the carriage house with me. Maggie knows everything.

With that thought in mind, she fell into a deep sleep. Malindi slept soundly too.

❀

samdogbaba walked into a dark and noisy cave and disappeared. He did not respond to Malindi's calls. She rose and flew from the strange place. Skimming above the ground, she sailed over speeding cars until she came to a wide river. She jumped in.

She swam underwater past a big fat hippo, the river horse, munching on grasses anchored to the river bottom. Her calf did a somersault and flashed the pink soles of his feet, inviting Malindi to play. Soft and slimy aqua grasses brushed against Malindi's sleek pelt. The river narrowed, she surfaced, pulled herself up on the bank and found herself in a subterranean tunnel lit by sparkling fireflies.

Primitive stick drawings covered the rock walls. Pictures of men with spears killing herds of animals. Their screams and bellows were terrifying and hurt Malindi's sensitive ears. She bore ahead, running faster, anxious to reach the end of the tunnel.

Farther on, the side walls were overlaid with pictures of suckling baby animals. A nursing chimpanzee cradled in its mother's arms. A newborn giraffe bumping against mother's belly. An elephant calf tucked under mother's trunk-like forelegs. Gradually, the animal pictures faded, replaced by portraits of human babies and human mothers.

Faint at first, becoming louder, childlike laughter echoed through the chamber. Malindi stopped, turned around and saw a dark-haired toddler approaching with short, unsteady steps. Her plump arms reached out to her, fingers wiggling. Malindi lowered her body and allowed the child to climb onto her back. Clutching handfuls of fur for support, the little one laughed with glee as they raced toward the light at the end of the tunnel.

CHAPTER TWELVE

"Still in bed, Caitlin? It's five o'clock here. Mary and the girls are getting dressed." Sam was hot and tired, the temperature was already soaring over one hundred degrees.

"How are they doing, Sam?"

"I think they're still in shock. The service will be rough on them. I'm making breakfast."

"They're so lucky to have you. I'm lucky too. I love you."

"Love you too, Caitlin."

She burrowed underneath her lightweight comforter. Strange that Sam was in the dark and she was waking up to a bright, sunshiny day. Could time travel be just a matter of moving the hands forward or backward on a clock?

Maggie was willing to switch her regular day at Cogslea. Caitlin was working on a third cup of coffee when Maggie arrived whistling, "The Bridge on the River Kwai."

"One of my clients has an African gray parrot that whistles that song straight through." Maggie pursed her lips and whistled the first two bars again. "Just like that. Isn't that amazing?"

"Mmmm." Caitlin slid the security bolts into place.

Maggie cracked a crooked smile. "He says a few other things that I won't repeat. Now, sit, Malindi. I have a biscuit for you." Malindi sat, took the eight ounce, homemade bone-shaped crunchy wheat cake into her mouth, lay down and demolished the treat in record time.

"Did you know that poachers smuggle macaws from South America into this country in suitcases and inside nylon stockings or cardboard tubes? Almost all the birds die before they get here. I saw a program about it on Channel 12. It's criminal."

"Yes, it is."

Maggie whistled herself to the closet where her muffled voice cited statistics on the number of rhinos killed for their horn. "To make dagger handles for men in some middle eastern country. A whole rhino killed for a knife. Isn't that awful?" She emerged from the closet and lapsed into her Irish brogue. "Wiv your leave then, missus, I'll be startin' upstairs."

"Listen, Maggie, have you ever been in the carriage house?"

"Sure and I have, missus. When the lord and lady keeps tenants, I've cleaned the carriage house too, I have."

"I'd like to see it," Caitlin said, making an effort to sound casual. "Would you mind going over there with me? Maybe after lunch?"

"Sure and I'd be glad to. I brought my lunch today." She went up the steps singing, "I'm Only a Bird in a Gilded Cage."

Ten pages into Ann Tyler's, *Celestial Navigation*, Caitlin realized she'd read the book before. She had to take her mind off the visit to the carriage house She attacked the picture puzzle. Only two pieces of complicated ground cover surfaced; she gave up and leaned back in the chair, sighing. Malindi sensed an opportunity for a walk and got her leash.

"Okay, girl, you have the right idea. We need to walk. Let me tell Maggie we're going out." She listened at the bottom of the steps and heard Maggie imitating a parrot. Or was she talking to the ghost of Violet Oakley?

"Okay, missus. We're almost finished the bedrooms, we are. *Ta, ta.*"

We? "Come on, Malindi, let's go."

❀

A group of cyclists neglected to warn of their approach and whizzed past an elderly couple strolling on the path's edge. "Young whippersnappers," the old man grumbled. Caitlin shook her head and *tch tched*. At Harper's Meadow, she turned around and headed back to the inn. Several people asked her what breed of dog Malindi was. She knew the public's desire to own exotic species was on the rise, so she gave her standard answer: "She's mixed." Not that anyone could acquire an African wild dog: worldwide, only zoos and a few educational institutions housed the species.

While Caitlin waited for a coffee and toasted bagel at the inn's take-out window, Malindi sat still, mesmerized by the peeping of barn swallow chicks huddling in mud nests plastered to the roof and walls of the adjacent park guard horse stalls.

"Come on, Malindi, forget the swallows, watch the ducks and geese instead."

Below the park bench where Caitlin sat, the waterfowl soon gave up their quest for tidbits and paddled to where a boy with a bag of bread held more promise. On the opposite bank, a golden retriever jumped in to retrieve a stick: an act he repeated over and over and over.

"Here's for your good behavior," Caitlin cooed, and popped the last of her bagel into Malindi's mouth.

❀

"Just finishing my lunch," Maggie said. "Did you have a nice walk?"

"Yes, we did, didn't we Malindi? I had something to eat at the inn, so anytime you're ready to go over to the carriage house is fine with me." Caitlin wanted to scream and jump up and down

99

because Maggie was chewing and chewing and chewing.

When her jaws stopped moving, Maggie said, "You should chew every mouthful fifty-six times. For your digestion."

It seemed to take forever for her to brush the crumbs from her lap and get up from her chair. Meanwhile, Caitlin removed the loop of keys from the key board in the pantry and waited by the door for Maggie. Malindi sensed the excitement of the adventure and paced from kitchen to pantry.

On the way to the carriage house, Maggie talked about the former tenant, an eccentric old woman who was once a dancer in the Ziegfield Follies. "Says she was Bert Lahr's sidekick. Always dressed to the nines. Never saw her without face paint and tons of gaudy jewelry. Just like Joan Crawford. La dee dah."

Maggie flipped her hand to the garage underneath the upstairs apartment. "Nothin' to see in there. We'll go right upstairs. I haven't been up in a few months." She lifted her nose and sniffed. "Probably dusty. 'Tis a sweet, tidy little abode. Wouldn't mind livin' here meself." She waited while Caitlin struggled with the lock. "Here let me do it. See, you have to push the key in a little further 'til it clicks. Now, there it is." The heavy door swung open. Caitlin peered over Maggie's shoulder, half expecting to see the woman in white standing inside.

They faced a narrow, steep stairway with a thin iron railing on one side. Malindi ran up the steps and sat at the top. Warm, dusty air smelling of old wallpaper paste and vinegar wafted down. A spicy scent of roses drifted past. Maggie ascended first and moved about, still rattling on about the former tenant.

Caitlin went up and turned into a charming Victorian room, rich in velvety reds and gold trim. A flash of silver in the corner of the room caught her eye. She spun around and came face to face with the woman she had seen in the window, in the train station, and in her painting. The last thing she remembered was the floor coming up to meet her.

Two piercing blue spots in a ruddy circle floated over her. When her eyes focused she saw Maggie's face.

"My, you gave me a scare. I was in the bedroom moving a lamp to the other side of the bed—where it belongs, by the way—when I heard the crash.

"What happened?" Caitlin tried to sit up.

"Don't move." Maggie pushed a velour pillow under Caitlin's head. "You must have had an attack of the vapors from the stuffy air. Or *ennui* as it used to be called." Maggie pronounced "ennui" with a French flair. "You're not pregnant are you?"

"No, I'm not." Caitlin made another attempt to sit up. She didn't resist when Maggie pushed her back down and adjusted the wet cloth that slipped from her forehead.

"Hmmm," Maggie said, sitting back on her haunches. "Still in all, I think you should go to Chestnut Hill Hospital and have somebody look at you. I read in a magazine that syncope can be a symptom of..."

Caitlin cut her off. "No! No hospital! I'm fine, really." She relaxed and tried to look fine.

"I don't know. How about seeing a doctor. Do you have a doctor here?"

"No, I don't. I didn't think I'd need one. Can I get up now?" Caitlin was afraid that Maggie would force her down again, but Maggie helped her over to the sofa. Cautiously, she scanned the room. When her eyes came to rest on the object that caused her to faint, she gasped.

In the corner, tilted to reflect the open doorway at the top of the steps, a full length, freestanding oval mirror stood in shadow. Maggie followed Caitlin's line of vision and walked over to the mirror. From force of habit, she ran her fingers over the smooth oak finish of the antique frame, testing for dust. She angled her stance to see Caitlin's reflection. Caitlin sat on the edge of the sofa with a rigid back; her face was pale, her thumbs were tucked inside clenched fists.

In an even tone, Maggie said, "Okay, Caitlin, you saw

something in the mirror, didn't you?"

Caitlin nodded.

"Was it one of the ladies? One of the Red Rose Girls?"

"No, I've seen their photographs. Definitely not one of them." Despite the warm air Caitlin felt cold. "When I got to the top of the stairs I saw that mirror. And in it I saw...I saw a woman in a long white Victorian dress. She reached her hand out to me and smiled. She seemed friendly but it was such a shock. Then, I fainted, I guess."

"Ah, well, that's all it was then."

Caitlin's mouth flew open. *That's all?*

Maggie lowered herself onto a Queen Anne chair brocaded in red silk. She threw her leg over one arm, crumpling a lacey antimacassar. She fidgeted and swung her free leg. She reached in a jean pocket, found a pack of peppermint lifesavers, popped two in her mouth and held the pack out to Caitlin. Caitlin shook her head. Maggie insisted, Caitlin knew it would be futile to refuse again and took one.

"You know," Maggie said, rolling the candy to the side of her mouth, "I used to smoke three packs of ciggies a day. Coughed like a sailor. Two years ago I stopped, and from all the reports in the Journal of the American Medical Association, I just added seven years to my life. But I gained fifteen pounds. One of these days I'm gonna start using Lee's exercise equipment to get rid of it."

"Good for you." Caitlin wondered how long it would take Maggie to get back to the subject of the mirror.

Maggie blew out a puff of peppermint air as if she were smoking a cigarette. "Did you ever crunch up a bunch of wintergreen lifesavers, stand in the dark and see the sparks fly?" She chortled. "I can always get my nieces and nephews going on that one."

Caitlin sighed and relaxed. Maggie was in control of the situation. "I never smoked. Do you ever miss it?"

"Ha," Maggie retorted. "Only every day of my life. But anyway, let's get back to what you saw. Did you recognize the woman?"

Good grief. They were discussing an apparition; how could

Maggie be this nonchalant? Her cavalier attitude helped to calm her nerves though. "No, Maggie, I didn't recognize her, although..."

"Although?" Maggie's rust-colored eyebrows rose to a point on her forehead.

"Well, I thought I saw her once at Allens Lane train station.

"Uh, huh. And?"

"And I saw her at night, up here in the window holding a candle." Caitlin looked toward the windows.

Maggie eyed the window sills. "I could check for candle wax, but there won't be any." To make sure, she got up and looked quickly at both sills. "Could use some paint, though." She settled back on the chair. "Anything else?"

This isn't so bad. Talking about it certainly helped. "I saw the hem of her dress swishing past the door in the library." Maggie looked wise and nodded her head. "Yesterday, one of the women in my painting group posed and my portrait turned out to be the woman in white."

Maggie's eyes grew round; she whistled a long screechy note that made Malindi's ears twist. "Well, then. Let's go see what this lady looks like. Come on."

Caitlin stood up too fast. She felt a little woozy but followed Maggie down the steps. A soft breeze scented with roses caressed her face. A soft voice whispered in her ear.

"*Help her. Help Nessa find her child. Where we failed, you can succeed.*"

Startled, Caitlin lost her balance and tumbled into Maggie. Maggie struggled to keep upright but her legs gave way and they both spun down the last few steps and landed on Malindi.

Maggie straightened up. "Whoa, what happened?"

Caitlin sat on the bottom step and put her hand to her head. "Ugh. I don't know. I slipped or something. I'm sorry."

"No problem." Maggie ran her hand over the Malindi's head and body. "Malindi seems no worse for wear. Are you sure you're all right, Caitlin?"

"I'm fine." Caitlin stood, moved her limbs to make sure. Are you okay?"

"Don't worry about me, I'm built of iron. But you look a sight. Come on, let's go back to the house and I'll fix you a good, strong cuppa." Maggie pulled the door shut and locked it.

In the kitchen, Maggie swizzled a dollop of honey into a large mug of steaming Twinings tea and put it in front of Caitlin. The soothing brew helped to warm her icy insides. Maggie tapped her spoon on the side of her cup. Soon her foot began to jiggle. Caitlin watched Maggie and was glad she never smoked nor had to pay penance for giving it up.

"Now, who could this mysterious woman in white be?" Maggie asked. "And how can we find out?"

And what does she want from me? Caitlin pondered. She suddenly realized that her head hurt; she put her hand to her forehead, pushed back her hair and rubbed her temple.

"Holy cow. You've got a giant goose egg on your head." Maggie jumped up, got a dish towel and wrapped it around crushed ice. "Hold this on. Phew, you really whacked yourself. Okay, that's it. You need to go to the hospital. You could have a concussion. I'll run you up there right now."

Caitlin resisted. Her hospital stay in Nairobi was still horribly fresh. "I'm really okay, Maggie. Besides, you have another appointment."

"Posh, tosh. I'm gonna call Ed. He goes to a doctor close by." Maggie found Ed's number and dialed. The conversation was brief: she told him that Caitlin had banged her head and she thought a doctor should look at her. She listened for a few seconds, said "Okay," and hung up. "Ed's coming right over."

Up against such a formidable force, Caitlin surrendered. She'd see a doctor. She took a sip of tea and studied the unflappable woman. "Maggie, have you ever seen a ghost or had a vision?"

Maggie stirred a spoonful of honey into her tea and then another. "Yeah, I have. Or I should say didn't see. I was about twelve years old, baby-sitting my niece in Fishtown and watching television when the steps in the living room creaked just like someone was walking up them. Then an unseen ball bounced down the steps. It happened several times but I never told my aunt."

Caitlin leaned forward in her chair as Maggie continued.

"Then one summer I was waitressing at the Doylestown Inn—a place that's notorious for their resident ghosts. I had a little room on the third floor. Every single night, I would hang my clothes on the clothes tree and every single morning they would be in a pile on the floor. So were the towels in the bathroom. Strangest thing."

"But, did you ever actually see a ghost?"

"No, but I know they're there."

"How about in this house?"

"I talk to Miss Oakley all the time," Maggie said, without blinking an eye.

"But, do you see her? And what do you talk about?"

"No, I don't see her because she's always behind me. We talk mostly about women's rights, that sort of thing. She encourages me to be independent, think my own mind, be my own person. You know—like her."

Most people would think this type of conversation surreal, but Caitlin knew what it was like to hallucinate. Were these experiences such a stretch? The words burst out, "Maggie, do you think I'm crazy?"

Maggie's response was one of puzzlement. "Why in the world would I think that? Somebody said, 'There are more things in heaven and earth than man has ever dreamed of.' Was it a poet? Walt Whitman? I can't remember, I'm gonna hafta look it up. "

Caitlin sighed.

"So, Miss Caitlin, we need to find out who this woman is. We could start in the library and look for her picture. And you have to show me the painting you did of her."

"Right." Caitlin rose to retrieve her painting, but at that moment Ed came to the door. "Maggie, don't tell him about the woman in white or anything else, okay?"

Maggie circled her index finger and thumb, winked and opened the door.

Ed did not comment on Caitlin's pallid face nor the bump on her forehead. He sat down at the table and Maggie poured him a cup of tea.

"I talked to Dr. Truet. He'll see you in twenty minutes. His office is only five minutes away on Wissahickon Avenue. The doctor's in his early nineties, a bit old fashioned, yet up on all modern medicine. He doesn't see many patients now, but he still makes house calls, and I don't know any doctor who does that anymore. Last winter when I had the flu, he came out in a blinding snowstorm to see me."

Caitlin eyes brimmed with tears. "Thank you, Ed. You too, Maggie. It's nice to have people like you to rely on, especially while Sam's away."

"Have you heard from him?" Ed asked.

"Yes, he's called several times." She glanced at the clock, and reminded Maggie of her next cleaning job. Maggie said she could cancel, but Ed and Caitlin thought it unnecessary.

"All right, I'll go then." Midway across the room, Maggie stopped and tossed her keys up in the air. "How about if I come back this evening and spend the night? We could go over the books and look at that painting, Caitlin."

Ed's eyes shot from Maggie to Caitlin who was nodding her head. "We should go, now," he said. "I'll drive. Come on, Malindi."

CHAPTER THIRTEEN

The doctor lived in a rambling three-story house on a large corner lot with medical offices on the first floor. The yard was richly endowed with Greek statues, gazebos, and scattered patches of bright wildflowers. Two opposing wooden benches flanking the front door were meant to seat an overflow of patients, but Caitlin was the only patient today. Ed walked her into the waiting room and dinged a silver service bell on the unmanned receptionist's desk. The doctor materialized immediately in the doorway of his office.

"Hello, Ed. How are you?" he said, pumping Ed's hand.

"I'm good, John. Real good, thanks to you. How's the family?"

"Splendid. My grandson's taking the wife and me to Egypt. This will be my fifth trip. Can't wait to try out my new camera." He turned to Caitlin. "This must be the patient."

"Yes...." Ed began, but a scratching noise at the front door made them all turn in that direction. "What the devil?" Ed opened the door and Malindi walked in carrying a red rose in her mouth. She walked up to Dr. Truet, lay the flower at his feet and sat down.

"Malindi, what did you do? How did you get out of the car?" Caitlin felt the room closing in on her. Was she dreaming? What was going on here?

"I'm sure I closed and locked the car door," Ed said, his face pinched. "I'm sorry, Caitlin; this is the second time she got away on my watch."

Caitlin was beyond puzzled. "Malindi, why did you break off that rose?"

"Oh, I don't think she did; I must have dropped it this morning." Dr. Truet picked up the rose and added it to a vase filled with roses on the receptionist's desk. "I cut a few every morning when they're in bloom. Been doing it for years."

"Yes, well, we'll go out to wait in the car," Ed said, leading Malindi out the door. His hand trembled on the knob.

Caitlin followed Dr. Truet through his consulting office into the adjoining examining room where everything was worn, white, enameled, and sparkling clean.

"I hear you took a fall and bumped your noggin. Let's take a look."

Caitlin climbed on the examining table and pushed aside the lock of hair that fell across her forehead.

"Mmm, that's quite a lump you have there, young lady." He pressed his fingers lightly around the perimeter of the raised area. Gently, he raised each eyelid with his thumb.

He smiled and patted her knee. "I think you'll live, but you'll have a mighty colorful bruise for a week or so. Put ice on it through tomorrow and don't go to sleep until around eleven tonight. Will someone be there with you? Wouldn't want you going into a coma or anything. Just kidding." He chuckled. "Don't worry. You'll be fine."

Nonetheless, Caitlin was glad that Maggie offered to stay over night.

"Let's check out the old ticker and take your blood pressure while you're here." He pressed the stethoscope to her chest, asked her to cough, then cocked his head, apparently listening for sounds that the instrument could not pick up.

The doctor's face was close to hers. What a lovely pink complexion he has, she could not help thinking. So few wrinkles and crinkles.

"Everything okay there. "Let's check your blood pressure." He wrapped the cuff so tight around her arm she thought she'd have to ask him to stop pumping. Still, she'd rather pass out than hurt the good doctor's feelings.

"Hmm. A tad low, nothing to worry about. Better than being on the high side." Her pulse was slightly fast, her temperature normal.

She felt his eyes on her clenched fists.

"Suppose we go into my office. All this white is making me snow blind," he said.

The office walls were covered with framed medical degrees, citations for service in the first and second world wars, a copy of the Hippocratic oath, family pictures, photographs of the doctor with former presidents and dignitaries. Caitlin sat down on a tattered green leather desk chair. Her eyes moved to an engraving of The Doctor by Samuel Luke Fildes: a famous Victorian print depicting a bedside scene of a doctor tending a little girl. The doctor looked serious and Caitlin just knew the little girl was going to die.

Dr. Truet absorbed the creaking jolt of his rickety swivel chair with familiarity. He tapped the tips of his fingers together in a prayer-like position and cleared his throat.

"Suppose you tell me what happened, young lady."

I'm in for it now. He reminded her of her grandfather, the one person in her family who could read her mind. He even looked like him, with crisp white hair side-parted in a line straight as an arrow. He wore similar clothes: black pants, bow tie, and a white shirt with sleeves rolled to the elbow.

"I climbed a flight of stairs into a stuffy room and passed out," she said.

He continued to tap his fingers together. "Eat anything today?"

"Half a bagel with cream cheese. And a lot of coffee."

"Hmm. You're not pregnant are you? We could cut to the chase if that were so."

Caitlin said she was certain she was not pregnant.

"Drink plenty of water? In this humid weather you need to be mindful of that."

She thought for a minute. "No, maybe not. I did go for a long walk this morning."

"Mmm, hmm, need I say more? How'd you get that bump on your head, anyway?"

"I felt a little dizzy when I went downstairs and I tripped. Maggie and my dog broke my fall, thank goodness, but I must have banged my head on a step or the wall or something."

Dr. Truet's cornflower blue eyes held Caitlin's. Self-conscious, she unwrapped her arms and tried to make her hands look relaxed. She knew all this did not escape the doctor's attention. He had the wisdom of decades of medical practice and observations of the human character.

"Caitlin, I'm concluding that you are a healthy young woman but a little on the nervous side right now." He paused, then he said, "Ever have mental problems?"

Sinking back in her chair, Caitlin sighed. There was no denying grandfather the truth.

"Yes. When I was in Africa two years ago, I happened to be in Rwanda when genocide broke out." Her voice cracked and she took a moment to regain her composure. "We were airlifted to a hospital in Nairobi and I was treated for shock. They misdiagnosed me with malaria and gave me huge amounts of Luriam—not the brand of anti-malarial drug I had been taking. I began to hallucinate. They kept me for over four weeks and my episodes grew worse. It was horrible, frightening. A friend finally checked me out. It took months for the drug to wear off. When I returned to the states, I saw a psychiatrist for post-traumatic stress disorder. So far, I've been able to deal with it. I'm okay now."

"Hmm, Luriam." Dr. Truet narrowed his eyes and rose from his chair. He opened the door of a glass covered bookcase and ran his index finger over plastic covered journals. He drew one out, closed the cabinet and sat down. Seconds later he tapped his finger on a page, laid the journal flat on the desk, adjusted his glasses and read the article.

"Mmmn hmm," he said, easing back in his rickety chair. "Just as I remember. That's a powerful and dangerous drug, Caitlin. Common side effects include, but are not limited to those of post-traumatic stress disorder. Luriam has been linked to neuropsyciatric adverse events such as emotional problems, seizures, and visual and auditory hallucinations, depression, and suicide.

Her voice trembled. "I know."

"Afraid of hallucinating again?"

"Yes."

Dr. Truet pursed his lips. "Yup, fear of recurrence can do as much harm as the problem itself. Do you stay in contact with your psychiatrist?"

"Yes."

"Ever take antidepressants?"

"No, I don't like to take medications."

He smiled broadly, showing all his perfectly preserved teeth. "Didn't think so."

She smiled back and felt better.

"I don't think I can do any more for you, Caitlin, except to give you a bottle of B12's. Do you take vitamins?" She shook her head. "You might be a little anemic, but I don't see the need for a blood test. B12's will give you a boost." He rose from his chair and went back into the exam room. She could hear him rummaging through a cabinet, still talking. When he returned he was expounding the benefits of proper diet and vitamins. He handed her a huge bottle of B12's.

He waved his hand when she asked for the bill. "A courtesy for my old friend, Ed. Just take care of yourself. Call me in a day or two, or anytime. Call me in Egypt if you want."

She assured him that she would. On the way out, she paused, noticing for the first time the artwork in the waiting room. All the subjects were children. There were popular prints by Renoir, Degas, Mary Cassatt, plus several originals by local artists unknown to her. One, a watercolor, pulled her in like a magnet.

The subject was a toddler with shiny black hair and a sweet expression. She was eating an apple in an orchard. At her feet sat a calico cat.

"Charming, isn't it?" Dr. Truet's voice came from behind. "I knew the artist."

Caitlin's heart fluttered. She tried to make out the signature. "Laura Enfield," the doctor said.

She turned around. "What can you tell me about her?"

Dr. Truet's eyes looked sad. "She lived at Cogslea one summer, studying art with Violet Oakley. I was often invited to their afternoon teas; that's how I met Laura."

"Did she ever wear long white dresses?"

"Funny you should ask. Yes, she did. The Cogslea ladies strongly resisted conformity to modern dress and frequently wore Victorian styles. Laura adopted the habit." He tipped his head toward the painting. "Too bad she never received recognition as an artist. I bought this painting from her for a paltry amount of money."

"What happened to her?"

Dr. Truet looked even sadder. "I don't know. I courted Laura that summer, but towards the end, I felt it my duty to join the army. I was shipped off to France to fight the huns in the Great War. I had hoped that Laura would understand and wait for me, but she didn't. She went back to England and I never heard from her again."

Caitlin waited for the doctor's sadness to pass. "Who was the child in the painting?"

"I don't know; I never saw her at Cogslea." A small sigh escaped his lips. "When I bought the painting, I asked Laura about the child. Her response was strange; she acted as if it was a mystery or something. As a matter of fact, she asked *me* if I knew who the child was. I had assumed it was one of the artists' models, but then I heard that they more often painted from photos." He chuckled. "I believe the ladies did not like children very much."

Caitlin's hand went up to touch Laura's signature. She withdrew it and felt obligated to explain her interest.

"I'm doing research on the Red Rose Girls and their protégés."

Without hesitation, the doctor lifted the painting from the wall.

"I'd be happy to lend it to you. These pictures all have to come down anyway; I'm having the office painted while I'm in Egypt."

❊

Caitlin skipped down the path to the car. Ed wondered why she was clutching a large flat package wrapped in newspaper so tightly against her chest.

CHAPTER FOURTEEN

S am called that evening. They were about to leave for Seattle, he told her. The memorial service and burial would be tomorrow. Caitlin told him she would order flowers for the service.

Shortly after the call, Maggie arrived with bags of food and dumped them on the kitchen table. "I stopped at the Ac-a-me and the Chinee take-out on Ridge."

Caitlin breathed in the sweet, steaming fragrance of brown paper bag, shrimp, and soy sauce. "This is wonderful." A pinch in her stomach told her that she hadn't eaten in a while.

"I know you don't eat meat—except for fish. I hope you don't mind if I eat all the grandfather chicken."

"Goodness no, Maggie. There's plenty else." Caitlin heaped fried brown rice, shrimp with cashews, and Mu Shu vegetables on her plate and pushed it all to one side to make room for a leek cake.

"*Hamlet!*" Maggie spat out and threw down her chopsticks.

"What?" Caitlin thought Maggie was cursing the chopsticks.

Maggie changed to a fork and speared a piece of chicken. "Hamlet, Hamlet. 'There are more things in heaven and earth,' blah, blah, blah. It's from *Hamlet*. I just remembered."

"Oh. Right."

"So what's this picture you told me about over the phone,

Caitlin?"

"Talk about coincidence, Maggie, I'll let you see for yourself."

Her rule of fifty-six chews before swallowing forgotten, Maggie scraped the last morsel out of her carton before Caitlin was half way through her dinner. A few shrimp landed in Malindi's bowl, Caitlin covered her own plate with waxed paper and put it in the refrigerator.

"Good idea. We hafta save room for candy and ice cream," Maggie said.

Earlier, Caitlin had removed from the living room wall two large oil paintings. She then hung, side by side, her clothesline painting and Laura's orchard scene on loan from Dr. Truet.

"Phew," Maggie exclaimed. "I'm no art critic, but I know what I see. Those two kids are one and the same."

Caitlin flopped on a sofa in front of the paintings and Maggie followed suit.

"What do you suppose it means?" Caitlin asked.

"Dunno. Who's the artist?"

Caitlin told Maggie everything that Dr. Truet had told her. "Did you ever hear of Laura Enfield, Maggie?"

"Nope, but the next step is to find out more about her and see if there are any other paintings of that little tyke."

"There are books in the library on the Red Rose Girls. We could start there."

For reference, they propped the two paintings on the wide window seat under the front window in the library. Caitlin added the portrait she had done of Birdie/Laura.

They scanned text for any mention of Laura Enfield. They examined every photograph for someone who resembled her or the dark-haired child. Two hours later, they came up empty handed, disappointed, and bleary eyed.

Maggie snapped shut a thin volume and placed it on top of the "finished" stack. "Let's have ice cream," she said. She crumpled up an empty bag of licorice allsorts and walked stiff-legged to the kitchen. "Not used to sitting so long."

Caitlin made a pot of coffee and Maggie scooped large portions of ice cream into bowls.

At the table, Maggie divided the fortune cookies. "Two for you and two for me." She cracked one open and straightened the paper. *"Man of great wisdom go far,"* she quoted. "Well, they got that half right. Ha, women go farther. Here's my next one." She laughed and handed the tiny slip to Caitlin.

"Beware the chives of March?" Caitlin laughed. "The chives? I love it. Here's mine. What? *'Play cards right, win a Brazilian dollars.'* Brazilian?"

Maggie chortled. "Wonder what the exchange rate for that is. What's your next one?"

Caitlin unrolled the last fortune and cleared her throat.

"What?" Maggie said.

Puzzled, Caitlin recited, *"Sampler the clues around you."*

"Are you sure you're reading that right, Caitlin? Let me see it." Caitlin slid the fortune across the table. "Humpf. I know the Chinese are inscrutable, but what the heck do they mean by this? Do they mean *sample*? Sample the clues around you?" The corners of her mouth pulled down, and she folded her arms across her chest. "And how in the name of all that's holy do the Chinese know we're searching for clues?"

"I don't know Maggie, but we certainly looking for clues around us."

"Yeah." Maggie licked her spoon. "Darn, I wish I'd gotten pretzel sticks to go with this ice cream."

"I love that combination. There might be a bag in the pantry. I'll look.

Caitlin climbed a small step stool in the pantry and found a bag of salted pretzel sticks on the top shelf. As she was stepping down the doorbell rang. Startled and off balance, she grabbed the shelf's support beam and knocked to the floor a few tins and a small dark picture that hung on the wall.

"Jeez, you really are accident prone aren't you?" Maggie said, standing in the doorway. "Are you all right?"

"Fine." Actually, she felt stupid. "Would you get the door

please?" She bent to pick up the items on the floor.

"It's Ed," Maggie called.

Ed put his flashlight on the dryer and looked up as Caitlin was brushing cobwebs from her hair. "Just checking to see how you're doing."

"I'm good Ed. Come on in and have some ice cream with us. We're taking a break."

Ed folded his legs under the kitchen table. "A break from what?"

Maggie looked up from the counter where she was scooping out ice cream and gave Caitlin a hard look.

Ed waved away the bag of pretzels. "Hope you're getting some rest and not straining yourself."

Caitlin had not fully explained to Ed her interest in the painting she had carried out of the doctor's office. "Oh, just doing some research, that's all."

"Anything I can help you with? Research is my profession you know."

What harm was there in telling Ed about Laura Enfield. She just didn't want him to know that she was seeing ghosts — or whatever — because he might tell Sam.

"We're trying to find out about a Laura Enfield. Apparently, she was a protégé of Violet Oakley's. Do you know anything about her, Ed?"

"Hmm." Ed pulled on his nose and thought. "Can't say as I have. You might go through the books in the library."

The women exchanged a look. The paintings were still sitting on the window seat.

"Actually, that's what we were doing," Caitlin said. "But we didn't find anything."

"Did you check through the Hillman's historical data on Cogslea? It might include articles and photographs of the women."

"That's a good idea," Maggie piped in. "It's all in a file cabinet in Lee's office downstairs."

"We'll do that next."

"I have a friend at Bryn Mawr College Library you might

want to contact. They have a fine archival collection on the Red Rose Girls. Would you be interested in taking a run out there?"

"I would, Ed, yes." Caitlin felt hope rise.

"I'll call her first thing in the morning. Then you can contact her and set up an appointment."

"Thank you, Ed."

After a moment's pause, Ed asked, "Have you heard from Sam?"

Sam knew nothing of what was going on. Not of Laura Enfield, not of the research, and not of her fall.

"Yes, Ed. Sam called a little while ago."

Ed did not respond. Whatever he was thinking he kept to himself. He pushed back his chair and headed for the door. "I'll call you in the morning. Thanks for the ice cream."

Maggie locked the door. Pumped up with sugar and caffein, their interest did not flag, even though the remaining books in the library revealed nothing.

"Let's tackle the downstairs stuff." Maggie grabbed a bag of Mary Jane's and ripped it open with her teeth.

Malindi roused from her nap when she heard Caitlin moving away. "Come on, Malindi, we'll go down together. Don't worry, we won't use the elevator this time." Fat chance she'd ever do that again.

Maggie insisted on going down first. "To block your fall— should that happen again," she joked. "No ghosts down here. Except maybe in there." Maggie directed her flashlight beam under the open staircase and into the corner room, the oldest part of the house. "Hello, in there. Anybody home?" Maggie ducked under the steps, located a single exposed light bulb hanging from the ceiling in the center of the room. She pulled the string. "Any ghosts in here?"

Eerie figures danced on the whitewashed walls. Unease overtook Caitlin until she realized it was only their own shadows animated by the swinging light bulb.

"Don't even joke about it, Maggie."

"Sorry." Maggie sobered up. She waited for Caitlin to leave before switching off the light.

There was little room for Malindi in Lee's cluttered office, so she lay down outside the door.

"Believe it or not, there's a method to this madness, but Lee's the only one to understand it," Maggie said. They put one foot in front of the other and crossed the room through a narrow aisle to a small clearing in front of the file cabinets. "At least Marny had a hand in compiling the Cogslea information. It's well organized."

They started with a cabinet drawer marked "History of Cogslea." Maggie handed folders to Caitlin; she made a pile of them on the floor. Another drawer held rolled up schematics of architectural plans for remodeling Cogslea. "I think we can skip this, agreed?" Maggie asked. Caitlin nodded.

A third drawer contained the deed, the leases, the Woodward Company files, and an album of photographs of the house and grounds. Putting their heads together they perused the album but found nothing of value. They skimmed through the legal documents but found nothing useful there. They cleared two desk chairs, sat down and started on the history folders.

"Okay, we're still looking for the same thing," Caitlin said.

"Right-o, Boss." Maggie buried her head in a folder.

An hour later they concurred that there was no sign of Laura Enfield anywhere down here. Disappointed, Caitlin slumped in her chair and felt hope escape in an exasperated sigh.

"Maybe you'll find shumthing at Bryn Mawr," Maggie said, chewing on a piece of Mary Jane. "They'll hab more shtuff there, ah bet. Don gib up."

"I hope so." They put the materials back in the file drawers and trudged upstairs.

Caitlin went into the yard with Malindi and stared into the dark. There was nothing there. Nothing, nothing, nothing. She felt lost. Why am I bothering with this? It's a waste of time. Well, maybe not. I've learned more about the artists, the era, the house. Nothing is ever lost.

"Come on, Malindi. Stop dawdling," she said.

❀

"I'm going to sleep on the third floor under the eaves, if you don't mind," Maggie told her before retiring. "What with them slanted walls and gabled windows, I feel like I'm the poor, orphaned maid in a Dickens novel. Mistreated and underpaid but lucky to have a bed b'neath me. G'nite, Miss. I'll be leavin' at seven in the mornin', but I'll call later in the day to see if you've uncovered any clues."

"Goodnight, Maggie. Thanks for your help."

Caitlin closed the bedroom door. She gazed out the window, hoping to see Laura Enfield floating across the grass. Nothing. She pulled back the covers, slid into bed, and slept soundly without dreaming.

Malindi, on the other hand, had a vivid dream.

A sea of golden grass stretched toward the horizon where purple tinged clouds hung beneath an aquamarine sky. Even from afar, the skilled eye, seeking the out-of-place shape, could distinguish the living form from the landscape.

Suddenly, in one swift and uniform motion, heads lifted from grazing, prides from dozing, troops from foraging. Frightened eyes turned toward the unseen menace. Before the wind shifted and the acrid smell and crackling sounds carried on the air, instinct intercepted. Before the gray smoke rose, every living creature ran, crawled, or flew from death.

High atop a termite mound, the alpha male studied the situation. Formulating a plan of action, he calculated time and space. He gathered his pack, nipped at the heels of juveniles, guided and encouraged the old, found carriers for every pup too young to run.

Nearby, deep in an abandoned aardvark hole, a female African wild dog huddled with the sole surviving pup of her litter. She had an ugly tear on her side, ripped open by a hyena's yellow teeth during the pack's defense of their kill. The infected wound would soon cause her death.

The leader stood at the den's entrance and observed the ailing female. Abruptly, he turned, gave a silent command to Malindi, standing behind him. Malindi understood. Gently, she picked up the whimpering black and white mound of fur and backed out of the hole. The pup went limp, making it easier for Malindi to carry her burden across the scorched earth and biting flames. Smoke billowed up in front of Malindi; she lost sight of the pack. Panic welled up inside her. Then she heard the bell-like *hooing* of the alpha male: the communication call of her species. Malindi followed the sound and soon reached the refuge of the woodland. There, she delivered her sister into the safety of their extended family.

Footsteps pounded down the hall. Caitlin woke and saw a blurry figure standing in the doorway holding a large red object. The figure was shouting.

"Where is it? Where is it?"

Her vision cleared. Maggie was searching the room with her eyes, waving a tubular red metal object about.

"What?"

Maggie slowed down. "I thought I heard you cry, 'Fire.'"

Caitlin sat up in bed and shook her head to clear the fog of sleep from her brain. "No, Maggie, I didn't. Unless I was dreaming."

Maggie put the fire extinguisher on the floor and plopped on the chaise. "Jesus, Mary, and Joseph." She crossed her hand across her chest. "Had me scared for a minute. I was about to call 9-1-1. All we need is a fire and burn down *this* house just like the farmhouse that used to be here." She jumped up and left, taking Malindi with her. "I'm gonna leave now," she said from the hallway. "Call me later, okay? Come on Malindi, I'll let you out and get your breakfast."

Before it slipped away, Caitlin tried to remember if she had been dreaming about a fire. Nothing came to mind. She was grateful for that: the nightmares had all but disappeared since she and Sam were together.

When she heard the laundry room door clang shut, Caitlin

put on a wraparound sundress and went downstairs.

Caitlin's favorite coffee mug, cream, and an Entemann's crumb cake with a large section cut away sat on the kitchen table. A full pot of coffee sizzled on Mr. Coffee's warming plate.

Thank you Maggie. First thing every morning, Caitlin needed coffee. "To get my head on straight," her Aunt Jane used to say. Maggie had left a note: "Remember to drink lots of water. Look at the paper." Glaring headlines reported that there had been three heat-related deaths in the city yesterday. The temperature today would reach one hundred degrees and the humidity was rising.

Yes, she must remember to take a bottle of water with her if she went out. She opened the paper and spread it on the table. The phone rang.

"Hello, Mrs. Hillman?"

"No, who is this?"

"This is Megan from Jack's Tree Service. You wanted us to come out and trim some limbs. Could we set up an appointment?"

Oh right. Marny had told her about this. She grabbed the appointment book out of a basket on the counter and set up a date for the following week.

The phone was still rocking in the cradle when it rang again.

"Jenny?"

"Jenny? No, you have the wrong number."

She was expecting Ed's call about the visit to Bryn Mawr Library and grabbed the phone when it rang yet again.

"Mrs. Hillman, this is Gwen from Robertson's Florists. Would you like to order your fall plantings?"

"I don't understand."

"Your yearly delivery? Would you like to set up an appointment? I would suggest some showy shrubs like glossy abelia, clethra, or summer sweet, hypericum, or stewartia for the bare spots around the greenhouse."

"I'm sorry, could we do this at a later date?"

"Of course, there's plenty of time. Thank you, Mrs. Hillman. And thank you for using Robertson's."

The phone rang again. "Dear God in heaven." Caitlin was not used to this.

"Hi, Caitlin. It's Carolyn."

"Hey. Good morning."

"I just couldn't wait any longer to tell you. Guess who I ran into yesterday at Frank's Bar?"

"Carolyn, you know I'm not good at guessing games. Who?"

"Jess Miller."

Jess. Jess was a serious suitor of hers in college.

Carolyn waited for a response and received none. "He's so good-looking Caitlin and really very sweet."

"Yes, I know."

"Caitlin, he asked me out. I said yes. We're going to the Keswick to see Mary Black."

"Carolyn, that's lovely. Have a wonderful time."

"I've got to go; my boss just came in. I'll talk to you later."

Caitlin's elbows rested on the table, her head in the palms of her hands. She tried to ignore the phone but the jangling grated on her nerves.

"What?" she snapped.

"Caitlin?"

She sucked in her breath. "Sam. Oh, Sam. I'm sorry, but the phone's been ringing all morning.

"Are you all right?"

"Yes, yes. I'm fine."

"You sound funny."

"I'm fine, Sam. Tell me what you've been doing."

"The service is this afternoon, but as soon as I hang up, I'm going to make my plane reservation for tomorrow."

"Oh, good, let me know when you get in and I'll meet you."

"I love you."

"I love you too, Sam."

Malindi abandoned her favorite bone and trotted to the door to wait for the feet that were treading down the street. Minutes later there was a knock on the door, Ed and Toby on the other side.

"Good morning, Caitlin. I've been trying to call but your phone's been busy. I got in touch with the librarian at Bryn Mawr. She'll be happy to accommodate you today. Here's her name and phone number."

"Oh, Ed, thank you. I'd like to go this morning."

Toby and Malindi were wrestling on the floor. "I can stay with Malindi," Toby said. "It's too hot to take her with you."

Caitlin thanked him and said she'd be ready in an hour.

"Ah'll be bock," Toby did a silly strut out the door and across the courtyard. "My, he's cute," Caitlin said aloud. She could have sworn that Malindi grinned.

CHAPTER FIFTEEN

Caitlin showered and tossed her wet towel on the growing pile of dirty clothes on the floor. She needed to wear something cool but smart and dressed in a pale yellow *kanga* and white T-shirt. Outside, she leaned the two paintings against the steps. Photos could be useful at the library; she used up a roll of Polaroid film.

"Come on, Malindi," she called when finished. Malindi didn't come. The garden gate was open. "Now what?"

In the garden, at the corner of the house, behind rows of hollyhock and feathery butterfly bushes, Malindi was half submerged in a hole, digging frantically, clumps of dirt flying.

"Omigod. Malindi, what are you doing? Come away."

The damage could be repaired later: fill in the dirt and replant. For now, lock the gate and tell Toby to keep Malindi out of the garden. Her behavior was odd though. Like she was on a mission. Something more important than just chasing a small animal down a hole.

❀

The Philadelphia Story and Katharine Hepburn were Caitlin's only points of reference to the prosperous Philadelphia suburb of Bryn Mawr. Kate had actually attended Bryn Mawr College—one of several select schools on the main line within sight of each other, and one the "seven sisters" promoting higher education for women.

The college had the courtly look of an English school campus. Pairs or groups of women conversed quietly on their way to classes held in gray stone citadels. Caitlin parked and asked one of the students for directions to the library and received the information from a polite young woman who had a canny resemblance to Ms. Hepburn.

In the archives on the second floor of the library, three file boxes waited on a table for Caitlin to examine. They were from Special Collections and contained correspondence and photographs from the Henrietta Cozens Papers. A folded card on the table stated the library rules: "No food, no drink, no gum. Use pencils not pens. Sit at a cleared table with items to be examined laid flat. Use white cotton gloves, provided."

Caitlin opened the first book of photographs and turned a few pages. Omigod! How good is this? she wanted to shout to the timid looking student in the far corner reading. As fate would have it—like finding the perfect dress on the first rack that you reach for in Loehmann's—Laura Enfield surfaced early in her search. There was no mistaking those piercing eyes that looked at Caitlin as if to say, "Well, here I am. What took you so long?"

Laura stood with three other unidentified young women near Violet Oakley who was poised at an easel demonstrating a painting technique or something. Laura was the only one facing the camera. There was no caption or accompanying description, but Caitlin was certain that the picture had been taken in the living room at Cogslea.

"Do you know anything about this woman?" Caitlin asked the librarian.

The librarian placed Caitlin's Polaroid photograph of her Birdie/Laura painting next to the photo in the book. "No, but I'd say they are one and the same person. Would you like me to xerox our photograph for you?"

"That would be great, thanks." Caitlin leaned back to allow the librarian to remove the picture from its protective plastic sleeve.

"I'd like to look through the rest of these photographs to see if I can find anything else."

Beyond the staged poses and fixed stares typical of photographs of the time, traits of personality shone through. Jessie: large-boned and vigorous, serious, dignified. Elizabeth: petite, pretty, a good natured twinkle in her eye. Violet: graceful, intense, passionate, dramatic.

Their attire was conservative yet elegant. Early photos showed them in austere, manly outfits. As time passed, waistlines expanded, hair grayed, features relaxed. Their clothing softened to filmy tunics, lightweight free flowing dresses. If fashions changed, so did additions and deletions in Cogslea's landscape and furniture. A photo taken out front on St. George's Road showed a rural, unpaved street.

She put the album aside and examined the other materials but none yielded anything useful. She checked the correspondence inventory list and concluded that, according to Dr. Truet's background information on Laura, the "Incoming: subseries, Edith Emerson to Henrietta Cozens, 1917 to 1920" would be a good start." She opened the box and put aside several folders before selecting one titled, "Letters from England."

Edith Emerson was Violet Oakley's former student and assistant who later became Oakley's companion and roommate after the other Red Rose Girls moved out of Cogslea. The two women traveled to Europe quite often and Henrietta Cozens, who disliked travel, was the recipient of numerous letters from Edith.

Caitlin lost herself in detailed and vivid descriptions of the countryside, European churches, museums, operas, gala parties, and lectures and almost missed a post script on the reverse side of one of the earlier letters.

Edith wrote: "Violet has been charmed by a lovely and talented young girl named Laura Enfield. Her parents have agreed to let us bring her home so that Violet may advance Laura's artistic skills in her summer workshop. See you soon. Love, Edith."

"Yes, yes, there it is."

The reader in the corner jerked her head up.

"Sorry, I got carried away. Sorry."

Caitlin replaced the folders in the proper boxes, paid for the xerox copy and thanked the librarian for her help.

※

The brutal heat in the closed car nearly knocked her over. She rolled down all the windows, uncapped a bottle of water and gulped it down. Okay, so there's the photograph of Laura proving she did exist. And the letter confirms that she studied with Violet. But what did that actually reveal? And what's the next step? And would this ever end?

Caitlin pulled into heavy traffic, rolled up the windows and turned on the air conditioner. Sam would be home soon and she would forget this wild goose chase that was making her crazy. Then they would relax and enjoy their stay at Cogslea.

On City Line Avenue the car in front of her braked abruptly. In that moment an image jumped into her head. Excited, she turned to reach for the briefcase on the rear seat, but traffic began to move again and drivers behind her honked in irritation when she didn't go with it.

"Shut up." She gripped the steering wheel and turned into the first gas station and parked. She retrieved her briefcase and with trembling hands, removed the photograph from its folder.

"Yes, yes. Why did I not notice that before?" She couldn't wait to get home.

※

Barely able to contain herself, Caitlin parked at a crazy angle in the courtyard. She jumped out of the car, fumbled with the keys, swung open the door and banged it against the wall. In her haste to get inside she tripped over Malindi, waiting to greet her.

Toby called from the library. "Caitlin, hi."

"Hi, Toby, it's me."

She ran to the pantry. Hanging above yellowed photographs

of Cogslea and local homes of interest, there was something out of place, something that did not fit in with the rest of the subjects. She climbed to the top step of the step stool, reached up and retrieved the object.

Dusty and brown with age, it had a charred spot in the upper right corner. The eight by ten inch sampler looked insignificant, but it made Caitlin want to weep.

"What'cha doin'? Toby asked.

She climbed down and nudged him with her elbow. "Toby, come into the kitchen and I'll explain." She put the sampler on the table and placed the Bryn Mawr Library photograph next to it. "Look," she said. "Tell me what you see."

Toby saw it right away. "This sampler is the one on the wall in the photo. I'll get a magnifying glass from the library to check out the words." Toby was eager to join in Caitlin's adventure and sped away and back.

To get the best reading, Caitlin rotated the magnifying glass over the sampler in the photograph. "The words aren't real clear, but I'll read what I can aloud; you see if we have a match." She stumbled over the first few words but soon caught on to the old-fashioned shape of the letters.

"Gosh, Caitlin," Toby said.

"Now you read the words on the sampler, Toby."

"*For Nessa. See me in the leaves above. Feel me in the summer breeze. Hear me in the robin's song. Remember me. Destiny Wickham, Age fifteen, 1800.*"

"You only missed a few words, but it's the same, Caitlin. What does it mean?"

For Nessa. For Nessa: the words in her ear when she fell down the carriage house steps. "I'm not sure, Toby."

Caitlin cleaned away some of the dust and grime with a damp paper towel, making sure that moisture did not creep under the glass. There were butterflies and bees in the sampler's borders. The verse had been worked with white threads but, emphasized beneath the colorless heading and text, a rosy breasted robin sat on a branch full of red berries.

The clocks chimed six o'clock. "Toby, can you stay a few more minutes and help me look for something?"

Toby nodded. "Let me call Granddad first. Hey, Malindi, isn't this exciting? Just like the Hardy Boys looking for clues. Come on." After his phone call, Toby joined Caitlin in the library where Caitlin was sorting through a pile of books.

"Maggie and I already went through these, and we stuck a paper in the page in case it was something that could be important."

"What are we looking for Miss Marple?"

"Okay, Sherlock, we're looking for a photograph of a woman with her back to the camera. At the time, I wasn't sure if it was Laura Enfield."

"Laura Enfield?"

Caitlin explained that she was doing research on the woman in question. Silently, they checked the marked pages.

"Found it. Here it is Caitlin. Look." Toby put the opened book on the table. The photograph showed a young woman in Victorian dress standing in front of an easel with her back to the camera. Her right arm was outstretched, index finger pointing to the wall. Pointing to the sampler.

"Toby, where's the magnifying glass?"

"Right here, Caitlin. What do you see? Is it the same sampler?"

"I'm sure of it Toby, and there's something else..." On Laura's canvas there was a faint image of a toddler eating an apple. "This sketch evolved into Dr. Truet's painting."

Toby picked up the painting. "Wow, Caitlin. This is awesome."

"Mmm, hmm."

The doorbell rang. "That's probably Granddad. I'll get it."

"Did you find what you were looking for at Bryn Mawr, Caitlin?" Ed said, stepping into the house.

Caitlin brought the sampler with her. "Yes, I did. Now I need to know more about this sampler? Can you help me?"

Ed took the sampler from her. "Mmm, superb cross-stitch.

Embroidering white threads on a white background is hard on the eyes and difficult to achieve a detailed interpretation." Ed's lips moved slightly as he read the words to himself. "Such a nostalgic and sad verse for a fifteen year old girl." The back was covered with brown paper, most likely done when the sampler was reframed, Ed told her. "Would you mind if I removed the backing? It can't hurt."

At Caitlin's request, Toby went and got an exacto knife from Caitlin's paint box. "Here you are Granddad."

Carefully, Ed cut around the edges and peeled away the brown paper. He studied the reverse side of the sampler. "The stitched ends are expertly tied. This was the work of an experienced and talented stitcher."

"Do the words mean anything to you, Ed?"

"Not really." He sat down at the kitchen table, laced his fingers behind his head and closed his eyes.

"Think, Granddad, think. You might have come across something like this at the historical society."

Ed opened his eyes. "You know, Caitlin, there's something familiar about this young woman's work. The society has a collection of samplers out on loan." Caitlin frowned. "But there are more in storage." He picked up the sampler. "This one was damaged in a fire."

"The fire at the farmhouse — here," cried Toby.

"Mmm, I was thinking that. The date is applicable. Well, Caitlin, do you feel like another field trip? I'm scheduled to volunteer at the society tomorrow. Want to go?"

"Oh, yes, of course."

"Can I go too, Granddad? Please?"

"You have soccer practice tomorrow, remember?"

Toby pleaded with praying hands

"Okay, grandson. Only if you go an hour early next week for extra kicking exercises.

"What about Malindi?" Caitlin asked. "It's too hot to keep her in the car. I miss my open jeep sometimes. In the southwest, I was able to leave her alone in it."

Ed stroked his chin. "There's a little fenced in yard in the back that's not open to the public; we could take turns staying with her."

"Okay, let's do it. What time, Ed?"

"I'll pick you up at nine o'clock."

Caitlin walked them to the door. Toby said, "I'm a good detective, Caitlin. We'll crack this case together. Oh, I forgot to tell you Maggie called. She wants to know what's going on."

"I'll call her now. Goodnight." Caitlin closed the door and went into the kitchen to phone Maggie. The red message button on the answering machine was blinking. She pushed the button and listened to Sam's voice telling her that he wouldn't be able to leave as planned. He would call again later.

Oh, dear. I hope nothing's wrong.

She checked Sam's sister's number tacked to the message board and dialed. Maybe it's just a glitch in plane schedules. No one answered; she left a message on voice mail. Then she called Maggie.

"So, what did you learn Caitlin?"

Caitlin told her all that had happened and of tomorrow's planned visit to the Germantown Historical Society.

"Good luck, Caitlin. I'll rub the belly on my Buddha charm for extra measure. Call me."

"I will. See ya." Malindi nuzzled her head against Caitlin's thigh. "Wish you could talk, girl. I bet you have all the answers." Surely, the sampler will solve the mystery of Nessa and that would be the end of that.

❁

In the middle of the night, Malindi crept out of the bedroom and climbed the stairs to a third floor bedroom under the eaves. There, a woman sat in a white wicker rocking chair next to a narrow cot. The woman smelled good and her posture was non-threatening.

"Hello, Malindi. My name is Laura and this was my room when I stayed here in the summer of 1918. Would you like to hear my story? Yes? Please lie down and I will tell it to you."

Malindi obeyed.

"That was the most extraordinary summer of my life. When Ms. Oakley saw my art work and offered to take me back with her to attend her art classes in Philadelphia, I was overjoyed. I could not abide one more boring summer in stuffy old Clopsdale, England. My dear old parents were visibly relieved to have their boisterous seventeen year old daughter out of the house for a while.

Aside from improving my artistic skills, there were two noteworthy events that took place that summer: One: I was involved in a mystery. Two: I fell in love.

I shall elaborate first on the mystery.

Among the books on proper etiquette for young ladies that my parents packed for me, my elder brother slipped in a book titled *The Woman in White* by Wilkie Collins. The story was awfully exciting and influenced me to the point that I dressed in long white dresses like the protagonist. This was not unusual at Cogslea though, as Ms. Oakley and her friends did the same. They despised conformity in dress and traditional customs.

My mystery began one day when I was alone, painting down by the creek, working on the effect of light and shadow on water. A young woman dressed in animal skins approached me. I attributed the strangeness of her appearance and her ways to the eccentricities of the Americans. She said her name was Nessa and she was searching for her three year old daughter, Fiona.

I told her that I had not seen the child but would be happy to keep my eye out for her. "I see you are an artist," she said. "Would you mind copying, for future reference, a few of my portraits of Fiona." She removed from a sack several charming watercolors of a chubby, smiling little girl. I asked her where she had received her tutelage in art but she did not answer.

I filled my sketchbook with the child's image and made notes of her colouring: black hair, dark brown eyes, light brown skin. She thanked me, packed up her belongings and disappeared into the thicket like a wisp of smoke.

I had almost forgotten the incident until two days later one of Ms. Oakley's friends permitted her daughter to pose for us. The girl was similar in age and stature to Nessa's child, but with light hair and fair skin. I retrieved my sketchbook and showed Ms. Oakley and the students my drawings. None were acquainted with the child and soon lost interest, eager to get on with the lesson.

Our model sat in a white wicker chair in the garden reading a book. She wiggled and squirmed and her mother soon took her home. The point of the lesson was, Ms. Oakley stated, to finish the painting from memory. But, instead of the model, I had painted Fiona. I was astonished, as were the other girls. Ms. Oakley said that I was merely expanding my imagination. Pleased and encouraged, I executed several more paintings of the dark haired child, Fiona. My paintings were like advertisements for a lost child, if you will. I hoped that someone will recognize her.

I saw the strange woman in the woods only once more. One evening, Prince, Ms. Oakley's dog, and I were walking through the woods on the other side of the creek, when I heard someone singing. Prince sat and didn't move from the spot. I followed the sound and found Nessa sitting on the ground, rocking back and forth, repeating a verse over and over. She held in her arms a rag doll. I took out a notepad and pencil from the pocket of my smock—Ms. Oakley always wanted us to be prepared to make notes on our artistic observations—and wrote down the words:

"See me in the leaves above. Feel me in the summer breeze. Hear me in the robin's song. Remember me."

The melancholy words were familiar, but I could not place them at the time. I was deeply touched by Nessa's sorrow and vowed to try to find her missing child, as it was all so wonderfully gothic. I moved forward to tell her so, but tripped on a tree root and fell. When I looked up she was gone. I never saw her again. I inquired of everyone I met thereafter if they knew the missing child, but none had.

There is one more interesting piece of the puzzle in my mystery. A photographer from the *Bulletin* came to photograph Ms. Oakley at work. He was good-looking and I did flirt with him more than a little. As he was taking our picture with Ms. Oakley at my easel, I happened to notice for the first time a sampler on the wall. It had Nessa's verse on it. I'm afraid I made quite a scene and frightened off my handsome photographer, although I did enjoy being the center of attention. I always did. There would be other men, I would never be short of admirers.

Which brings me to my tale of romance. Unlike the uneventful summers in my stodgy and sleepy hometown, that summer was filled with laughter and dancing, soirees, afternoon teas, and outings. Ms. Oakley inspired me to be a free spirit like her. I answered to no one here. Well, maybe with the exception of my mother's friend, mean old Mrs. Stevenson. But, I was not above claiming a severe headache in order to escape her tedious company.

At one of Cogslea's afternoon teas, I met John Truet. He was tall and handsome with eyes the color of the cornflowers in the garden. I fell in love with him immediately and knew that he reciprocated my feelings. He escorted me to the theater, took me for carriage rides in the park, boating on the river. At each meeting, he never failed to bring me one red rose which I would tuck into my hair or pin on my bodice.

My handsome suitor was in his first year of medical school. Now this might have been detrimental to any plan for marriage, although he never expressed such a thought. It was of no matter to me: I lived for each glorious moment of every day and did not think of tomorrow.

One evening, at a grand and lovely party on Washington Square, ugly old Mrs. Stevenson poured poison in my ear. She told me that I had a rival and pointed with her ivory fan to the woman John was dancing with. I recovered beautifully and smiled at the nearest man. Dancing in his arms near John, I swooned, pretending to faint. This brought John to my side. He carried me to a chaise on the outside porch and loosened the buttons of my dress. I drew him to me and begged him to take me home. I was such a pretty sight, with flushed cheeks and heaving bosom. We left for Cogslea in a cab. In the doorway, we had our first kiss. It was delicious.

As summer drew to an end, John brought me terrible news. He had enlisted in the army. Although I stamped my little foot prettily and summoned all my feminine charms, John was not deterred and left.

I cried for days. Well, at least half a day. I consoled myself with the vision of John, on furlough, resplendent in his uniform, calling on me at my home in England.

But then I received a letter from my brother telling me that a former beaux of mine from London was planning to ask for my hand in marriage. To live in London had always been my dream.

I returned home, wiser, more worldly, even prettier. As for Nessa's loss, my heart ached. I never forgot my promise to help her find Fiona. You see, Malindi, I am not entirely vain and self-centered."

CHAPTER SIXTEEN

During the fifteen minute ride from Cogslea to the Germantown Historical Society, Toby entertained Caitlin with historical trivia.

In a grave voice he said, "It was a dark and foggy morning in October of '77, when the Battle of Germantown took place. The soldiers in the Continental Army wore white pieces of paper on their hats so as to identify themselves as Americans. General Howe's men were strategically scattered around Germantown. General George Washington's troops attacked the British holed up in Cliveden, a house a few blocks up on Germantown Avenue. But confusing orders and several other plans went awry. One commander fell asleep in a farmhouse and missed the entire battle. One got drunk and wandered about in the woods. A local guide got lost in the fog and arrived an hour late. Thinking they had won a skirmish, one unit started shouting and gave up their position in the dense fog. They were, of course, shot. The final straw came when a lieutenant approached the British general with a flag of truce and was killed with a bullet for the effort. General Washington ordered a retreat."

Caitlin chuckled over Toby's choice of events to tell the story of the historic battle. "I'm surprised we won the war," she said.

"Toby? Get on course," Ed said.

"Sorry, sir. General Washington and his brave, starving men survived the bitter cold winter at Valley Forge in threadbare, shredded clothing and rags tied around their feet for boots." Toby banged his fist on the headrest in front of him. "With sheer determination and a little help from the French, we won the war."

Caitlin murmured an approval.

Toby tapped Caitlin on the shoulder. "See that park on the left? With the Civil War monument and cannons? That's Market Square. As early as 1703, people came here once a week to buy and sell their produce and stuff. Sort of like a colonial shopping center."

Caitlin's skin pricked. She could almost hear the vendors calling out their wares. "Sweet cream butter. Pots, crocks and silverware. Tea from England."

"There's the historical society," Toby said, pointing to a three story brick building across the park.

Ed turned off the avenue into a small side street and pulled into the visitor's parking lot. They got out of the car; Ed unlocked a wooden gate; they entered a private courtyard.

"Toby, I'll get Caitlin started, then I'll switch places with you. Wait on the verandah in the shade," Ed said.

To get to the curator's office, Ed and Caitlin went through museum rooms elegantly designed and furnished in colonial revivalist style.

After a brief introduction, the curator, Daisy, said, "Come in please, sit down. I know what you're talking about, Ed, but that collection of samplers is in storage."

"I don't mind getting them out."

"As you know, they are recorded on film," Daisy continued. "You could look at the slides."

Caitlin watched Ed's face; she'd rather get her hands on the samplers.

"Are they in the attic or basement?" Ed said.

"Let me check my files." Daisy put on her glasses that hung from a beaded chain around her neck. She slid out a card drawer and removed a few cards. "Attic. Aisle two. Oversize box numbers seven and eight. You're welcome to look, Ed, but it's a mess up there."

"We don't mind, do we Caitlin?"

Caitlin shook her head. Mind? She'd dig through piles of trash in the dump if necessary.

Daisy tapped the cards on her desk. "While you're doing that, I'll look through the stacks for accompanying documentation."

Caitlin followed Ed to a narrow staircase, darted around him and flew up the steps. Expecting to be hit with attic heat and dust, she was pleasantly surprised at the air-cooled temperature, regulated to preserve the artifacts. There were rows of neat aisles containing hundreds of storage boxes arranged in clear and orderly categories. If this is a mess, what would Daisy call my housekeeping habits, Caitlin wondered.

Ed found the cartons without trouble and placed them on pullout shelves to verify the contents. Then, they each carried a box to the second floor to the closed stacks room. Caitlin reached for the box of cotton gloves, but Ed told her they wouldn't be necessary. They unwrapped the samplers from their archival storage papers and lined them up on a clean white sheet covering a library table. Nine. Caitlin placed the tenth—the one from the pantry at the end. She felt like a kid looking at gifts at her birthday party.

"I found the file for these pieces," Daisy said, emerging from an aisle. "They are all the work of Destiny Wickham." She frowned and pointed to a penciled notation scribbled in the margin of her crisp white paper. "Hmm, most irregular. Someone has written, 'one of the last residents at Cloverhill Farm on Cresheim Creek.' I wonder who did that. Anyway, several years back, a Germantown resident spotted this collection at a flea market in New Jersey, bought the lot and donated it to us. We had them reframed, using UV protected glass, acid free matting and spacers to separate the inside surface of the glazing from the face of the sampler." She wiggled her finger at the tenth sampler. "You should have that one redone, by the way." She took a step backwards. "That's all I have. I hope it helps."

Caitlin sighed. It did and it didn't. Only statistics. "I guess I need to know more about Destiny. What was she like? Did she die in the fire? What does that poem mean?"

Daisy smiled and removed her glasses. "I run into that

predicament all the time when I try to trace a person through an artifact. You can get a match with date and location of origin, but all too frequently the provenance is lost along the way. When people do their genealogy, in addition to facts, they should record the interesting stories, the personal stuff. Did the individual like to fish? Play cards? Were they afraid of cats or thunderstorms? Were they disappointed not to have gone to college or have children? Everyone should keep a diary, a journal, write a memoir. These are the real heirlooms of a life." Daisy lifted her shoulders and lowered her head. "Sorry, sometimes I get carried away."

"No, you're absolutely right."

"I can, however, tell you more about samplers in general."

"Please," Caitlin said.

Ed excused himself to trade places with Toby. Daisy sat at the table opposite Caitlin.

"Samplers date back at least four hundred years. Traditionally, they were a means to prepare young girls in stitching skills for use in later life. The girls employed alphabets in two types of script and numbers, together with different motifs and symbols along the borders and in horizontal divider lines. During the eighteenth and nineteenth century, the stitches became more complex. Biblical, moral, and inspirational verses were added. Theme pictures expanded. Maps became popular in the late eighteenth century."

Daisy picked up one of the samplers and put her glasses back on. "This one reads, 'Abhor that which is evil. Cleave to that which is good.' That kind of message was typical of its day. Strawberries were used a lot; since they have no rind or pit to dispose of, they were considered to be the perfect fruit. In this border, strawberries signify righteousness and purity of spirit."

Daisy paused and Caitlin encouraged her to continue.

"Samplers come in all sizes, often bigger and longer than the nine by twelve ones we see here. These are done on natural linen with cotton threads instead of silk, indicating that expensive materials were not available or affordable to the family. They are neatly and evenly stretched. The colors are good and strong with no noticeable fading or color run. Only minor stitch loss. No organic stains or holes. It's unfortunate that they suffered scorching."

"What about the motifs, especially the white on white?"

"Destiny used this poem on three of her samplers. I don't recognize the text; it was probably personal. As for the borders, bees represent hope, butterflies resurrection, liberation, new beginnings. The robin, and birds in general, stand for spirits of the air." Daisy got up and stood over the other samplers. "Destiny frequently used apples and apple blossoms which stand for love and fertility. Weeping willow for sorrow and dejection of the bereaved; pineapples were a hallmark of Philadelphia cabinetmakers and stand for hospitality; roses for love; the dove for peace and charity; honeysuckle for enduring faith. I don't know the meaning of some of Destiny's spot motifs. Something personal, I'm sure.

Toby, came in on the tail-end of the conversation. "Any luck?" he asked. "Who's Destiny?"

Caitlin shook her head and patted the seat next to her. Toby sat down.

"Hi, Toby." Daisy removed her glasses, rubbed her eyes and sat down again. "We had a volunteer here once by the name of Betty Green. Unfortunately, she had a stroke and retired a year or so ago. She was ninety years old. A remarkable woman. Dedicated, tenacious. She would take on an assignment and pursue it like a pit bull. As I recall, she was cataloging samplers at the time of her attack. I'm quite sure Betty is still alive and if anybody can help you, she can."

"Do you have her phone number?" Caitlin asked, feeling hopeful.

"The last I heard she was a resident at Alden Park Manor Apartments on Wissahickon Avenue, not far from here. I'll get the number and call her while you wrap up the samplers. You may leave the cartons on the table, I'll have a volunteer take them upstairs."

"What did you find out, Caitlin?" Toby asked.

As they wrapped samplers, she filled him in on what Daisy had told her. When they went downstairs they learned from Daisy that Betty still lived at Alden Park. And, though pretty much incapacitated by the stroke, she would be happy to receive them.

"Thank you so much for your help, Daisy. Ed said to tell you he'll be back later to work on pewter steins."

🌸

They pulled into one of the parking lots of a castle-like collection of rosy brick buildings adorned with numerous turrets and balconies of coral-colored cement. From the honeycomb configuration of the buildings, Caitlin guessed that all of the apartments afforded spectacular views in all directions.

Toby and Malindi waited by the car.

Ed and Caitlin registered at a hotel-like reception desk in the lobby. They were then directed to the elevator where a uniformed, white-gloved attendant took them to the tenth floor. They padded down a thick hall carpet and were met at the door of Betty's apartment by a chubby woman with dark skin and a Jamaican accent. She invited them inside.

Betty sat ramrod straight in a wheelchair under a yellow smiley-face balloon. "Here, take this ridiculous thing away, will you," she said to no one in particular. "I don't know what they want me to do with it."

The balloon's string wrapped around two fingers of Betty's right hand, her left hand was paralyzed. She was neatly dressed in a white blouse and khaki pants. Her hair was exactly the same as Ed had described it to Caitlin: pure white and pulled back in a french twist. Missing, however, was the pert black bow she always wore in the back. For some reason, that made Caitlin very sad.

Ed released the balloon and let it float to the ceiling. The Jamaican woman brought canned pepsis with napkins wrapped around them before disappearing into another room.

"I don't know if you remember me, Betty. I'm Ed McGregor and this is Caitlin Gilbert. I volunteer at the Germantown Historical Society. I'm a Tuesday person like you."

"Of course, I remember you. You dropped that seventeenth century sterling silver teapot and put a big ding in it." Betty laughed, her mouth went lopsided, her left eye drooped.

"You never let me forget it either," Ed said in a wry voice.

"Sorry, I can't offer you a real drink. I do miss my martinis every night. They won't let me have any, you know. You don't happen to have a cigarette, do you?" she asked, raising a shaking right hand to her mouth.

Ed shook his head with a knowing look.

"Smoking and drinking is what's kept me alive this long, you know? So, Ed. Why are you here?"

Caitlin really liked this woman. She didn't mince words. Maybe she felt there wasn't much time to waste.

"Remember Violet Oakley and that group of artists at Cogslea?" Ed asked. Betty nodded as far as her frozen muscles would allow. "Ever hear of Laura Enfield?"

"Never heard of her. Couldn't stand that Oakley person, though. Met her at a few events in town and thought she was a pretentious bore. Always wore violet clothing even though the color looked dreadful on her." Betty managed a half grin. "Talk about a contradiction in character: her logotype was a bunch of shy violets under an ambitious and mighty oak tree. Violet Oakley—get it?" A little noise rumbled in the back in her throat. "Didn't know any of the other women in her group."

"You're sure? Laura Enfield?"

"What did I just say?" Betty said, a puritan sharpness in her tone.

"Well, okay then. Remember those samplers you were cataloging at the historical society?"

"Of course I do."

Ed chuckled under his breath and winked at Caitlin. "Caitlin is doing research on the young girl who made them. Apparently, she lived at Cloverhill Farm on Cresheim Creek."

"Cloverhill Farm? Oh, drat, here comes Miss Sunshine with my meds."

"Now, now, Ms. Green. We must not complain. Doctor says this medicine is working wonders on you," the Jamaican woman said.

"Then let him take it if it's so great." Between gulps of iced water, Betty downed all her pills. She turned to Ed and Caitlin. "If you don't mind, I'd like to use the ladies room. Such an inconvenience, you know."

"I'll go down and let Toby come in for a while," Ed said.

Caitlin waited politely outside the door and was glad to see Toby coming fast up the hall. She felt bad that he was missing out on the story. "How's Malindi?" she asked.

"She's fine. I walked her through the gardens, past the tennis courts and indoor swimming pool, out to the street and back again. Did you know that Grace Kelly's mother used to live on the top floor suite above Ms. Green's? The elevator man told me."

"I have heard that, Toby. Looks like we can go in now." She introduced Toby to Ms. Green.

"Please sit down," Betty said, waving her good hand. "Let's see, where was I when I was so rudely interrupted. Oh, yes the samplers. All had some scorching," she began.

In detail, she described each sampler. Caitlin checked her notes and was amazed at the clarity of Betty's recall.

"I did research at the Philadelphia Free Library, The Library Company of Philadelphia, American Philosophical Society, Historical Society of Pennsylvania, and the Chestnut Hill Historical Society, but found only dates and such, things that I already knew. I wanted to find out more about the family, especially the girl who made those samplers. There was something so poignant about that poem called 'Remember.' Something about that young girl. Like she was trying to reach out to me but just couldn't cut through time and space."

Caitlin's hands trembled and Betty's milky eyes looked into hers. Her voice softened and she said, "I think you know what I mean, don't you?" Caitlin didn't need to speak. An acknowledgment passed between them that was as clear as the written word.

Betty continued. "Well, let me tell you, since my stroke I've had plenty of time to sit and think. You can only watch so much television, you know. I did remember something important."

Caitlin leaned forward, Toby glugged.

I come from a large family. Eight boys and four girls. I

was the youngest. Every last one of us went to college, thanks to our hardworking parents. Kids today don't appreciate things." She looked at Toby and narrowed her eyes. He withstood her gaze with polite tenacity.

"We all lived well into our nineties and I'm the the last of our clan. But I don't mind. I'm not afraid of death. When I was little, we had big family meals every Sunday night. After dinner we'd sing, recite poems, play the piano or violin, and listen to our elders' stories of 'the good old days.'"

"Now here's the, eh, what's the word? Oh, yes, the 'zinger.' I vaguely remembered my great-great-grandmother telling us about a terrible fire that occurred when she was a child. Believe me, after her story I had nightmares about fires well into my teens. I called David, my older brother, and asked him if he remembered anything about that fire. He did.

"Seems a young girl by the name of Destiny claimed that she had visions. And she kept reciting that poem that's on the sampler over and over. Neighbors accused her of being a witch, of causing people to become ill, of making crops fail and cows' milk to sour. People jeered at her. Eventually, her parents prohibited her from going out. In the early nineteenth century, you see, they were still yoking women who were accused of witchery in the public stocks in Market Square. Fortunately, it never came to that for Destiny, because most of the time her parents had her locked up in the root cellar, feeding her bread and water only. A terrible fire at the farmhouse killed her as well as her entire family. Neighbors blamed it on Destiny, but there was never any proof of it."

"Goodness," exclaimed Toby, shivering.

"Goodness and mercy, people can be so cruel," Betty said. She looked at Toby. "Such a nice young man. Are you a doctor? Please don't tell me I need another MRI." She turned back to Caitlin. "You must come and visit me when I get back in my apartment at Alden Park. I'm only here temporarily, you know. I believe we are playing bingo tonight."

Betty had occasional lapses in dementia. "We'll come back to visit," Caitlin told her. Lowering her voice she added, "Maybe we can take you out for a walk in the garden. I'll bring cigarettes and gin."

"Bless you."

"I hope you don't mind my asking, Ms. Green..."

"Fire away. Oh, what a terrible pun." Betty's chortle cracked with growing fatigue.

"Were you ever married and what did you do for a living?"

"No, I never married. There were too many things I wanted to do without being tied down with kids and housework. And I'm proud to say that I taught art at Girl's High for forty-five years."

Caitlin smiled. It was becoming clear that there was a link between the women involved in this mystery.

CHAPTER SEVENTEEN

Caitlin invited Maggie and Toby over for the evening. She was still reluctant to include Ed but had decided to let Toby in on everything. He looked about ready to jump out of his skin with excitement.

"You have to promise not to tell anyone the part about my seeing ghosts, Toby. Not even your grandfather. Promise?"

"Cross my heart," Toby moved his hand across his chest. "Maybe we should cut our fingers and mingle our blood."

"To-bee," Caitlin said.

Maggie snickered.

Toby furrowed his brow and put on a serious look.

They sat at the kitchen table with the paintings and the sampler propped up against the wall, the Polaroids and the Bryn Mawr photo on the windowsill. They had just finished eating ice cream and were nibbling on salted peanuts. Malindi was licking the ice cream carton Toby had placed on the floor under the table.

"Let's review what we know," Caitlin said.

"I think we should list the facts on a blackboard like the detectives do on *Mystery Theater*," Toby said.

Maggie said, "We don't have a blackboard, Chief Inspector, but we have plenty of legal pads and pencils. So let's get to work." She popped a handful of peanuts in her mouth, chewed and swallowed.

"Uh, just what is it we're trying to find out anyhow?"

Caitlin lifted her shoulders. "Good question. I'm really not sure, but maybe if we go over what we know we'll find out."

Maggie and Toby sat with pencils poised over their writing pads.

Caitlin began. "Laura told me to find Nessa."

"Say what?" Maggie's jaw went slack.

"Who's Nessa?" Toby said.

"I don't know who Nessa is. Her name never came up until Laura mentioned her."

"Laura mentioned her?" Maggie's eyes bugged.

"I'm sorry, I guess I didn't tell you. Before I fell down the steps in the carriage house, a voice whispered to me, *'Help her. Help Nessa find her child. Where we failed, you can succeed.'*"

"Wow!" Toby's glasses slipped down his nose. "This is big."

Maggie screwed up her face and shook her head. "There's a huge gap here somewhere. Let's go over the facts like you said."

"It all started with my seeing Laura Enfield in the Allens Lane train station." Toby started to write. "No, wait. It was the hem of her skirt in the library doorway first. Then the train station." Toby added the information. Maggie folded her arms across her chest and listened.

"Oh, wait. Number One. When we arrived here, I saw Laura at a garden party in the front yard."

"You what?" said Maggie. Toby nearly jumped out of his chair.

"I'm sorry, I forgot." Caitlin described the lawn party scene.

"Put hem as three, station as four and the next as number two. When we had our first painting group, I thought Gina was dressed in a long white gown like Laura."

Toby's mouth flew open. "You're kidding? I didn't know that. Wow. I was right there. I wish I'd seen her."

"Then, I painted that picture of the little girl by the clothesline. Then I saw Laura in the carriage window. Then I painted Birdie like

Laura." Caitlin passed her hand across her forehead. "And there's something about that calico cat. It keeps popping up. It must mean something.

Toby wrote furiously. The tip of his tongue protruded from the corner of closed lips.

"Then I saw her in the mirror in the carriage house." Maggie grunted. "I found a painting of Laura's at Dr. Truet's that was similar to mine." They turned their heads to look at the paintings.

"And the photo at Bryn Mawr led to the sampler," Maggie said.

"Right, and the sampler is leading us to something further back in time."

At that moment the phone rang. Caitlin picked up the receiver.

"Caitlin?" It was Sam. "I called earlier, but the line was busy. Then you didn't answer. Did you get my message?"

"Yes, is everything all right?"

Maggie tugged on Toby's sleeve. "Come on, Toby. Let's take Malindi out back for a while."

"But..."

"Scoot, young man."

"Lieutenant."

"Lieutenant young man."

Sam spoke. "Mary and the girls are talking about moving to Sacramento. Most of their friends are there."

"Maybe that would be best, don't you think?"

"I do, but I'll have to help them find a house."

"Maybe I should come out."

"Caitlin, sweetheart, we'd probably pass each other in the air at this point. Besides, it's really not a pleasant situation here with Howard's father so sick."

"Do what you think is best, Sam. I'm sure Mary would be lost without your help."

"I'll call tomorrow."

Caitlin hung up and reflected on what Sam had said before summoning her team.

"Okay, where were we?"

"Maybe we should think about what you all have in common," Maggie suggested.

"Artists," Toby said.

"Women," Caitlin added.

"Ms. Green is a woman and an artist," Toby said.

"Independent," Maggie said. "Although you are married," she added quickly.

And independent, thanks to Sam's understanding. "But I only see Laura when Sam isn't here."

"Maybe ghosts don't like men," Maggie said.

Toby tapped his pencil on his notepad. He smacked his forehead. "Maybe there were others beside Laura and Destiny and Ms. Green that we don't even know about."

Caitlin had been thinking the same thing. "Could be. But no one's been able to break all the way through." She looked at the little girl in the paintings and then off into space. "But maybe I can." Her voice was no more than a whisper.

Her assistants looked puzzled but received no clarification. Caitlin changed the subject.

"Have you noticed Malindi acting differently?"

"You told me she was digging under the house," Toby said.

Caitlin nodded, "Right."

"And she ran off to the art center and lay down in the field. You said that was unusual for her," he added.

"Yes, I don't know what that was all about. And she simply will not go into the old apple orchard. When I was painting there, something or someone pushed me to the ground, but I saw no one."

"Spoooky," Toby drew out the word for effect.

Maggie hissed and looked wise. "Something awful must have happened there. Dogs sense those things."

"I'm sure she knows a lot more than we do," said Caitlin, patting Malindi's head. "Right, girl?" Malindi chuffed.

They stared at their yellow lined pads, Caitlin and Maggie at their blank ones and Toby at his pages of carefully written notes.

"Well, I don't think we can do any more tonight," Caitlin

said. "Let's keep thinking about it though. I'll walk you home Toby— Maggie, call me tomorrow."

✿

The air pressed thick and heavy on Caitlin. Toby didn't seem to mind the heat and humidity; he zigzagged and bounced yards ahead of Caitlin with Malindi trotting by his side.

"This is a real adventure, isn't it, Caitlin?"

"Yes, Toby it is."

"I could be the hero, and you—I mean Destiny, could be captured by the Borg, or lost at sea in a raging storm, or tied to a runaway train, or Godzilla about to devour you—I mean her, and I would rescue her.

"You're very brave, Toby."

Suddenly Toby stopped and pranced in front of her.

"Caitlin, remember Ms. Green said something about Destiny's parents banishing her to the root cellar? We should look for the root cellar."

"You're right, Toby. Good thinking. Let's do it tomorrow."

"I have an appointment with the orthodontist in the morning. Promise you'll wait for me?"

"I promise, Toby. My painting group is coming anyway." She felt encouraged. Surely, the root cellar would reveal all. And that would be the end of that. But hadn't she said that before?

✿

Caitlin had forgotten to fill Malindi's water bowl in the bathroom. When Malindi woke up thirsty, she trotted downstairs to get a drink from the one in the kitchen. Reentering the hallway after her drink, she heard someone calling her name. She followed the sound: through the open cellar door, down the steps, and into the original farmhouse room in the corner of the house.

A single beam of light fell from a lone window high on the wall and pooled around a young woman sitting on a bed of straw.

151

The rest of the room was bathed in darkness. Patting a spot on the floor next to her, she beckoned to Malindi. Malindi lay down and nestled her head in the girl's lap.

"Hello, Malindi. My name is Destiny Wickham. I'm fifteen years old. I lived here a very long time ago. When my parents had reached their fortieth year, they had relinquished all hope of producing children for the Lord. Thus, in 1785, they were astonished and bewildered by my arrival on God's good green earth. Perhaps that is why they named me Destiny and not a more pious name like Hope, Faith, or Charity.

I was a dutiful daughter, yet I continually displeased my parents. They destroyed my drawings of farm animals I did as a child, saying I had blasphemed God by worshipping idols. They forbade me the use paper and pen ever again.

Old Somes, a farmhand, taught me the fundamentals of reading and writing. I was devastated when Father turned him out, accusing him of insubordination in trying to educate me. Somes had been with the family all his life, coming over as an indentured servant with my grandparents from Devonshire. Nevertheless, I continued to improve my reading skills, as Father did permit me to read from the Bible after that.

During the daylight hours, I was occupied with improving my skills at baking bread, churning butter, cooking, sewing, sampler making, so that my parents could offer me as a desirable marriage prospect. I prayed that my future would hold a far less restrictive life. I longed to be able to express myself freely.

I was rarely allowed off our farm except on Sunday to go to church, three miles away in Germantown. There, I had the opportunity to absorb the hustle and bustle on Main Street, the ladies' fashions, the animated children. I envied with all my heart the unfettered lifestyles of other girls my age. In church I felt that the minister was speaking directly to me, preaching that I would be damned forever to the fires of hell for my irreverent thoughts. One day, Mother told me to collect wild strawberries on the other side of the creek. I wandered too far in the woods and came upon a girl, perhaps three years old, playing with a frog. She was barefooted and dressed in buckskin, her hair was black and shiny, her skin like that of an Indian. I presumed her to be an Indian, although the Lenni Lenape were almost gone from here by then. She helped me gather the berries, laughing the whole while. She spoke not at all. I called her Robin because she could imitate the chirping sounds of that darling bird perfectly. When I told her I had to go, she waved and disappeared into the thicket.

I made the mistake of telling Mother about the child. She told Father and he sent me to the root cellar without supper. He swore that God would strike me down for my lies and heresy. The following day, Mother made me rip out the verse on a sampler and do it all over again without a thimble. "Hear the instruction of thy father, And forsake not the law of thy mother."

I stole into the woods to play with the child as often as I was able, sometimes in the night while my parents slept. I fabricated stories to tell Robin of a fantasy land, without adults or religion, where children, faeries, and tamed beasts lived in harmony, and where no harm ever came to them. We played tag, hopscotch, jackstraws, and other games that we made up.

One day, Robin composed a picture on a flat rock using bits taken from nature: a piece of pure white birch bark for the face; violets for eyes, rose petals for lips, and shiny black stones for hair. It was me and I wept.

On every visit thereafter, she would *paint* a picture on the rock for me. They were charming scenes, made with bits of shells, colorful pebbles, twigs, flowers, stones, and feathers. I memorized each picture and, afterwards, I would copy them into my samplers exactly as she had made them. Embroidering was no longer an unwelcome task confined to unimaginative motifs and text taken from the scriptures. This way I could keep Robin close to me. I reveled in the thought that I had a secret. I concealed my work from my parents by hiding and switching samplers whenever Mother or Father came near.

One day, a neighboring farm boy followed me into the woods. He hid behind a tree, watching me play with Robin. That evening, he approached me in the barn and tried to kiss me. For his insolence,

I slapped his ugly face and drove him away with a pitchfork. Soon after, he took his revenge. He spread gossip that I was a witch and that I talked to an invisible friend. After that, whenever our neighbors' milk soured or their crops failed, they blamed it on me, the witch.

Eventually, my parents forbade me to go off the farm altogether, even to church. Every Sunday, I was forced to kneel on the stone floor and read the bible from sunrise to sunset. But on other days, I still managed to sneak out to visit Robin. Occasionally, my parents would find out and they would banish me to the root cellar. I didn't care, because I could work on my samplers there. It was in the root cellar that I heard a woman singing. Her voice was sweet and sad, and her words so beautiful, that I used the verse in three of my samplers.

"See me in the leaves above. Feel me in the summer breeze. Hear me in the robin's song. Remember me—Nessa. I am Nessa."

Matters grew worse when the elders in church began to insinuate that I was possessed and should be yoked in the public stocks in Market Square with other witches. I would not have feared the humiliation or pain as long as I had Robin in my heart.

I knew that our clandestine meetings would eventually come to an end. It all began when my left eye twitched all day. Then a bat flew in the house, a rooster crowed at night, and I saw an owl in the middle of the day. But when a raven sat on our roof and croaked for over an hour, the portent of these bad omens became clear to me.

I went to our meeting place one last time, knowing that Robin had already gone for good. On our special rock I found, fashioned from wildflowers of every color, the outline of a heart. In the center, made with wild strawberries, bark, and tiny pebbles, there was a picture of a robin sitting on a berry branch.

My Robin was gone, but she had given me such joy that no matter what happened, I could bear it."

Destiny leaned down toward Malindi. "You have a good mistress, Malindi." Malindi raised her head. The girl put her face close to Malindi's and looked deep into her eyes. "What's that? Yes, I know you agree with me, Malindi. We can trust her to do the right thing now, can't we?"

CHAPTER EIGHTEEN

Caitlin pulled the brim of her straw hat down to shade her eyes. She scanned the grounds, trying to figure out where the root cellar might be. It could be in the basement. Or it could have been filled in. All evidence of a root cellar could have been removed entirely. She sighed.

The timer beeped. The model relaxed his pose, donned a black silk robe and sat down to read a book. Joy, Birdie, and Gina were in attendance. Also a newcomer.

"That's great, Bridget," Gina said. "Are you sure you don't want to try my watercolor pencils?"

Bridget declined. This was her first attempt at drawing; she felt more secure staying with charcoal.

Gina adjusted a pink passion flower tucked behind one ear and poured herself a glass of iced mint tea. It was a hot day. She wore orange flip flops and a shocking pink two piece Esther Williams bathing suit "You're off to a slow start, Caitlin. Are you lost without Sam?"

"Hmm, no. Well, yes, I do miss Sam terribly. I just feel droopy, that's all."

The weather was horrible, everyone agreed. More than one drawing had been discarded over the course of an hour. After the break, the model stretched his spindly torso and limbs. Bridget couldn't get the whole figure on a page, half her sketch book was filled with poor starts. Caitlin told her that she was probably trying too hard.

"Loosen up, just get the gesture. May I?" Bridget nodded

and moved aside. Caitlin drew a flowing line down the paper, made a correction, stood back and whispered in Bridget's ear. "He's really easy to do—he has an elongated S shape like a flamingo." Louder, she said, "You only need to capture the gesture, the expression. Later, when you have more experience the full figure will be a snap."

"Thank you," Bridget said, relaxing her shoulders.

Birdie gave up altogether and moved to the shady patio. With grim determination, Joy persevered. Ultimately, Caitlin couldn't salvage any of her drawings and was glad when the time came for the model and the others to leave.

When they were gone, she went in the kitchen, dabbed cold water on her face, neck and arms. She gave Malindi an ice cube and ate a yogurt. Toby arrived earlier than expected.

"I'm so excited about this, Caitlin. It's like a treasure hunt. Where shall we begin?"

"We'll start in the garden at the corner of the house."

Toby peered into a purple flowered butterfly bush. "What are we looking for, Caitlin?

"Something that looks out of place, different. A bump on the ground, a plastered up hole in the wall. Anything that suggests 'root cellar.'"

"Well, this sure is out of place. Is this where Malindi was digging?" Toby held up a broken branch of butterfly bush.

"Oops, I forgot. Maybe Robertson's can replant it. Just kick the dirt into the hole for now."

Under a pantry window, where the old farmhouse wall joined new, there was a noticeable difference in the plaster's color and texture. "Look, Caitlin. The root cellar might have been downstairs in the basement." He jabbed his finger on the stucco. "Maybe poor, starving Destiny was imprisoned down there. Wretched and begging for help, crammed in between barrels of inventoried potatoes and carrots that she couldn't touch for fear of a beating."

Caitlin chuckled at Toby's vivid imagination. She pulled back a thorny rose branch and looked behind it. "I've thought of that, but I didn't see any sign of a door or sealed up opening when I was down there."

They inched their way along until they came to the dividing wall between garden and pergola. They exited through the center gate and walked to the end of the pergola. Here, they were up against a stone wall. Literally.

"There's no way of knowing if the root cellar is behind this."

"Got a jackhammer?" Toby joked.

She was afraid he might be serious. "Let's stand back and see what we're up against."

Like surveyors at a site, they stood by the fishpond and studied the area. Where the patio ended, the ground sloped sharply downward and wide stone steps divided it up the middle. The banks were covered with a mixed hedge of holly and rhododendron.

Toby threw his shoulders back. "I read up on root cellars last night. That's a perfect place for one. It's rocky and it must be forty degrees cooler inside. Good for keeping meats, milk, and cream at the right temperature in the summer and above freezing in the winter to preserve fruits and vegetables."

"But how to get in there, Toby. The vegetation is so thick. Maybe the architectural drawings would show exactly where the root cellar is—or was."

Toby jumped forward. "Let's go."

Toby took the elevator; she took the stairs. In Lee's office, Caitlin found the architect's renderings. They unrolled the blue scrolls and spread them on the desk, each holding down one stiff end. No root cellar.

"Maybe in the architect's notes," Caitlin said.

They divided the folders. They flipped through dozens of crinkly onion skin pages, skimming words that had been carefully typed by Mr. Day's secretary on an early Underwood upstrike.

"Here it is. Here it is. Look, Caitlin. Mr. Day says, 'stone patio built over the root cellar.' It's under the patio. Whee."

"Then that's where we'll look." They raced up the steps, out to the lawn, and stared at the impenetrable jungle.

Undaunted, Toby approached the thicket. "We'll find it." He tried to wedge himself between the resistant branches, but Caitlin pulled him back.

"Toby, you'll hurt yourself. If we could just see a door or something, we could cut our way in. I'll get a flashlight, you go to the potting shed and find shears. Get gardening gloves too."

Caitlin retrieved the heavy-duty flashlight she kept by the side of the bed and waited in the yard for Toby. He brought with him two sets of gloves, two denim shirts to protect their arms, two bandanas to tie around their heads, and industrial pruning shears.

He snapped the tool in the air as he walked. "I'll cut."

Caitlin began to have second thoughts about hacking up her friends' garden. "Let's try to find the entrance to the root cellar with the flashlight first."

Toby put down his lethal instrument and Caitlin shone the light through the hedge. Starting at the left side, they systematically worked their way across. Nothing.

"It's got to be there, Caitlin. Let's do it again."

Going from right to left this time, they resumed their search. They both saw it at the same time: a straight corner—a shape not of nature's design.

"Looks like a door." Caitlin's heart raced.

"I see it too, That's it, Caitlin. Ah'm goin' in," he said with the dramatic air of a super-hero. He grabbed the pruning shears.

"Wait, Toby. Be careful. Try to cut the branches on the inner side in a zigzag fashion. That way, maybe it won't show so much."

"Ouch!"

"What?"

"Leaves of holly."

If the scratching and biting branches hurt, Toby did not complain again. He chopped his way through ten feet of entanglement.

Toby's voice was muffled. "Shine the light in here Caitlin." A rustling and thumping sound followed. "It's it, Caitlin. It's a door. Come on."

Caitlin picked her way toward him. Indeed, it was a door of some sort. She helped him brush and scrape away dirt and debris from a wooden door imbedded into the bank of sloping ground.

They tried to pry it out, but it wouldn't budge until Toby dug around the edges with the sharp end of his pruning shears. Finally, they loosened the door and flung it aside. The damp smell of earth and decay wafted out.

"Omigod."

"Whoopee."

An iron gate barred them from entering the dark hole. Caitlin shone the flashlight inside and saw steps descending into an underground room.

"Root cellar, root cellar," Toby cried.

"Root cellar."

They pulled on the bars but the gate held firm.

"We need a crowbar."

"I'm sure there's one somewhere. Probably in the basement."

"I'll go," Toby said.

They extricated themselves from the hedge. Toby ran off to fetch a crowbar. Caitlin brushed herself off and pulled twigs and leaves out of her hair. Enthusiastic weathermen had been yammering for days about excessive heat and humidity, now in the danger zone. She went back into the house to refill their thermoses with lemonade.

❀

During this entire episode, Malindi lay near the fishpond watching them with her head resting on crossed paws. Had they been more attentive, they could have saved themselves a lot of trouble in finding the entrance. All they had to do was follow the direction her nose was pointing. But then they were only human. Only when they uncovered the hole did she rise, stretch, and join them.

Toby and Caitlin twisted their bodies to conform to the hedge's cutout opening and worked their way to the gate. Taking turns, they pried around the edge with a crowbar while the other dug away dirt with a pronged gardening tool. After many attempts, the gate gave way. They peered into the hole.

"Shine the light in there Caitlin. I'll go first, in case there are snakes or spiders." With the light directed on his feet, Toby scraped away dirt and leaves from each stone step with the gardening tool.

His voice floated up. "There are eight steps. Be careful Caitlin."

While she picked her way down, Toby scratched at the dirt floor. "Floorboards, Caitlin. Strong, too."

"Good." She turned the flashlight on the broad overhead beams that supported a wood ceiling.

"They often lined the ceiling and walls with tin." Toby poked overhead with the tips of the pruning shears. A few clods of dirt fell down.

"Careful, Toby."

Malindi sniffed every inch of the room then laid down at the bottom of the steps.

"It's cold down here, isn't it? But I think it feels good, doesn't it?"

"Mmmm." Caitlin shivered, not from the temperature but from something else. An entity? A presence? She directed the light around the room. A few corroded tins and several blackened canning jars of questionable content lined the shelves around the room.

Toby's voice quavered. "Looks like witch's brew with eye of newt, bat saliva. Hee hee. So this is where they sent Destiny when she was bad. I wonder if she had a bed or something to lie on."

"Maybe just a pallet of hay. Poor Destiny."

"Or a light?"

"I hope she was able to bring a candle with her."

"Caitlin, just for fun, turn off the flashlight and let's see how dark it is."

She pushed the switch and the room plunged into blackness. Instinctively, they turned their heads toward the welcoming rectangle of light at the top of the steps.

"That's enough." Caitlin turned the flashlight back on. "I don't think we'll discover anything more here."

"But we found the root cellar."

Caitlin felt deflated, but Toby's enthusiasm was still switched on. They climbed the steps and propped up the wooden plank against the opening without bothering to replace the iron gate.

"What now?" Toby asked, rocking back and forth on the balls of his feet.

"I don't know." She felt a little dizzy. "Toby, I didn't have much for lunch. Would you like to have a bagel and cream cheese with me?"

"Sure."

They piled their excavating tools on the patio stones and went into the kitchen.

Caitlin sliced and toasted bagels while Toby mixed up a pitcher of gatorade. She gulped down a glass of the lime green liquid. Dr. Truet would be displeased if he knew she was neglecting her intake of liquids and skipping meals.

Toby looked up from spreading orange marmalade on his cream cheese bagel. "You think maybe Destiny will start appearing now?"

"I don't know, Toby." All of a sudden she felt tired. She let him chatter on a bit about Julius Kelpius, the hermit of the Wissahickon.

"Remember I told you about him? He lived in a cave on the ridge. Early settlers lived in caves while they were building their houses. His had a cot, table, lamp, and lots of books in it. It's still there but empty, of course. Granddad and I hiked over there to see it. Want to go sometime? I can show you where it is."

While they were eating Maggie called. Caitlin told Toby to tell the root cellar story. "Give her a full report, Toby."

Exaggerating more than a little, Toby described the event in minute detail. "Okay if Maggie comes over?" Caitlin nodded. She didn't feel much like talking; she let Toby prattle on, jumping from one subject to another.

❈

A short time later, Maggie bustled in chattering about the natural preservation of foods.

Caitlin sat outside while Toby showed Maggie their discovery. She scarcely heard their enthusiastic comments because of the buzzing in her ears and the blunt pain behind her eyes. They came out and clucked around her like a mother hen and her hyperactive chick and she was happy to see them go.

CHAPTER NINETEEN

Caitlin washed down two migraine pills with gatorade. She peeled off her grimy clothes and took a long lukewarm shower. She tried to nap, but inane thoughts ran around in her brain like squirrels in a cage. What did Sam say in his last conversation? When was he coming home? What did Carolyn say about Jess? What would she say to Sam when he came home?

She gave up. It was too late for a nap anyway. Too close to bedtime. Eight o'clock? Would Sam call again? Her mind clicked back to morning. Did he call then? The phone on the bedside table rang; she looked at it before picking up the receiver.

"Sam?"

"No, sorry to disappoint you. It's Carolyn."

"Oh, Carolyn, I'm always happy to talk to you."

"Are you expecting Sam to call? I can call you back later."

"No, it's okay. He doesn't call at this time, anyhow. What's up? How goes your budding friendship with Jess?"

"That's what I wanted to talk to you about. Here's the thing. You and Jess had a relationship once, and that's all in the past, but..."

"But, you want my permission." Caitlin laughed. "I'm happily married, and I don't have ownership tags on past or probable lovers. And I couldn't be happier that Jess asked you out."

"Well, I just wanted to clear the air so that nothing could ever come between our friendship."

"Never!"

She stared into the refrigerator. What am I looking for? I feel a bit nauseous. I should eat something, if only to please the good Doctor Truet. Wouldn't want to pass out and end up in his office again. She shuffled containers around on the crowded shelves. Leftover tuna salad. Good. Protein. She needed protein. She spread the tuna on whole wheat bread, added lettuce and tomato, poured a glass of milk, and took her dinner out to the patio.

Dusk was her favorite time of day. A peaceful time. A brief respite for prey animals— a changing of the guard between diurnal and nocturnal predators. Caitlin closed her eyes and listened to the orchestral sound of insect and amphibian, punctuated with hoot and screech of owl.

Her mind wouldn't relax. She was confused. Why didn't Sam call? Was he mad at her? Maybe he was on his way home. No, no, he said he was going to help Mary find a house. In any case, she needed to finish this business once and for all. Sam musn't see her all crazy and hallucinatory.

She laughed. The interruption was as disruptive as a cough from the audience is to the Philharmonic. It caused the animal orchestra to pause for half a beat before picking up exactly where they left off.

An idea began to tap-dance around in her head, but it was so scary that she dared not acknowledge it. "Come on Malindi, let's go inside. I'll try reading in the library.

❀

Reading was a chore; she soon gave up. She picked up the television remote and tuned in the classic movie channel. *Indiscretion of an American Housewife* was in its last melodramatic throes and she managed to lose herself in the soulful eyes of Montgomery Clift for a short while. *The Lady Vanishes* followed. Though she had seen the movie several times, she never could remember the ending. Bored with *The Thin Man*'s constant guzzling of alcohol, she turned off the television and went to bed.

But sleep—that blessed commodity, evaded her. What had happened to the lovely cool air that used to drift in through the window at night? For the first time since arriving at Cogslea, Caitlin shut and locked the bedroom door, closed the windows and turned on the air conditioner.

There's no one breaking into the house. I'm not missing anything happening outside. It's not really noisy. Damn, damn, damn, the air conditioner really, really is noisy.

"I give up." She turned off the air conditioner, put on a long sleeve cotton shirt, a pair of khaki trousers, sneakers and socks. Malindi stood by the door, waiting. She had been expecting this to happen.

❁

Caitlin pulled a backpack from the closet and filled it with the necessary articles: sweater, flashlight, matches, water bottle, collapsable water bowl for Malindi, aspirin, notepad and pen, chapstick, house and car keys. She placed the bag by the patio door. She stuffed a bed pillow into a trash bag and retrieved a plastic tarp from the greenhouse. Now where did she see that camping equipment? She turned on all the downstairs lights and descended the basement stairs. Without warning, the hot water heater turned on with a clang and she almost fell down the steps.

Don't be silly, there's nothing to be afraid of down here. Her eyes turned toward the empty corner room behind the staircase. Except maybe in there. She entered the room on wobbly legs, pulled the string on the hanging light bulb. Shadows on the wall began to dance.

"Destiny? Destiny, are you here?" Her jaw clenched; the hair on her arm lifted. What would she do if someone answered? But wasn't that the whole point? Didn't she want to see something? Someone? Bring it on. Get this over with. On a hunch, she shut the door and turned off the light. "Destiny?" The room closed in on her. She pushed her arms outward and searched for something solid. There was only Malindi leaning heavily against her legs. She turned on the flashlight and left the room, more than a little shaken.

Camping equipment lay piled in a corner in the exercise

165

room. She took a sleeping bag and a rolled-up exercise mat, hooked them under one arm, and picked up a Coleman lantern with her free hand.

"Come on, Malindi. Upstairs."

Fresh batteries were in a kitchen drawer. She slipped the pack on her back, carried the other paraphernalia in her arms and made it outside in one trip. In the dark, she dragged her stuff through the hedge opening, pulled aside the wooden door and rolled the sleeping bag, mat and pillow down the steps. With her hands freed, she turned on the flashlight.

"Come on, Malindi. As Toby says, 'Ah'm goin' in.'"

She placed the lantern on a shelf displacing a daddy-long legs that scuttled away. "Oops, sorry. If you're the only kind of creepy-crawly thing in here, that's fine with me. We can share."

She spread the tarp on the floor, unrolled the mat on top, put the lantern within reach, the flashlight inside the sleeping bag. Any creature wanting to venture through the uncovered door would surely change its mind when it saw Malindi.

"Light's out, Malindi."

Her eyes remained fixed on the rectangle of dim light at the top of the steps. Gradually, her night vision kicked in. Patches of light sifted through the hedge; she tried to imagine objects in the patterns.

The dank, earthy smell inside the root cellar was not unpleasant and not unlike sleeping on the ground in Africa after a day of tracking African wild dogs. But where were the deep, belly-rumbling calls of lion? The hippo grunts and grinding of teeth as they fed in the nearby river? The soft *pat pat* of treading feet of curious hyena investigating their campsite? Exposed and vulnerable, fear never entered her mind there. Never recovering from hallucinations — now that was fear.

Curled up at the foot of the sleeping bag, nose tucked securely under her tail, Malindi was the first to fall asleep.

Many people have recurring dreams. You're back in high school and you can't remember your locker combination; you're naked at a black-tie party; you're falling from an airplane. Malindi had her own recurring dream.

She was in a wooden crate in the back of a jeep. There were bars on one end of the crate and holes on the sides and top. Hay covered the floor. The air smelled like petrol. The jeep's wheels kicked up choking dirt as it bounced over ruts. The jeep stopped. She saw a field where stiff birds with wings that never folded sat. Some flew away, carrying lightning bugs in their bellies.

"*Matata*, Malindi. *Matata.*" caitlindogmama reached in and touched her nose with her fingers. And disappeared. The crate was lifted onto a cart and wedged between boxes that reeked of dead cow and crocodile. The cart rolled past strange and unfamiliar smells. Foreign words skimmed past her ears. Then all was quiet. And dark. And hot. Hotter than the plains in Ah-free-kah.

A biting stench of fear hung in the air. Malindi was not alone. A carrier containing a domestic cat had been placed next to her. The pitiful yowling ceased, the terrified animal flattened and crept into a corner where it curled into a compact, trembling furry ball.

Malindi sniffed the air. Dog. But not her kind. It was one of the silly creatures that lived on farms. Always yapping and spinning in circles. Another smell. One that raised the hair on her nape and along the ridge of her back. Deep in her throat, a low growl issued. The urge to attack was strong, but she couldn't do it without her pack. Hyena was lucky today.

Malindi peered through an air hole and located the source of a soft mewling sound: Yes, she had seen those fuzzy cubs with black underlined eyes before in a place that caitlindogbaba called 'dewildt-south-ah-free-kah.'

Trouser bottoms, heavy work boots, and the wheels of a wooden box passed the front of her crate. "Phew, this thing stinks like a skunk. What the hell is it?" snarled one man.

"Label says civet cat. Destination, Philadelphia Zoo. Should fit right in with stinky Philly." The men laughed. A bloodcurdling scream ripped from the crate and the men left in a hurry.

Malindi was limp from the heat. After what seemed like

the passage of one full moon to the next, the men came again. She braced her legs as her crate swung through the air and was dumped with a thud onto a moving hill that carried her up toward the sky and into a dark, cold den. The hyena, the civet cat, and the cheetah cubs joined her. An enormous box with iron bars took up the remaining space in the rear of the cargo plane. In the box, a partially sedated rhinoceros stood on shaky legs beside a veterinarian sitting on a stool monitoring its vital signs.

Behind an open cockpit, half a dozen people dressed in khaki sprawled across five rows of seats that extended across the forward section of the cabin.

Civet urine permeated the air. Objects fell from place. The noise from the plane's engines became an unbearable assault on Malindi's sensitive ears. She knew that she would run no more. She pawed at the hay and piled it into a corner. With Caitlin's sock in her mouth, Malindi crept under the hay to wait for death.

During the night, Caitlin woke and saw the unmistakable outline of a skunk in front of the entryway. It paused to investigate the changes in its well-established trail before scuffling away, leaving a musky odor of scent glands in its wake. Caitlin waited and watched the rectangle of light. Nothing happened, she drifted in and out of semiconsciousness.

The rectangle of light moved; it was not fixed at the doorway. It shifted, it floated.

"Destiny?" Above the pounding of her heart, Caitlin heard a humming sound. She sat up, strained her ears, rotated her head to funnel the sound. Faint, then louder, the sweet voice of a young girl singing reached her through the thick darkness. Caitlin caught enough of the words to put together the now familiar verse:

"See me in the leaves above. Feel me in the summer breeze. Hear me in the robin's song. Remember me." Like a wisp of smoke, the apparition disappeared through the open door. "Wait." Frustrated, Caitlin struggled with the zipper on her sleeping bag. Awkwardly,

she crawled out like a newborn chick from its shell. She grabbed the flashlight and stumbled up the steps, Malindi ahead of her.

The hedge tore her skin. She tripped, but kept her eye on the light as it turned the corner of the house. Breathing heavily from exertion and excitement, she reached Malindi, who was looking into the depths of the orchard. The air was heavy with the sweet scent of spring apple blossom.

"What is it? What can I do?" Caitlin cried.

A cacophony of night noises answered. A transient breeze took her by surprise as plants swayed and bobbed, elongated leaves of willow waved their strands of hair, oak trees rubbed their limbs together, creaking. Everything around her was moving. Everything except the interior of the orchard. And that was as still as a photograph.

Caitlin penetrated the orchard and moved with caution toward the light. The center of the vapor adjusted, defined itself, taking the shape of a girl. She began to dance. The girl bowed and twirled, silently clapping her hands to joyous music that only she could hear. Caitlin was entranced by the beauty and elegance of the performance.

Suddenly, sparks ignited at the girl's feet. Flames groped her twisting body. Like a shooting star, the figure streaked upward and vanished into the icy brilliance of space.

Caitlin fell to the ground, sobbing. Minutes later, she sat up and held her breath. There was no mistaking the clear, innocent laughter of a child. She turned toward the source. Outside the orchard, Malindi's head was raised. Her mouth formed a circle. Malindi was *hooing*.

✳

Murky rays of early light reached their fingers into the root cellar. Tucked halfway inside her sleeping bag, leaning against the wall with a pillow at her back, Caitlin wrote in her notebook. Always take notes, her psychiatrist had advised. Right away.

She sipped water, wishing it were coffee. *"Where we have*

169

failed, you can succeed," Laura Enfield told her. Caitlin Gilbert had a role to play in this story and she would let it happen. She would open the gate and let the "plan" that had been stewing on the outskirts of her mind come in. It was all a matter of timing.

CHAPTER TWENTY

Sam said over the phone, "We've looked at several houses and Mary has decided on one. I can come home as soon as the papers are signed."

"Oh, Sam. That's wonderful. So..." She looked at the calendar on the kitchen wall. She could not do this thing with Sam here; he would never allow it. "Day after tomorrow?"

Sam's voice was warm, husky. "Hope so. I'm looking forward to our reunion, Caitlin. Let's spend the rest of the summer with no more than two feet between us. Or, better yet, no space at all."

"Mmm, Sam. Shall I meet you at the airport? I have a silky blue thing from Victoria's Secret that you haven't seen."

"Will you wear it to the airport?" He laughed, sounding better than he had in days. "I'm not sure I could endure the ride home. I'm getting — impatient."

Her eyes were fixed on the calendar. She would need time to recover. "If I don't answer the phone, please don't worry — Maggie, Toby, and I have plans." (Not entirely false.)

Next, she called Maggie. She caught her on the way out the door. "I'm expecting company," Caitlin told her. (Also true — Sam was coming home.) The could get together midweek. That was fine with Maggie.

Over a second cup of coffee, she debated how to handle Toby and Ed. There could be not be any interruptions. If she remembered correctly they were free this morning.

"Hi, Toby, how are you?"

"Great, Caitlin. What's up? Anything new?"

"Mmm, not really." (I'm such a liar.) "I was wondering if you and Ed could come over for lunch today. I've got to finish up some stuff for my exhibit later (true), and I'll be busy all weekend (uh, huh). Sam is coming home early next week, so we probably won't be able to get together until after that."

"Let me ask Granddad." After a short, muffled conversation, Toby came back on the line. "Sure, Caitlin, we'll be over."

"I'm making sticky buns for dessert."

"Yummy. Granddad wants to know if we can bring anything."

"Nope, just yourselves. See ya later."

"Get your ducks in a row," her Aunt Jane used to say. She called Carolyn and left a message on her answering machine telling her that she wouldn't be home. Just in case Carolyn took it into her head to stop in on her way to or from the theater with Jess.

The recipe was filed under *C* for Caitlin's Sticky Buns in Marny's recipe box. She checked the clock and ticked off the steps in her head: Mix the dough, let it rise; steep Stash's licorice tea, let it cool; make tuna salad; set the dining room table with good china and linen napkins; assemble the sticky buns and put them in in the oven.

With those tasks out of the way she called to Malindi. "Let's go outside, Malindi. I want to pick fresh mint for the tea and cut some flowers for the centerpiece."

Strange how calm she felt, arranging yellow day lilies in a PortMerion vase, expecting company like any normal person. Things will be different tomorrow. Fortunately, the forecast called for clear, dry weather. The timer on her Ironman watch reminded her to take the sticky buns out of the oven. She put them on a rack to cool just as Ed and Toby arrived.

Toby brought a marrow bone for Malindi. Little hussy,

Caitlin thought. You accept that bone like a lover receiving a box of chocolates.

"We're eating in the dining room," she told them

Ed took a seat at the elaborately set table. "This is nice, Caitlin, but you didn't have to go to so much trouble."

"It's nothing. Just tuna salad and potato chips on expensive dinnerware, that's all."

Toby took a sip of iced licorice tea. "Ooh, this is good. It tastes sweet, but you said there's no sugar in it."

Caitlin smiled, nodded, passed Ed a croissant.

"Does Sam know yet when he's coming home?" Ed asked.

"Soon." She sipped her tea.

"Tell him I'm ready to add the final details to the canoe, but I'll wait for him."

"That's nice of you Ed. I know he'll be pleased."

"Toby told me about the root cellar you two discovered. That's a pretty significant piece of history, Caitlin. I wonder when it was built."

"I don't know exactly, but it did exist when the architects renovated the house early this century."

Ed stirred his tea and stared at his plate. "Wouldn't be surprised if it goes back to the early eighteenth century."

Toby and Caitlin's eyes met.

"I'll make coffee and get dessert." Caitlin gathered dishes, Toby helped. In the kitchen, Toby pinched her arm and whispered, "Early eighteenth century."

"How about that?" Caitlin whispered back.

Toby cut up sticky buns and tore a sugary piece off the top, shoved it quickly into his salivating mouth. Caitlin didn't stop him. "Oh, these are so, so, good," he said.

"Come on." Caitlin carried a sterling silver coffee service into the dining room and poured coffee. After second helpings of sticky buns and two glasses of milk, Toby pushed back his plate.

"I'll wrap the rest up for you to take home," Caitlin said, smiling at Toby. "I'd rather you have them."

Malindi leaned heavily against Toby's legs. "Can I take her

for a walk, Caitlin?" he asked.

Timing was everything. Caitlin chewed her lower lip. "Okay, a short one—half an hour. Just as far as Devil's Pool. And don't let her off the lead, okay?"

"Okay, come on Malindi. Get your leash."

An awkward silence stood between Ed and Caitlin. She suggested that they finish their coffee outside. At least on the patio there would be something to look at besides embossed chinese wallpaper.

"It's been a very hot summer," Ed said, making conversation on the patio.

"Awful."

"I don't know how Toby and his teammates can play soccer in this weather.

"The heat doesn't seem to bother kids," said Caitlin. "They're lucky."

"Yes."

"I hope he drinks plenty of water."

"Yes, he does."

They watched the busy work of bees on the potted geraniums for a while.

Ed spoke first. "Sam called me."

"He did?"

"He said he couldn't reach you and he was worried."

"Oh."

"He's your husband, Caitlin. It's only natural that he would worry about you."

"I know." She slid her eyes toward him. "What has he told you about me, Ed?"

"Nothing, Caitlin." He hesitated and studied her expression. "But sometimes—because of the way you react—I wonder what you're hiding."

Ed was a nice man who, along with her husband, was simply concerned about her health. She blurted it out. "Before I met Sam I had a bad experience in Africa. Afterward, I saw a psychiatrist and she helped me through my—my difficulty. Sam did too."

"You have nothing to apologize for," Ed said, talking to the tops of the trees.

Seconds dragged into minutes. It had occurred to her that Ed might wonder why she didn't accompany Sam. For Sam's sake, to support him. She said softly, "I didn't think Sam would be gone this long. Do you think it's weird that I didn't go with him, Ed?"

"No, not really. My wife and I were often apart. She was an archaeologist and spent weeks at a time on digs in foreign countries. As a teacher, with summers off, I was able to join her on my vacations." He coughed, took a sip of water. "She died twenty years ago."

"I'm so sorry, Ed."

"Yes, well, life goes on."

"Oh, Ed."

Ed straightened and planted his coffee cup on the patio table. He faced her and said with a smile, "Shall we talk about the weather?"

"The weather's always a safe subject, Ed."

Toby and Malindi came romping back from their walk. Caitlin wrapped up the leftover sticky buns, said goodbye to her guests and promised to call if she needed anything. With her back to the closed door, she sighed as if a huge weight had been lifted from her shoulders. She was resolute. It had to be done. Dr. Truet would understand. "Say hello to my friend, Laura," he'd probably say.

Where did all these dishes come from anyway? she asked herself in the kitchen. She loaded the dishwasher and left the remainder in the sink.

She filled four buttered slices of whole wheat bread with American cheese, put them in a frying pan on the stove over an unlit burner. Whenever her stomach was queasy, a grilled sandwich was about the only thing she could manage to eat. She moved two bottles of coca-cola to front and center of a refrigerator shelf.

She gave the drooping impatience in the garden a good soaking before going into the root cellar to retrieve her things. She lugged these, along with a folding lounge chair and a small cooler filled with water bottles and gatorade, out to the apple orchard.

After showering, she dressed in loose cotton pants, a T-shirt, and a cardigan tied around her shoulders, all the while trying to avoid the burgeoning pile of clothes on the floor. "My God, I'm such a slob." Sam had been doing all the tidying up and he never once complained. She promised herself she'd be a better housekeeper in the future, bundled up the mess and crammed it into the clothes hamper. Downstairs, she gathered the scattered newspapers and shoved them in the recycling bin.

For the tenth time, she looked at the clock. It was time.

In the powder room she questioned her judgment. "Are you sure you want to do this?" she asked her reflection in the mirror. Of course I do. It's the only way. What's the harm? After all, didn't Sherlock Holmes use cocaine to gain insight into solving mysteries? She thrust her arm into the medicine cabinet, grabbed the prescription bottle and twisted open the lid. Before changing her mind, she tossed a Luriam tablet into her mouth and washed it down with a full glass of water.

✿

Four hours passed before she felt anything. She had been working on a new puzzle—a maddening tri-color Andy Warhol picture. Poor choice but no time to switch. She looked up and the room shifted. Plates below the earth's upper crust slid ever so slightly along fault lines.

Did I wait too long? I should eat now. When she stood up she felt dizzy, disoriented. She walked to the kitchen on legs that felt like wet noodles.

She turned the light on under the cheese sandwiches and poured a glass of coke. Damn. Should have made coffee for later. Coffee would help her head if not her stomach. Let's see, stomach—head, stomach—head, she weighed the two in her open palms before putting coffee, filter and water into the automatic coffee maker and setting the timer. The sandwiches turned to golden brown; she ate one with little discomfort, the other she wrapped in wax paper and left on the counter. Meanwhile, the tea kettle whistled. She brewed a strong, sweetened pot of English Breakfast tea and poured it into a thermos.

She teetered back to the library and worked for a while on the puzzle. As long as she did not make any sudden movements with her head, it wasn't so bad.

Then it hit. Surged through her body like a tornado. The room spun, every muscle in her body ached, she broke out in a sweat. She bit her lips, dug her fingers into the leather cushion of the chair. Minutes — or was it hours — passed. As suddenly as it came, it went, along with relief so welcome that she almost felt good. Now, get back to the powder room.

Was it possible that she was so sensitive to this drug that she wouldn't need a second pill? She laughed — a rabid, hysterical sound that startled her. "How do you do, Dr. Jekyl," she asked the face in the mirror. "Let's see if you turn into Mr. Hyde. Or is it the other way around — Dr. Hyde into Mr. Jekyl? Can't remember. Never could remember that. And, is it a wooden stake for a vampire and silver bullet for a werewolf, or vice versa? One should get those things straight because you never know when you'll need that important information. She placed a second pill on her tongue and drank a full glass of water.

Caitlin explained to Malindi that no matter what happened she should not leave her side. "That sounds like something out of an old movie. 'Whatever you do, don't open that door! You stay here, I'm going on alone!'" She giggled and clutched the rim of the sink. A wave of nausea quickly sobered her up. "Mustn't throw up and lose that pill." Like a child in a fun house, she staggered past pulsating walls and over a rolling floor.

"I think we better go outside now, Malindi."

❀

She watched the stars brighten in a ultramarine sky and waited for the second attack to strike.

This time it came full force. The invasion started with micro-soldiers parachuting into her respiratory system where they launched their pitchforks, cherry bombs, poison and hatred, causing her to hyperventilate. Platoons regrouped and marched through her digestive tract with combat boots that dug into her soft tissue with painful, grinding steps. The troops then fanned out to the very tips of her fingers and toes, forcing those digits to curl in upon themselves in pain. Seasoned warriors, they worked in unison to lift her up, spin her in circles and dump her limp body onto the bucking deck of a ship that pitched in a roiling sea. Her equilibrium was gone; she could not differentiate sky from earth, up from down.

Commanders barked their orders: "The enemy must not be mortally wounded, just incapacitated. Save the head for last. Only when the victim loses all mental faculties will we celebrate complete surrender." Jackhammers went to work behind her eyes, a vice clamped around her brain.

With extreme effort, Caitlin tried to focus on where she had put the migraine pills. Yes, side compartment—backpack. She must economize every move. In her mind, she repeatedly enacted how to reach the pills. Why, oh why did she close the buckle on her backpack?

Damn! She moved wrong and rolled out of the lounge chair into the icy sea. Her teeth chattered, she shook; her body began to freeze from the inside out.

Too weak to crawl into it, she pulled the sleeping bag over her quivering body and closed her eyes. The stars came with her, spinning faster and faster until she disappeared.

Victory was complete. The soldiers raised their bloody red flag.

❈

MALINDI, GERMAN TOWNE, PENSILVANIA, 1707

Following instructions, obedient Malindi remained at Caitlin's side. Until Caitlin fell asleep. Then, to make sure that her mistress was not in danger, she ventured forth to scope out the area. She moved to the apple orchard, took a tentative step inside.

In that instant, the dismal, variegated grays of canine monochromatism vanished and an unlimited palette of brilliant color opened like a flower before her.

The sky was cobalt blue with streaks of peach and lavender. Yellow buttercups and purple gentian tickled her ankles. In a velvety meadow of emerald green and gold, rosy-breasted bluebirds mingled with butterflies splashed in rainbow hues. Pink and cream petals from flowering crabapple, black cherry, and apple drifted down, filling the air with their spicy scent.

Absent in this lovely, peaceful landscape were the guttural, wrenching noises of modern machinery, replaced by diverse birdsong and hum of insect. Malindi's round ears picked up the rushing sounds of Cresheim Creek. Not the trickling sound that she was familiar with, but a crush and a thunder. She trotted in that direction, expecting to find the chain link fence that ran around the yard, but only a flock of surprised wild turkeys stood between her and the summit of the ravine. They scattered as she circled around them. A twig cracked, she froze. The strong musky odor of wolverine permeated the air.

Silently, Malindi picked her way down the slope where she saw tracks and scat of marten, mountain lion, gray wolf, deer, and elk on the muddy bank. She hid behind a boulder. Downstream, a moose stood in a diverted pool of water grazing on plants, casually ignoring the tawny gray lynx that hunkered down at the creek's edge, drinking. A black bear lumbered past, crossed the creek, and disappeared among American elm, black walnut, butternut, and chestnut trees.

She heard a soft whirring sound in the distance. The racket gained momentum and became a crescendo as the phenomenon roared overhead and the ravine went dark. Malindi raced up the incline. The sky was painted with dense streaks of blue, slate gray, and wine red moving in one direction, accompanied by the beating of thousands upon thousands of wings. Passenger pigeons racing toward extinction.

Malindi raised her head and cried for the pigeons, for the Xerces blue butterfly, the Santa ataline monkeyflower, Stellars sea cow, the blue pike, the relict leopard frog, the Gull Island vole, the dusky seaside sparrow. Her cries went on and on, name after name, but not a living person heard her lament.

❁

Caitlin occupied the same space as Malindi, but her attention was focused on a lovely young woman sitting beneath an apple tree, writing. The woman put down her pen and journal and rose to greet her.

"Hello, Caitlin. My name is Nessa Stewart."

❁

THE JOURNAL OF NESSA STEWART

Belfast, Ireland, Apryl 12, 1703
My name is Nessa Stewart. I am fourteen. I am from Ayr in Scotland. Father and I are aboard the vessel, Belfast Lass. In a wee bit we depart over the watter to Amerikie. Many of the passengers are indentured, but father sold our farm animals and tools to pay for our passage in full. We shall abide in German Towne, Pensilvania. Farewell dear Scotland. I'll not be comin' back ever again. Farewell me darlin' Calico cat. I shall miss you a heap and love you forever. I'm sorry you cannot go with me, but Sine loves you and will give you good care.

Apryl 13, 1703 Father stood on deck with me 'til the sight of the bonnie shores faded, then he went to his bedfast in the crowded quarters below. He's unwell with a cold. I'm hopin' the bracin' sea air will do him good. This venture is very excitin', and I pray to the almighty God that Father will come out of the darkness that took him when my dear Mother and her newborn babe died one year ago. When we received a letter from Paddy invitin' us to join him in Amerikie, I was taken aback and surprised when Father suggested that we start afresh in the New Warld.

Apryl 14, 1703   Once a day, at midday, we get vittles. Two jugs of watter, two pints of beer (I trade the beer to the tars for more watter), a bit of butter, two collops of peas, flesh four times a week and salted haddie the other three days. Nauthen at tea time. Father and I are savin' our parcel of dried meat, biskits, and lemons for later.

Apryl 15, 1703   I have never been to sea afore and I want to lairn everthin' about the ship. But I fear I'm mak'n a pest of meself with the tarry-breeks by my chatter and questions. They think they can quiet me with their cursin', but I've heard warse from the lads in Kilmarnock. Today, Danny — one of the tars — and I watched a large ink fish blacken the watter around us. Twas an awesome sight.

Apryl 16, 1703   Last eventide, on a quiet sea under a blankit of stars, the children and I gathered around auld Barnaby to hear his sea yarns aboot kelpies and craturs what eat wee bairns. He told us of his travels with Captain Kidd on the pirate ship, Adventure Galley. He was with Kidd when the pirate buried his treasure in Nova Scotia and Barnaby says he's goin' back some day to dig it up. He members seein' the rogue a-swingin' on the London gallows and swore his black body is still sittin' in an iron cage there today. I'm afeart the children had no sleep after hearin' that.

Apryl 17, 1703   The day was merry. The children and I played quirks and twisters. I'm yet laffin' at "She sheared six shabby sick sheep" that the wee Inglis Thomas spoke. At day's end, we gathered on deck and Danny tooted his tin whistle and the tars sang sea chantys. We danced jigs and reels with the whistle a-blowin and Patrick drummin' on a barrel like a bodhran. For the children's sake the boys obleeged me with no cursin'.

Apryl 18, 1703   The vessel came through bluffart and bluthrie weather. We were more under the watter than on. Most tied themselfs to their bedfasts, but I love the foamin', heavin' waves, the keenin' of the wind and the jabble of the sea. Danny says I would make a good tarry. We saw a pod of bou-backit whales jumpin' and jelpin' in the watter. 'Tis bitter cold and I'm gladsome to have Mither's warm wooljaiket and tam.

Apryl 21, 1703 I have acquainted meself with a daicent Inglishman, Jonathan Payne by name. He's a painter and makes wee pictures of folks. He will paint miniatures of the rich Amerikers. Father will not eat. Cook takes pity on me and gives me warm broth, but Father takes narry a drop.

Apryl 24, 1703.   Father has flux and fevver. The jabble of the vessel is makin him warse and I'm afeart he will die.

Apryl 25 1703   Father is dead. Buried under a wattry lair with no cairn nor flower.

Mey 20, 1703   Captain Jones has been very good to me. Mebbe I put him in mind of the daughter he lost to Barbados Fevver. Lest I be robbed, he keeps my papers, gear, and purse 'til we land.

Mey 22, 1703   Jonathan Payne is tryin' to cheer me by teachin' me to draw and paint. He says I have a natural talent for it. I fill the long hours drawin' the other folk. He is also teaching me to speak proper English which will serve me well in the colonies, he says. Mebbe I can get a job teaching children.

Mey 25, 1703   Jonathan Payne has painted my portrait. He has erased the worrisome circles around my eyes and brightened my dour countenance. My green eyes sparkle and my dirty, limp, auburn hair looks bonnie again. The picture is in a wooden frame and I shall treasure it always.

Mey 29, 1703 With luck and a calm sea we shall make land in good time, Captain Jones told me.

Juin 15, 1703 At keek of day, we left the ocean and traveled up a shallow bay on a winding river channel. Our first sight of the new colony was a brick tavern with a blue anchor hanging out front. I had to laugh at ship's company (especially Danny) as they were eager to jump ship and join the colourful ladies waving from the shore. Jonathan said I should not look at such depravity, but I want to see everything. I did a quick watercolour sketch of the scene on shore.

Captain Jones wished me well and offered to take me back to Scotland in two months time when the ship returns. I thanked him for his kindness, but I would like to find a new life here. Perhaps I shall marry one of the dashy-lookin' men I see strolling down Dock Street. Phildelphie is a fair green countrie towne with tall pine trees and crisscross streets.

Without the jabble of the rolling sea, walking on solid ground makes me feel topsalteerie. I long to bathe. I am waiting on the wharf for Jonathan Payne to find some means of transportation, for he will accompany me to German Towne. My head is swirling from the unaccustomed activity and noise around me. More of the "frail ladies" (as the sailors jokingly call them) are hanging about. The crew is unloading bales of goods—tea, sugar, tools. Colonists are examining the indentured passengers. Merchants line the market street selling oysters, fresh vegetables, fruits, wares and such. Jonathan promised to purchase a few pieces of fruit. Here he comes now in a small nag-drawn cart. My new life is about to begin.

I hear that The Governor of Pensilvania, William Penn, welcomes and encourages new settlers to seek freedom and prosperity here. As he lay dying, dear Father told me to be brave. And Mother always said to make the best of what I have. I will endeavor to honour their wishes. With God's grace, I shall do so.

Dear, kind Jonathan saw me to my destination and promised to come back for a visit at his earliest.

Cousin Paddy is a kind man, a widower, but without

Father it would be improper for me to live with him and his two sons. A German family resides across from Paddy's mill. That is where I am now, with Herr Uchman, his wife, their sixteen year old son and two wee ones. The wife has not recovered from the birth of twin girls a few weeks ago. In exchange for room and meals, I am to do household chores and help Frau Uchman with the babes.

I fear I am in for a bad time. I know they speak English, but the family converse in German, and I am supposed to understand them. They are ugly hacksits with lint white hair, pale faces, and they smell. Herr Uchman is sullen, his son a lazy, daft oaf, and his wife mean-spirited, ready to give me the rough side of her tongue at every turn. The babes are like their mother, ill-willie, fretful little things. Haggis-headed dunderheads all. I shall call them the Uglies.

Their home is more suited as a barn. It is one room, a rude log and wattle structure, oilpaper in the windows, a dutch door open at the top to allow a snippet of air to trickle in, the bottom shut to keep out the animals. The heat of this country is suffocating. I miss the cool breezes of Ayr. Unlike my cozy home in Scotland, there are no pretty ornaments, fine pottery, nor clock. Meals are silent. We sit at a plank table on two low benches. Since I do not have a trencher, I must wait and eat out of the pot when they are finished. Utensils are wooden and crude. A bed in the loft serves the elders and the babes; the son sleeps on a jack-bed in the corner. I sleep on a pallet of straw by the door.

There are two scrawny red cows, one ox, one old horse, several pigs, and dozens of chickens that spend a good deal of time in the trees. Perhaps the silly cluckers go up there to escape the wild creatures that inhabit the surrounding forests. No barn and only a lean-to for the animals, I must round up the cows and stray pigs every evening.

The kitchen is a separate room with dirt floor and high ceiling. I sat by the roast all this morning, turning it while

I cooked vegetables, baked bread, churned the butter, and rocked the twins. Although it is hot and tiring work, I welcome the solitude.

My dear mother used to say, "It's good to dread the worst, for the best will be all the more welcome."

A stray calico cat has taken to following me around, bringing great joy to my dreary existence. She makes me laugh when I squirt milk from the cow's teat straight into her mouth. I am considering sleeping in the root cellar, then she can join me at night. I call her Thistle.

I have hidden my journal, painting supplies, money, flax seeds, and parcel of fine unbleached linen under the floorboards in the root cellar. I do not trust the Uglies. I am going to move down there. They do not like to go in it because they think there are snakes down there. So I will be safe. Ha, ha. And, from now on, I will make entries in my journal in Lallans."

Once a week, I take pleasure in gathering and loading up the cart with vegetables, butter, and cheese for market. Unlike my benefactors, I have given names to the animals. Old Bess, the mare, and I follow a narrow path by the creek to Main Street, a busy thoroughfare. I must take care that the wheels do not get caught in deep ruts nor that Bess trip in them. I enjoy the hustle and bustle of German Towne. Bargaining with vendors and conversing with shoppers on the greene is a treat after a week with the crabbity Uglies.

Between here and the original settlement of German families on Main Street, I pass a prosperous farm and enviable two-story wood frame house with a sitting porch. A barn too, and a fenced in herb and flower garden. One day, as I was returning from market, a lovely woman by the name of Mrs. Burnett invited me to join her and her daughter and grandchildren for tea. Sweet fragrance of rose potpourri and spices and the laughter of children fill the house. It is a most cheerful place. Now, every market day I pass half an hour with them taking tea and biscuits.

The good woman gave me two dozen candles. I hid them under my apron and smuggled them into my root cellar bedroom. Candles are scarce as hen's teeth and I would get a tongue lashing if I were selfish enough to want to illuminate my cave dwelling. Now I can see to write in my journal and sketch pictures of Thistle.

The Burnetts invited me to a flaxing bee. Upon hearing this, my captors gave me extra chores to do that day. They sent me to the paper mill to sell rags. But I executed my revenge and took my good sweet time to make the acquaintance of the Rittinghausen family. Since then, I frequently sneak away to visit them. I pretend I am weeding in the vegetable garden, then I slip past the cornfield and travel a narrow path through dense, uninhabited forest to get to the mill. The walk takes little more than a quarter of an hour.

I leave the dark wood and come upon a lovely, open scene where the mill sits astride a gurgling stream. Nearby is a bake house and a charming one room cottage for the elders, Wilhelm and Geetruid. There is a two-story home for his son's large family. All the buildings are built of sturdy blueish gray stone.

I have not yet sorted them all out, but I believe a dozen children belong to Nicolaas and his Dutch wife, Willemena. Occasionally, another son, Gerhard, a resident of German Towne, and a daughter, Elizabeth Papen with her brood of five daughters visit. When they do it is a very noisy affair.

On the lea between the mill and the hills that swell up on the settlement's edge, I often play hide and seek and blind-man's bluff with the older children, patty cake with the wee ones. Willemena brings us apple cider and tea biscuits. She speaks no English but is very sweet. Sometimes I take my painting sack and do landscapes and portraits of the children.

Pastor Wilhelm Rittenhausen is an industrious gentleman.

He is from Germany where he learned his skill and trade as paper maker. He has a friendly manner, but is stooped and round-shouldered from long years of bending over vats of mulching paper pulp. His hands are enlarged and red from plunging the paper mould into the warm water. He generously offered to exchange my unbleached linen from Scotland for his absorbent, unpolished paper in lovely pale shades of browns and blues. Excellent for watercolours he says.

The entire family engages in the making of paper. Sometimes, I join the small children in removing buttons from clothing, sorting the rags according to quality.

If an inlet or harbor is a safe haven for boats, the mill is my refuge. In my dreams, I hear the squeak of the wooden gears of the water wheel, the sound of water pouring into it, the stamper beaters pounding the rags to make the pulp. The acrid smell of soaking rags lingers in my nostrils.

Lately, on my trips to the mill, I sense that someone or something follows me. Once, I turned quickly and through the thick foliage saw the black eyes and gray fur of a wolf.

At last, I have seen my stalker. He is a tall, bronzed youth with long black hair pulled back and fastened with feathers. A gray fur piece drapes across his broad shoulders. He has beautiful dark brown eyes that fix steadily upon mine. The other day, I thought I saw him smile before he disappeared into the forest. It is not true that the natives are black and naked.

Each morning, outside my bedroom, I find a small gift on the ground: a piece of smoked meat, a bead necklace, a butterfly wing in a purple shell. When I go to the paper mill or to market, when I cross the creek to take grain to Paddy's mill, I know he is watching me. I told Paddy about him.

Paddy smiled and said, "Sounds like Temetet, the wolf. I've traded with him and I wager he follows you for protection.

The Lenni Lenape are a friendly bunch." Then Paddy scolded me for traveling through the woods unescorted. But what choice do I have?

One day, when I found a pretty blue bead on my doorstep, I decided to give Temetet a gift. I painted his likeness and put it outside my door before I went to bed. It was gone in the morning, but I did not receive another gift in its place. I thought perhaps I had offended him. That evening, while I was searching for Nelly, the cow, Temetet appeared before me in the apple orchard. My heart dropped to the bottom of my stomach. I had to remind myself to breath.

He is exceedingly handsome, a few years older than me, and with a gentle manner. "Thank you for my gift," he said in good English. Then he smiled. His teeth are perfect and white. He walked with me until we found Nelly by the creek. Then he left. My heart is full of him. I love him. I love Temetet, the wolf.

Temetet calls me Okwes. It means fox in his language. Because of my auburn hair and green eyes, I suppose.

Mrs. Burnett fears I will not survive nights in the root cellar over the winter. I told her I would not sleep in the Uglies house for anything. I have considered the kitchen, for it is covered, and at least warm during the day from the cooking. Two days ago, to my surprise, the Burnett men, their neighbors, Paddy and sons arrived before dawn. Temetet was with them. They cleared a small parcel of land on this side of the creek that belongs to Paddy and raised a little log cabin. For me. All my own. The women brought food, the men worked hard, and my heart is bursting with gratitude and love for these good people.

The Uglies and I have reached an agreement. I will do some chores for them in exchange for food and the use of their butter churn and other tools that I do not yet possess. When

I have my own garden, I can wean myself away from them entirely. Father used to say, "the Scot has never been very servile or supple at the knee." I will be independent yet!

Autumn: I cannot speak of what happened, but writing helps to ease the pain and diminish the shame. After all, it is not my fault. The twins were in my care, on a blanket in a patch of sun in the apple orchard. I was gathering windfall fruits when, all of a sudden, I was struck from behind and knocked to the ground. He tore at my clothes and tried to force himself upon me. I cannot erase the sight of his ugly face, the dreadful smell of him. I struggled, but he was strong. I wanted to die.

I heard the growl of an animal and then I was free, the vile body flung from me. Whispering in soft, threatening snarls, Temetet had a knife to my attacker's throat. He turned to look at me, waiting for the word. I managed to rise and told Temetet to let him go, he was not worth it. The cowering beast scrabbled to his feet and ran away.

I saw Frau Uchman crouching behind a bush, watching. She charged out, scooped up the babies, and ran into the house. In the back of my mind, I thought, "I'll cash this voucher in one day, you dreadful sow."

Temetet gave me a knife and made me promise to have it sheathed at my waist at all times. He is teaching me to fish and hunt game with bow and arrow. He says I have a good eye.

I sold a portion of my flax seed and used the money to buy pots and eating utensils. After much practice, I can spark a fire by twisting a stick in a wooden bowl like Temetet taught me.

By way of the Rittinghausens, I have received a letter from Jonathan. He is doing well painting the colonists in

Philadelphia and the upcountry. He will come to visit as soon as he is able. He says that there could be a market for my little landscapes, and that I should devote more of my time in producing them for sale. I would welcome the income. He suggests, however, that I sign the paintings with a man's name, as women artists are not generally accepted. I will compromise and use just my initial N followed by Stewart.

I am with child.

Dear Paddy has asked for my hand in marriage. He is a kind and generous man but I cannot accept, because I do not love him. And he is old. Fourty-five. Temetet wants me to marry him and move to his village, but I am determined to raise my baby here where it can be educated in the new Quaker school near the market place. I want my child to have the best of everything. I can do this. I do love Temetet so much though.

I sold most of Father's clothes to the paper mill. The rest I am wearing. I don't care what I look like, I am comfortable.

April 1704:   My belly is telling a tale, so I decided it was time to cash in my voucher. I made it clear to Frau Uchman that I wanted old Bess. Having purchased another mare, they have been neglecting her anyway. What could the stupid woman do but let me have her? Indeed, a wee mouse may creep beneath a muckle corn stack.

I love my dear Bess. She is fattening on sweet alfalfa hay that I purchased from the Burnetts at a charitable price. Her step is frisky once again like a young colt. Temetet fashioned saddle bags and baskets to throw over her back, and she and I are happy not to have to drag the cart over the treacherous main roads. We can take short cuts through the woods.

June 1704: When my time came, Grandmother Burnett stayed

with me. She said the delivery was as easy as a pea popping out of a pod. I will call my beautiful wee bairn Fiona, after my dear mother. She has thick, straight hair as black as a raven's wing and her eyes are sparkling ebony. Mrs. Burnett brought me blankets and clothing that her grandchildren have outgrown. Paddy made a lovely little crib out of black walnut, and Temetet made a clever leather bag that I can wear on my back or chest to carry my precious bundle.

Autumn 1704: My darlin' Fiona laughs and gurgles and waves her arms about. She is a joy. She watches our every move. Temetet built a sheltered stall against the rear of the house for Bess. I made dozens of candles from the beeswax that Temetet harvests from wild hives.

Winter 1704: Jonathan arrived on horseback with the first snow. Imagine his surprise when he found me in my cozy house. Of course, he knew about Fiona and brought her a sweet rag doll. He brought me a beautiful blue paint powder called Indigo from the West Indies.

Fiona in my backsack on Bess, Jonathan on his horse, we went for a long ride up the creek, following the Wissahickon up stream. The cliffs and glens are incredibly beautiful. I must go back to paint. Fiona gurgled and laughed the whole way. At home she fell sound asleep, curled up in front of the fire with Thistle.

Temetet brought venison steaks; I made corn biscuits, roasted root vegetables, and opened a pot of stewed apples. We all fell asleep under blankets and furs alongside darling Fiona.

When Jonathan departed, I gave him maple cream candy that I made last summer from the maple water Temetet and I collected in the spring. He took a few of my watercolours to sell, but I will never part with the pictures of Fiona.

Spring 1705: A warmth comes with the west wind, the

191

ice is breaking up, and the geese honk overhead on their way north. And, thanks be to God, I have eggs. A group of chickens found their way to my door and simply will not leave. I planted corn, oats, pumpkins, squash, potatoes, beans, and carrots, and have a small herb garden of parsley, sage, lemon balm, lavender, and chives. All courtesy of Grandmother Burnett and Willemena Rittenhausen. I shall have my first real crop this year and soon will be free of the Uglies entirely. Temetet fashioned a hoe out of a wooden pole and the shoulder bone of elk. He traded furs for sugar, salt, crockery pots, and bowls. He never ceases to entertain Fiona with the toys he makes. Her favorite is a necklace of dried deer hooves hanging over her cradle. He calls her his little Chiskuskus—Robin.

Summer 1705: In the spring, after my crops were planted, with Fiona on Temetet's shoulders, we walked to the river and traveled upstream in a dugout canoe to Conshohocken. We embarked and walked a short distance to a pleasant valley. Laughing children and friendly women poured out of their strange wigwams and longhouses to greet us. Men thumped Tem's back and said things that I could only guess the meaning of.

When it quieted down, Temetet and I knelt before the chief and the medicine man on a blanket strewn with meadow flowers. We made our vows, honoring our promises for life. One of the women placed a crown of red and blue bay leaves upon my head (which shortly ended up on Fiona's head). Temetet handed me the stripped shin bone of a deer, signifying that he would hunt and provide me with meat. In turn, I gave him an ear of corn, to show that I would always grow maize for our bread.

There was a grand feast of venison, turkey, corn, cooked pumpkin, berries, and beach plum, followed by dancing and music played on the water drum, flute, turtle shell, and gourd. The men played a game using netted sticks and a wooden ball. Fiona had a wonderful time with the children.

Best of all, they gave us a wonderful and generous gift. Three goats. Three playmates for Fiona, company for Bess and Nelly, and milk and cheese to come. Fiona must think they are cows because she has already named the black and white goat, Moo. I shall call the others Morag and Morna, good Scottish names.

Life is good. My goat cheese and butter are selling well at market. I wrap the cheeses in linen, my butter is indented with a robin made from the wooden mold that Tem carved.

Autumn 1705: Autumn blanketed the ground in a lush carpet of scarlet and gold. Fiona delights in covering herself with leaves. She says she is a tree. I gathered apples for the Uglies and myself, and stored my share in Paddy's spring house, along with my root vegetables. I've preserved meat and made pots of jams. We went to the Burnetts' corn husking bee. After the work was done we had a feast under a golden full moon. The children showed Fiona how to blow soap bubbles. We made corn husk dolls and my bonnie Fiona would not let hers out of her hands. She is sleeping with it clutched to her chest right now.

Winter 1705: I am beginning to look like an Indian or some sort of wild woman, for I dress entirely in skins and furs now. Fiona as well. We wear deerskin leggings, jackets and moccasins of soft skins and furs of bear, deer, and coyote. They serve well to protect us from the bite of wind and weather. In the evenings I sit by the fire making a quilt out of my old clothes and Father's. Temetet busies himself making cabinets and furniture. And of course, more toys for his little Chiskuskus.

Spring 1706   Jonathan came for a visit. He brought a pineapple, the first I have ever tasted. He gave me a hefty bag of coins in payment for my paintings. We all went berry picking for wild strawberries and raspberries. Little Robin is into everything. There was no stopping her from diving into the baskets of berries. She was covered in juice and we couldn't stop laughing.

I offered to take the twins to the Burnetts' flaxing bee, but Frau Ugly turned up her nose and the twins screamed. They are all so unpleasant.

Autumn 1706: The Uglies' crops failed. It is not the fault of this rich, fertile land, but theirs. They are terrible farmers.

Frau Ugly has a bad cold. I took her skunk oil, a Lenape remedy for curing colds, but I could have saved my breath to cool my porridge. I put a few drops in tea but she would not drink it, nor did she take the roasted onion syrup in warm milk that would have helped her. Stubborn woman.

I spent the rest of the day doing their laundry and mine. Fiona amused me by playing hide and seek among the sheets. I painted her picture, using the indigo blue that Jonathan gave me, for her apron. She wanted to paint too, so I gave her paper and a few little pots of color. She painted a funny little picture of Moo, the goat.

Winter 1706: Temetet made a sledge out of bent willow for Fiona. She wanted to take it out immediately, but we convinced her to wait for snow. When the first snowflake fell, she was at the door, ready to go.

The Uglies are faring poorly this winter. I take them food, remembering that Mother always said, "a bit is often better given than eaten." Temetet catches game for them. He cannot understand how they go hungry when there is so much food around. Germans live off the farmland, they do not hunt, I told him.

Herr Uchman demanded to be reimbursed for Bess. He said that I acquired her dishonestly. That did not sit well with me. I stomped over and plunked my butter money down on the table. They have no scruples; all they want is money while I have all that I need and want. Money is not everything.

Spring 1707: I am teaching Fiona and Temetet to read from the books that the Rittenhausens gave me. They are excellent pupils and we play a game to see who learns the most words in an evening.

Frau Uchman asked if I would mind the twins tomorrow at my house. I overheard her say to her son that they are having visitors, an old childless couple with money. I thought it odd, as they never have company.

This evening, listening to the gurgle of the stream and chirping of birds settling to nest, Temetet, Fiona, and I chased the first fireflies of summer. We are so happy. I cannot imagine a better life.

I want to die. Fiona is gone.

Temetet and I looked all day for Fiona. Tomorrow he and Paddy and the boys will scour the country to find her. They suspect foul play

T went again to search. Frau U. brought me soup. I heard her talking to Herr U. outside the door—something about taking me to the cornfield. Must tell T. He will hide my things—he knows where.

CHAPTER TWENTY-ONE

A searing light burned its way through Caitlin's eyelids and traveled into her brain where it exploded in a million pieces. Where was she? *Who* was she? In the empty tunnel of her mind, she gradually became aware of a sound. She could see the sound. Wings flapping. She opened her eyes.

She lay on her side with her head resting on one arm. A few inches from her nose a white butterfly landed on a blade of grass. The butterfly folded its wings and shifted position, minimizing its body and cast shadow. "Oh clever little one, I'm not a predator. I won't hurt you." A prism of sunlight washed over the insect's scaled wings, changing them to a blue so vivid that Caitlin could hear the color.

She looked deep into the butterfly's eyes.

How extraordinary. Your eyes are a mosaic pattern—like dots in a photograph. You have tiny hairs around your mouth. The insect wiggled its antennae, uncurled a long, slender tongue, and flew away, leaving a pleasant scent of cherry pie, vanilla, and cinnamon.

Caitlin turned her attention to the blade of grass, still quivering from the butterfly's flight like a sapling in the wind. Sage green. No, brighter—Viridian, DaVinci #D290. I shall curl up and sleep in that tubular sheath. Or, like a spider, stretch my limbs along the flattened edge where it unfurls and narrows to a point. She moved her hand to do so and the serrated edge sliced her fingertip. A single, glistening drop of blood—Cadmium red deep, DaVinci #D210—oozed up and rolled in slow motion like a bead of mercury to spill upon the ground.

Malindi rose and took a long drink from her water bowl. She stood over her mistress and let water drip from her mouth onto Caitlin's face. Time passed. Minutes? Hours? Caitlin stretched out her free arm and pulled her backpack closer, fumbled for the migraine pills. Hadn't she done this very same thing only a moment ago?

Someone was calling. Softly at first, then louder and with urgency. Yes, Caitlin was her name. Why couldn't people leave her alone? She wanted to lie here forever. She didn't need anyone; she had Malindi.

"Caitlin, it's Ed. Where are you?"

Her mind processed the information. Ed. What was he doing snooping around here. Old busybody.

"Caitlin, are you all right?"

His voice sounded nice. Ed. She needed Ed. He would lie down beside her and hold her. They'd die in each other's arms. What was she thinking? He'd spoil everything. She'd have to get rid of him. She'd have to kill him. With a rock? Her eyes traveled to the Belgian blocks lining the path. Too heavy. And she was feeling a bit weak. A kitchen knife. She would lure Ed into the house and stab him. Now where were the sharpest, longest knives? Yes—in the dining room, sideboard, left hand drawer. That dreadful carving set with the yellowed antler handles.

She rolled onto her hands and knees, testing the rotation of the earth. Not too bad. She tried to stand, failed, and fell to the ground. Gritting her teeth she tried again. When the world finally stopped spinning, she put one foot in front of the other and began the long journey toward the irritating voice coming from behind the courtyard gate. Fatigue dragged her down, but she reached her destination and concentrated on one last task. Thank God, the combination padlock hung free. She vaguely remembered opening it at some point in time. One bolt slid open, the second stuck. She began to cry and worked at the bolt, sniffling and cursing until her fingers were bloody. At last, the rusty bolt moved and the gate swung open.

She fell forward and collapsed in Ed's arms.

❀

She moved her heavy lidded eyes to half mast. A high square window behind her and an oil lamp on a table holding bottles of medicine provided the only light in the room. A string of laundry hung across the far wall; a flowered pitcher and a mortar and pestle sat on a small bench at the foot of the bed. Seated next to her, a black leather doctor's bag at his feet, a bearded man in a dark red Victorian jacket and vest leaned forward, pensively stroking his beard. Concern pinched his face. In a dark corner of the room, a shadowy figure looked on, worried and helpless.

Caitlin plucked at her rose-colored coverlet, closed her eyes and slept.

❀

She was dialing Sam but he did not answer. On the second attempt, a faint voice answered, but she was unable to distinguish the words. Next time, the line was busy. Again, she punched in numbers. "No one by that name here," snapped an angry, faceless person. She tried again; the recipient slammed down the receiver. As she grew more anxious, the touch-tone phone changed into an outdated dial face. She dialed but her fingers stuck in the holes. Frantic now, using a pencil, she rotated the dial. Midway, the pencil broke. With shaking fingers, she tried again, but for the life of her, she could not remember Sam's number.

❀

During the twilight of her sleep, the doctor pulled a quilt from the bottom of the bed and covered her with it. He was the kind, thoughtful doctor from the famous painting that hung in Dr. Truet's office.

"Are you still cold?" the kind, thoughtful doctor asked.

She nodded. He pulled the bedclothes aside and laid down beside her to share the comforting warmth of his body.

🌺

They studied each other. "How long have I been asleep?" she finally asked.

"Twelve hours," Ed said. "How do you feel?"

"I'm not sure. Why are you here?"

"You didn't answer the phone, so I stopped by to see if you were all right."

"Oh."

"Do you think you could eat something?"

"I could try."

"I'm afraid I ate your grilled cheese sandwich. How about soup and crackers?"

"That would be good. And coke please. I feel like I have a terrible hangover. Would you mind feeding Malindi?"

"I will do that.

Malindi seemed unwilling to leave Caitlin. "It's okay, Malindi. Go with Ed."

Caitlin inched her way into the adjoining bathroom. She looked in the mirror. Yikes. Not a pretty sight: her face was drained and gray, eyes glassy, mouth a rigid slash. Like death warmed over. A shower and a change of clothes would help, but she was afraid of passing out. She staggered back to the bed and collapsed.

Ed brought dinner on a tray and placed it on the bedside table. He helped her sit up, plumped up her pillow, and put the tray on her lap. He pulled out bureau drawers, found a T-shirt, shorts, and underwear, and stacked them neatly at the foot of the bed. He brought a basin of warm water, a washcloth and towel, and placed them on the bedside table. Without a word he left the room.

As she was getting dressed, the foreboding notes of the overture to "Tannhauser" played in the library. Holding tight to the railing, Caitlin crept downstairs. By the time she reached the bottom step, black dots were dancing in front of her and a raging river rushed through her head. The floor fell away.

Ed was standing over her.

"A little dizzy," Caitlin said. "Got up too quick."

"You need fresh air."

She nodded, moved to rise, but he picked her up and carried her out to the patio where he placed her gently on a lounge chair.

"Cold?"

"Yes."

"I'll get a blanket." He floated out of her vision, returned and tucked an afghan over her lap and around her shoulders.

"What happened, Caitlin?"

"I don't know." Honestly, she did not know.

"Caitlin."

"I'll try to remember."

"You're not much of a drinker and you don't do drugs."

"True."

"I don't mean to pry, but you must admit, Caitlin, this is all very strange."

She sighed and closed her eyes. Did she want to remember? It would be nice if Sam—no—Ed would stay with her. She was confused, irritable. Where the hell was Sam anyway? You can't trust anyone anymore. It was hot. Why did she have this stupid blanket on top of her?

"I'll stay the night Caitlin, but is there anyone who could come over tomorrow?"

"I'll be all right," she snapped.

❀

Hell, she wasn't all right but she could handle it. Always did. And if not, she'd go up to Ronksville and stay with her brother. Again. Her heart suddenly ached and swelled in size. She wanted desperately to go home. She felt like this in Nairobi when she had that awful feeling of homesickness, that need to get out of there. She could be home in less than three hours.

In the dark, she eased open a bureau drawer, removed several articles of clothing and tossed them on the floor. As she was rummaging around in the top drawer, selecting underpants and socks, her hands slid over something wonderful. Thrilling to the sensuous fabric, its smallness, she rubbed the cool silk against her cheek. Her nightgown fell to the floor and the midnight blue garment slid over her body with a whispering caress.

"*Starehe*, Malindi. Stay." She stepped into the hallway, turned on the light, adjusted the dimmer switch. In the open doorway, the curves of her body filtered through a blue, filmy haze, highlighted by a soft glow from the hall light. Her voice purred, her movements were airy. She was an ethereal being, drawn to him by his color, his shape, his chemical scent. Floating above him, her hair drifted across his chest, her touch as light as the tip of a butterfly's tongue.

Frozen in midair, she was suddenly rendered immobile — like a specimen on a insect collector's pinning board. Scarcely breathing, she listened to heavy footsteps padding down the hallway. Claws raked the carpet. At each door the beast paused. It was searching for her soul. Then, what had begun as a low rumble escalated into a thunderous roar that shook the walls. It bellowed through her quivering body and vibrated in the pit of her stomach. The tawny, panting beast rounded the doorway. Hot fetid breath blew past her, scorching her skin. Amber eyes glinted in the dark, piercing hers. One single swipe of a forepaw knocked her through a black hole in the earth and she fell into a turbulent sea where waves rocked so violently that she thought her bones would break.

"Caitlin."

Water filled her ears, but his voice, deep and sensuous, slipped through her watery grave.

"Caitlin."

Poseidon poked her with his trident. Ed. Ed was Poseidon. "Drink this."

The cola bit into her parched throat. "What happened?" Her mind was muddled. She felt sick.

"You passed out in the hallway. I called Dr. Truet. He prescribed rest and company. He's getting ready to leave for Egypt, but said he'd come over if you want him to."

"Not necessary." She felt vulnerable. Like a sick animal

pretending to be well and capable of fending off predators in order to survive. The attempt failed, she knew Ed saw through her.

"I didn't know you spoke Scots, Caitlin."

Imperceptible and dull, the words ploughed through the air before they hit her with the force of a flood bursting through a dam. She remembered.

"What did I say?"

"Before you passed out yesterday, you were babbling in Lallans. You did it again a few minutes ago. Something about finding Nessa's baby."

"Nessa," she whispered, crumpling in upon her self.

CHAPTER TWENTY-TWO

S unk deep inside a leather chair in the library, the gulping sobs less intense, she called her psychiatrist.

"This is India Buckingham. Please leave your name and number, and I'll call you back as soon as possible. If this is an emergen..." The message was interrupted.

"Caitlin, caller i.d. tells me it's you. What's up?"

"I'm sorry to bother you on your day off, but..." Caitlin's voice broke.

"Are you hallucinating again? Tell me everything."

Caitlin told her that she had taken Luriam.

"Now let me get this straight. You deliberately took the drug that caused you all that trouble in Africa. Are you crazy?" A silky laugh followed the absurd comment and India's counseling tactics once again centered Caitlin as they had in the past.

Caitlin recited a brief account of events, including seeing ghosts. India paused a moment to digest the information.

"Look, Caitlin, I'm just a mere mortal and don't have the right to judge whether or not ghosts exist. Your state of mind is more important. Have you told Sam these things?"

"No," Caitlin answered, sheepishly.

"And what happened last year when you told him about Africa and your hallucinations?"

"I got better."

"Well, it doesn't take a rocket scientist to figure out what you have to do now, does it?"

"I'll tell him everything.

"The Luriam should wear off in a few days, so I don't think you'll end up killing anyone." India chuckled. "But you might want to stay away from kitchen knives and rocks for a while. Now, dear patient, I know you don't take drugs—except for the kind that can kill you—but suppose I prescribe a light tranquilizer for your symptoms: nervousness, irritability, and nightmares. In case you change your mind?"

"Okay."

"And if you do take the tranquilizer, tell Sam. Wouldn't want you experimenting with Valium like you did with Luriam. And for God's sake don't get them mixed up." She clucked her tongue. "You've got to write a book about this someday. Call me."

"I will," Caitlin promised and hung up the phone.

Ed tapped lightly on the door frame. "May I come in?"

"Of course, Ed."

He sat down and she squirmed under his pointed look. "What's going on Caitlin?"

"I shouldn't tell you before I tell Sam."

He kept silent.

She raked through her memory. "What did you say I was babbling about?"

"You were talking about finding a child. And you were speaking in Lallans."

"What?"

"You were speaking in Lallans. It's a dialect spoken in the Scottish lowlands and in Ulster, Ireland. Quite different from Scottish gaelic, although I know both."

"You do?"

"Of course. I grew up in Scotland. Any Scot worth his salt can speak it. As a youth, I spent hours reading Rabbie Byrnes's poems aloud."

Her taut face cracked a smile as she pictured a youthful Ed, sitting in front of the fire, two mastiffs by his feet, reading poetry to his family. Or sauntering through the heather reciting romantic verses with his sweetheart on his arm.

"Ed, would you translate something from Lallans for me?"

"I will. What is it and where is it?"

"It's a journal but I have to find it first."

"Translate something you don't have? And how do you know where it is?"

She avoided his eyes. "Let's just say I have inside information."

"Look, Caitlin, I know you had a problem in Africa and that you're prone to hallucinations."

"Uh, huh."

"Tell me more, Caitlin."

"Things were revealed to me in sort of a dream."

"And before that?"

She sighed. Could he see into her mind? "I saw—I guess you would call them—uh, visions."

She did not expect an outburst of laughter and shrank back in her chair.

"Ghosts. You saw ghosts."

For a brief moment, she had the impression that he was making fun of her and she was offended. But he wasn't; he believed her.

"Caitlin, you're talking to the man who saw dead monks walking in the Wissahickon. Besides, Scotland is full of ghosts, faeries, wee beasties and things that go bang in the night. Almost every country house has some form of unexplained phenomena: a tapping in the walls, shutters that fly apart, latches that undo themselves, and doors that slam shut. In our farmhouse, an old woman in a white dust cap sat squeaking away in our rocking chair by the fireplace every night after we went to bed. Unafraid, my dog, Tennyson, would lie beside her until the cock crowed. Mother said it was a great, great aunt of hers: a spinster, whose fisherman sweetheart was lost at sea. She was a'waitin' his return."

In the light of day, discussing this odd subject with a friend, she felt better. She talked until both she and all aspects of the story were exhausted.

❀

"One minute," Caitlin called. She snapped closed the last tiny hook of several dozen hooks on a red satin boustierre before examining her reflection in the mirror. Too plain. She bent over, brushed her hair vigorously, puffed it out. When she stood up, she put her hands on her hips, tilted her head and made a pouty mouth. Much better. She opened a top bureau drawer, pawed through an assortment of cosmetics and tossed them on the floor. She found a cherry red lipstick and spread it on her lips, touched her finger to the tube and painted a dab on her cheekbones. She puckered her mouth. Appreciating the effect, the corners of her lips turned up in a seductive smile. One last touch: her fingers found a sultry French perfume on the cluttered bureau top, she sprayed the scent on her neck, shoulders, and inner thighs.

Downstairs, a player piano rolled out a tune that blended melodiously with the laughter of the other girls. Madame told her that this customer liked it rough. Well, she could accommodate him. She pulled aside the gaudy beaded curtain, stood in the doorway and beckoned to him. Ignoring his puzzled expression, she explained the rates: "Two dollars, plus twenty-five cents extra for each act, and another dollar for you know what," she recited, businesslike.

The customer picked her up in his arms, pushed through the beaded curtain and carried her outside where he laid her gently on a strange piece of furniture, shiny and hard. "This is nice," she said in a heavy voice. "I like doing it outside."

"Caitlin."

Arms encircled her, held her tight.

She pushed the man back to peer into his face. She put her fingers to his mouth. The man's face began to break up and splinter apart. From the fog of confusion, Sam's features emerged.

"Sam? It's you."

"I left you alone for one minute and you were gone. Malindi

found you. You were, of all places, in the elevator with the door locked. I had to unscrew the door from its hinges."

"I don't understand. I feel weird." Her head rolled back; she was slipping away.

"Caitlin, listen to me, look at me," Sam said firmly. "Ed called and I got the first flight home. All he told me was that you'd been hallucinating."

Her body felt leaden with fatigue. "Sam, I'm so tired. I'd like to go to bed."

❋

"You look much better this morning, Caitlin."

"I feel better. I'm sorry to have troubled you, Sam. That you had to come home."

"I was ready to leave."

"I talked to my psychiatrist."

Except for the slight lift of an eyebrow, Sam's expression did not change. From his patio lounge chair, he tossed the frisbee to Malindi before casually taking a sip of coffee. "You didn't eat your corn muffin, Caitlin."

"I will. Could you pour me more coffee, please."

He filled her cup, added cream.

She looked down and saw that she had shredded the sports section of the paper without realizing it. Would Sam accept her ghosts? The traditional Navajo—which Sam was not—believed in spirits, but they never talked about the dead nor spoke their name again. They would leave the hogan door open for the soul of the deceased to escape. Goodbye, that's it!

She stalled and bit her lower lip. In a tiny voice, she said, "Sam, I took Luriam."

The words hung in the air like Chinese symbols.

"You what?"

"I found Marny's bottle of Luriam in the medicine closet, and I took two pills."

She flinched back in her chair and closed her eyes to block

from her sight the fulminating black stallion. The beast reared back on his hind legs and tore at the air over her head with his forelegs. His eyes were like burning charcoal and steam pored from his flaring nostrils.

"Caitlin, Caitlin." Sam cradled her in his arms, his voice soft and tender. "What happened?"

"I don't know, I kind of blacked out."

Sam pored her a glass of ice water from the pitcher beside them. "Drink this."

She drank a full glass and pulled herself together. "Sam, please try to understand. I needed to find someone. I've been seeing things. A woman. A girl. They were trying to tell me something, but I couldn't get through to them. I didn't know what they wanted. I thought that taking the drug would give me a breakthrough."

Sam held her tight and stared off into the woods. "I understand Caitlin. I just wish you had confided in me. Suppose you tell me about it now."

Letting go, she released a heavy sigh. "I had a dream that revealed the story of a young girl who lived here long ago."

CHAPTER TWENTY-THREE

When she finished telling her story, Sam stood up and held out his hand. "I'd like to see where you had your dream."

As if on cue Malindi trotted into the apple orchard.

Caitlin gasped in surprise. "That's odd. She wouldn't go in there before."

Sam walked around the orchard for a bit.

"What do you expect to find, Sam? Clues?"

He shoved his hands in the pockets of his jeans. "Not really, Caitlin. As you said, it was a dream."

She put her arms around him and promised herself that she would never keep anything from him again.

"Now what Caitlin?" Sam asked as they walked back to the house.

"I have to find Nessa's journal. She said it's in the root cellar."

"Would you like me to help you?"

"Of course, but I should let Maggie and Toby in on it."

❀

Soccer practice had been canceled due to the rain, so Toby was available. Maggie had tickets for the Phillies game, but it was rained out. Sam was in the other room talking to his sister. He told Caitlin that he would stay in the background and give the full glory to The Three Detectives. He would join them shortly.

They sat at the kitchen table. Caitlin told her friends that she had evidence that there was a trunk buried in the root cellar.

"Holy Toledo," cried Toby. "Let's go. Let's dig it up."

Maggie's eyes crinkled in an accusing squint. "How did you find out?"

"Let's just say—for now—that I had a dream."

Maggie's expression changed. "Good enough. Let's go."

"I'm Inspector Clouseau and we need to find a reim. A reim with minkeys," said Toby, clumsily bumping into chairs on the way out.

Maggie chortled. "You're a card, Toby, you know that?"

"Wait. We're going to need shovels, maybe a pickax," Caitlin said.

"They're in the shed." Toby took off for the shed. Caitlin and Maggie got flashlights and lanterns. It was raining hard; they made a dash for the root cellar and squeezed through the hedge. Malindi followed.

Maggie lifted the Coleman lantern, illuminating the room in jerky splashes of light. "Where can it be?" Maggie asked.

Toby circled his fingers like binoculars around his eyes. "If I were Superman I could see right through rock."

"Sorry to disappoint you, comic boy, but you're gonna hafta use your muscles on this one. Where do we start, Caitlin?"

Caitlin stood in the far left corner of the room with her eyes shut as if in a trance. We're coming Nessa. We can do it, Laura. Thank you Destiny. She took a step backward and pointed with her shovel. "Right there."

They were archaeologists uncovering prehistoric bones: they dug and scraped off dirt, they removed leaves and debris with great care. They picked and brushed until Toby hit something hard.

"It's it. It's the treasure."

Maggie pulled on his arm. "Wait, let's not damage anything."

They scraped a little more and uncovered bare spots of wooden floor boards.

"Now what?" said Maggie.

Caitlin used her fingernails to scratch through the hardened dirt in the center of their handiwork. She let out a squeak when she felt a metal handle lying flat against the wood. She pried the handle up and tugged. A square section of the floorboards came up in her hands. They gasped in unison. The light from Maggie's flashlight shone on a flat slab of granite wedged in between two natural boulders. Caitlin slid her fingers underneath the thinner edges of the stone tablet.

"It's got to be underneath there. We'll lift together," Maggie said. "Bend your knees, don't hurt your backs."

They knelt around the opening, their fingers curled underneath the stone. Each took a deep breath and hunched forward.

"No, wait," Caitlin said.

"Huh?"

"I want to see if one person can do this. Or did it take two? Let me try."

"Huh?" Toby repeated, eager to lift.

"I getcha," Maggie said. "But it would be easier for one person to lay it down then to lift it up, right?"

"Right."

"Do it both ways," Toby suggested.

"Bend your knees."

Caitlin lifted and slid the granite slab along the floor out of the way. One person, one strong, young person could lift it out and replace it as well.

The lambskin duster shook as Caitlin brushed off the top of a small black metal trunk. Nearly three hundred years ago Nessa, or maybe Temetet, put this treasure, this box of memories in the ground. "Bigger than a microwave oven," she said, feeling giddy.

"Sweet Jesus," Maggie gasped.

"We have to do this very carefully in case it falls apart," Caitlin said. "Lift it straight up. Don't let the sides touch rock."

On their knees, with scant space between their arms, they reached underneath the box and lifted. The trunk weighed about twenty-five pounds. They handled it like a precious baby and placed it on a white cotton sheet on the floor.

Toby whispered, "Holy cow."

"I have chills," Maggie said.

Caitlin could not explain how she felt. She was overwhelmed.

"Let's open it," Toby said.

"Not here. In the house." Caitlin wrapped the treasure in a sheet and put it in a double strength trash bag for protection against the rain. Sam and Malindi, watching from the doorway, moved aside to let them by.

The storm had passed, bringing in its wake sunshine and fresh, cool air. Stepping outside, Caitlin felt like they were crossing a threshold from the past into the present. They carried the trunk to the living room where Sam had already cleared and covered a library table.

"I can't wait to see what's inside," Toby said.

"We really shouldn't touch anything," said Caitlin in a hushed tone.

"I have a pack of cotton gloves in my car that I use for cleaning silver." Maggie hustled out to her car and hurried back in.

Both ends of the trunk had metal handles, the lid was hinged with leather straps in the back. Caitlin slipped on Maggie's cotton gloves, put her fingers under the lid and tried to lift. She was met with resistance. She jiggled the lid but to no avail. She said a little prayer to Nessa and tried again. The lid raised. Sam propped it up with books so that it wouldn't break away from the fragile hinges.

A yellowed piece of linen covered the contents. Caitlin lifted the fabric. Centuries evaporated as the liberators came face to face with three miniature portraits in wooden frames: Nessa, Fiona, Temetet. And Nessa's journal. With beating heart, Caitlin removed the articles and laid them carefully on the table. Underneath, there were drawings, paintings, leather and wooden toys, baby clothes, a rag doll, a corn husk doll, a butter mold with an inscribed robin, bead, bone, and tooth jewelry.

When all the articles were on the table the group sat down. The time for rejoicing would come later; now was the time to respect and honor the past—an answered prayer too long in coming.

Caitlin held one very special item in her hands. Nessa's soft, brown leather journal, carefully tied with binding of cotton twine.

She pictured Nessa, bent over in the candlelight, writing on the fine linen pages in her neat rounded script. Always optimistic, forever courageous, she wrote of her hopes and dreams, of her love for Fiona and Temetet. Though the words were in another language, Caitlin knew exactly what they said.

❊

Later, when they were alone, Sam gestured toward the trunk's contents, and asked, "What will you do with all this, Caitlin? Will you give it to a museum?"

"I don't know. I'd like to find Nessa's descendants and give it all to them." Her voice caught. "Nessa wanted desperately to find her child, and she wanted to be recognized as a person of value. She was very talented.

Sam stroked her arm. "Finding her family could take a long time."

"Time's not a problem is it, Sam?"

He drew her to him and rested his chin lightly on top of her head. "Of course not, sweetheart. Whatever you want to do is fine with me. You've got plenty of stuff here for an exhibit. Nessa's drawings and paintings, the artifacts, the samplers, along with your paintings and Laura's."

"Maybe the Art Alliance could reschedule my exhibit and substitute one for Nessa. I'll call Anne this morning." Caitlin was getting excited.

Sam smiled and she felt encouraged. "What else?" he asked.

"Ed and Toby, Maggie, Gina and Carolyn would help. We could have them for dinner to discuss what we need to do."

"A planning committee?"

She laughed. "Yes, a planning committee."

"What can I do, Caitlin?"

"Oh, Sam, I'm so glad you'll support me. I do have something in mind for you, but let me call Anne and get this show on the road first."

CHAPTER TWENTY-FOUR

Anne was skeptical. "The fall program and scheduling brochures are at the printers, Caitlin."

"I'll pay for anything that has to be redone, Anne."

"The Board of Directors meets this Friday. It will be up to them. I'll put it on the agenda."

Caitlin was determined. She tried another tactic. Anne would not want to lose a significant and exciting show to a competing museum. An exhibit that was important to the history and culture of Philadelphia. "I could always call Woodmere," she said.

"Caitlin, please wait until after Friday. I think our board will approve your plan."

"Thank you, Anne. I'm having a small dinner party on Thursday evening to discuss the event, and I'd like you to be there."

"I'd be delighted to come, Caitlin. It's on my way home, and I haven't been to Cogslea in quite a while. Thank you."

"Please feel free to bring your fiancé."

"Thanks, but he's in New York until Friday. I'll see you Thursday. Goodbye, Caitlin."

"Well?" said Sam.

"Not sure. She has to run it by the board, but she's coming to our dinner meeting." She leaned back in his arms. "But now, I have to make some phone calls. How about if you invite Ed. He's been waiting for you to help finish the canoe.

He kissed the tip of her nose and let her go.

※

"We could call ourselves The Philadelphia Ten, Maggie said, cutting up a peach for a summer fruit bowl.

"Who's that?" Toby asked. He was helping Caitlin arrange cheese and crackers on a plate.

Maggie pointed her knife at Toby. "Did you wash your hands?"

"Of course I did. Who's The Philadelphia Ten, Caitlin?"

"They were a group of female artists who exhibited regularly in Philadelphia galleries and museums and later in traveling exhibits throughout the country from about 1917 to 1945. The membership did not include men.

Maggie dropped a handful of white grapes into a glass bowl. "You know why they were so special, Toby?"

"Why?"

"Because women were not taken seriously in the political and cultural world then. These women were far ahead of their time. They were giants."

"Giant women." Toby lifted his shoulders and puffed out his cheeks. Maggie swatted him and Caitlin giggled.

"Were the ladies that lived in Cogslea members of the group, Caitlin?"

"At one time, yes, but the group fluctuated in number and membership throughout the years, yet it was always called, The Philadelphia Ten in honor of the original members."

Toby pushed his glasses up the ridge of his nose. "We could call ourselves, The Cogslea Ten, since we're more than the Three Detectives now."

"Good idea, Toby," Maggie counted on her fingers. "But are we ten? We three, Sam, Ed, Carolyn and Gina. That's only seven."

"We should add Nessa," Caitlin said.

"And Anne," contributed Maggie.

"Malindi," Toby shouted. "Malindi makes ten."

Laughing, they high-fived each other. Malindi soaked up a hug from Toby.

"Are you ladies ready? Eh, excuse me—and Toby," Sam said, entering the kitchen.

"We're The Cogslea Ten," Toby explained.

"Okay, but is the food ready to take out? Ed and I have the tables, chairs, and bar set up."

"A few more minutes, Sam. Would you mind getting the door?"

It was Carolyn. She handed Sam a white bakery box. "Guess what I brought?"

"Canollis?" Caitlin wiped her hands on a tea towel and hugged Carolyn, noting that she looked particularly pretty this evening.

Everyone carried a dish outside and placed them on lace-covered tables with vases of fresh flowers and silver candelabras.

"Lovely," Carolyn said. "Did you make all this food, Caitlin?"

"Shirley's Catering did the entrees."

"Good for you girl. Don't knock yourself out; you have better things to do. Hang on to that man of yours, Caitlin. He's a gem."

"I know." She wanted to ask Carolyn about her love life, but the door bell rang. It was Anne, looking smart in a short-sleeved white suit and a summer tan. A few minutes later Caitlin admitted the last guest.

No spandex tonight, Gina was poured into a black strapless knit dress with side slits up to her thighs. Her hair was dyed jet black and cut in a chin-length bob with long bangs that kissed the tips of her thick lashes.

Caitlin did a double-take.

"Like it?"

"Love it."

"Makes me feel very sexy," Gina purred. "You should try it." She sashayed out to the patio and Caitlin watched, dumbstruck as Sam—her stoic, reserved Sam—seemed to melt under Gina's spell.

Carolyn nudged Caitlin and said under her breath, "Sex kitten. Watch out for that type."

"Please help yourself to food," Caitlin told her guests. She grabbed Sam's arm in passing, pressed her cheek to his, nipped his ear with her teeth, and whispered, "For flirting with Gina, I'm going to put John Denver on the CD player tonight and torture you."

He feigned retreat but could not hide the delight in his eyes. "Oh, no. Not John Denver."

"Yes, but this time you're the cowboy getting a Rocky Mountain high and I'm the eagle soaring."

"Oh, God," he groaned. "Oh dear God."

Gina took a seat next to Sam and engaged him in a one-sided conversation about Navajo art. His eyes kept sliding to Caitlin. Ed and Anne, discovering that they had mutual friends, mentally revised their divorce, birth, and death records. Eager to get on with the meeting, Toby bolted down his food and prematurely started clearing the serving table before Caitlin could stop him. At last, Sam carried out the ornate silver coffee service. Toby and Maggie brought the desserts.

"I saw you, Toby. You pinched that chocolate eclair, didn't you?" Maggie said.

"Did not."

"Humpff. Then why is chocolate smeared all over your face?"

"Why is there cream puff filling on your lip?"

"Smarty, I call dibbies on leftover cheesecake."

"Dibs on the canollis."

When everyone had coffee and dessert on their laps or on small serving tables beside them, Toby announced that the meeting was called to order.

Caitlin laughed. "Did you bring Roberts Rules, Toby?"

"No," he said, blushing. "But I brought pencils, pens, and legal pads for everyone."

"Good. Toby will be my right-hand-man in this operation. That's a big responsibility, Toby. Do you think you can handle it?"

"Yes, ma'm." He distributed the writing materials.

Caitlin explained her plans for the exhibit. When she was finished, Anne told the group that she felt optimistic that the board would push it through. "Three dimensionals can be displayed under glass and on stands or pedestals," she said. "I'll need an estimate on space required for each piece."

"I'll catalog everything and give you the sizes," Caitlin said.

"I can help," Toby volunteered. "That's what I do at the historical society."

"Good," Caitlin said. "I'll take care of framing the artwork and papers and write the accompanying text. I'd like to do portraits of Nessa and Temetet, plus a rendering of Destiny, so I'll be working here, but I can help you with your assignments if you wish. Ed is translating Nessa's journal. How's that coming Ed?"

Ed told Caitlin beforehand that the journal and her dream were a flawless match. With a poker face, he said, "Almost finished, Caitlin. Good story."

She stifled a smile and turned to Carolyn. "Now for Carolyn. This is exciting. Carolyn is going to write an historical novel based on Nessa's story, enriched with the history and ambiance of Philadelphia in the early eighteenth century."

Everyone made sounds of approval. Carolyn said that the project could take at least two years because of all the research involved. Plus she had to sell her first novel.

Ed said that he knew a publisher seeking new writers with completed manuscripts in the historical novel genre. "Would you like me to call him, Carolyn?"

"Would I? I've been dreading that ordeal. Thank you so much, Ed."

"If you like, I could help you with the research of Nessa's book," he added.

"Ed's knowledge of the Wissy, the Rittenhouse family and colonial era will save you time, Carolyn," Caitlin added.

"My lucky day has arrived." Carolyn was beaming.

"Now for Maggie." Caitlin winked at Maggie as all eyes turned to her. "She is going to find Fiona's descendants."

"No promises," Maggie said. "But, I'll do my best."

"If anyone can track down a person, it's Maggie," Caitlin said affectionately.

"Wouldn't it be great if they came to the reception?" Toby added.

Maggie put her empty plate on the table. "You know, I've been thinking..."

Toby wrote in his notes with a flourish, "Maggie's been thinking."

"Listen, Madame secretary, you can be replaced you know."

Toby chuckled and wiggled in his chair.

"What is it Maggie?" Caitlin asked.

"It might be fun to serve colonial and native American foods at the opening. You know, like blueberry slump and Indian pudding."

"That's a great idea, Maggie." Caitlin looked toward Anne. "Would that be all right?"

"Absolutely. I'll put you in touch with our staff chef."

"Mmmm, Indian pudding," Toby smacked his lips.

"Definitely Indian pudding," Caitlin said.

Gina's crossed leg jiggled, her fingers drummed on the arm of her chair. "What is it you have in mind for me, Caitlin?"

Caitlin turned her attention to Gina. "This may be a lot to ask of you; since you always have such a heavy schedule."

"Yes, but?"

"I would love to have you do a life-sized statue of Nessa and her child."

"Fantastic. I'll do it." No task too large for petite Gina. "As a matter-of-fact, I've been taking classes at a foundry in Bucks County and I'm dying to try my hand at casting in bronze. I'll put aside all my projects and get to work on it immediately." Gina's brow wrinkled beneath her bangs. "But what about a model?"

"Well, here's the thing." Caitlin drew up her shoulders and looked at Sam. "I have a job for you Sam. An important one."

"Yes, Caitlin?"

"Nessa was buried beside a sapling hemlock tree at the edge of the cornfield, now Allens Lane playing field."

Sam nodded. "Where we found Malindi when she ran away."

"Yes."

Toby said, "I knew Malindi was an important part of this group. Hooray for Malindi; she found Nessa." Malindi lifted adoring eyes to him and seemed to smile.

Caitlin paused, weighing the air.

"We have to dig her up."

"Wha...?" cried Toby, sending his pen into space.

Questions, some articulated, some not, jerked around the room like bumper cars. Creepy. Impossible. They needed permission. Who would do it? When could they do it? Where would the bones go afterwards? The expense.

"I'll take care of it," Sam said without ado. Caitlin wanted to hug him.

"Aren't you scared that the skeleton will come to life," Toby asked, half rising from his chair.

"I have no qualms about working with dead people, Toby. I've participated in numerous autopsies," Gina said confidently. "The bones will yield the information I need to determine size and shape of the model."

Ed looked at Gina over the rims of his glasses and smiled. "I have a friend in Washington, a forensic artist. He recreates faces, and reconstructs bodies from skulls and skeletons for the police department and the Smithsonian. Let me give him a call."

"He helped recreate Lucy. You know—the skull that was found in Ethiopia," Toby said.

Anne put her manicured fingers to her mouth, "But..."

"What is it, Anne?" Caitlin asked.

"Since this is, to some degree an archaeological find, I've been wondering if the University of Pennsylvania wouldn't be a better forum for this sort of thing." Their faces dropped. "I'm just playing devil's advocate here."

Caitlin responded. "I understand where you're coming from,

220

Anne, but this is really about women, their passion for art, and how it affected their lives. Helped them to survive, you might say."

Ed came to her defense. "I'm retired from U of P and, as much as I love the place, red tape and an orthodox mindset often get in the way of progress. I believe an art institute is the right venue."

The others agreed.

"I do have one concern," Ed added. "Perhaps it isn't my place to bring it up, but it's better to face it now rather than later."

"What's that?" Caitlin asked.

"Finances. Won't this cost a great deal of money?"

Caitlin turned to Sam. "How do we stand on that, Sam?"

"Unless the project costs more than a million dollars, our coffers can handle it. Shall I tell them where that money came from, Caitlin?"

"Sure." Sam took care of the money; she didn't much care for bookkeeping and check-writing.

"To make a long story short, last year, Caitlin befriended a man in a hospital who was dying of Aids. For her kindness, he left her a million dollars."

"Wow," said Toby.

"No big deal," Caitlin said. She didn't think she had done anything out of the ordinary then. And now, she was happy to rectifying a terrible injustice done to a young woman who deserved more from life than what was dealt her.

CHAPTER TWENTY-FIVE

Early the next morning, Caitlin and Toby took a run over to the historical society to pick up the samplers. Then they went up to O'Donnells stationary shop in Chestnut Hill for acid free tissue paper and boxes, archival plastic sleeves, and slide film. They spent the rest of the morning in the living room measuring, photographing, and cataloging. They both jumped when the phone rang.

"That's Anne." Toby trailed Caitlin into the kitchen.

It was the tree service reminding Caitlin that they were scheduled to trim the trees that afternoon. She winked at Toby and whispered, "How lucky is this."

"I have another little job that I'd like you to consider, if you don't mind," she said to the caller.

"Sure, ma'm, what is that?"

"It might require the consent of your supervisor."

"All our workers are experts, m'am. I'm Jack, the owner, and I'd be happy to come along for a consultation. The Hillmans are valued customers of mine. I'll see you this afternoon."

"Thank you," she said and hung up. "Tree people," she told Toby, walking back to the living room. "Sam will talk to them."

They spun from their work and raced to the phone when it rang again. Caitlin mouthed the word "Anne" to Toby. From the look on her face she was receiving good news.

"Thank you so much, Anne, for advocating our cause to the

Board of Directors. I'll get the measurements to you soon. Yes, and the text for the brochures. Thanks again."

After Caitlin called Ed and Sam with the good news, she and Toby hugged each other and frolicked around the room in a wild dance of victory. Malindi joined in the fun.

✿

Sam came home at noon. "We put the final layer of shellac on the canoe today," he said, helping himself to last night's leftovers. "A launching is in the near future."

"Hooray," Toby said. "We'll all go. Malindi too. Do you think she'll get in the canoe, Caitlin?"

"Not sure, she might have to stay on shore. Goodness, look at the time. They'll be here soon."

"Who's that, Caitlin?" Sam asked.

"Tree guys."

"Oh, right." Sam put the food away; Toby and Caitlin went back to work.

✿

At the appointed time, a green truck pulled up, followed by a green van with the identical logo of a spreading chestnut tree painted on the side. Sam unlocked the gate to allow the arborists to bring in their equipment, then he and Jack moved to the yard where they could watch the work. Caitlin served iced tea and cookies and disappeared. She and Toby hid behind the curtain of the opened living room window to listen to the conversation.

Jack was a large man with a thick neck, a barrel-chest, and bulging thighs. Caitlin and Toby later agreed that he looked like a vertical log — very appropriate for a tree guy.

His booming voice overriding the noise of the chain saws, Jack asked, "So, what can I do you for?"

"It's a rather delicate matter so bear with me," Sam said.

"Sure."

223

"We have reason to believe that there's a body buried in the playing field in Allens Lane Art Center."

Jack's bushy eyebrows twitched.

"The person in question was buried there early in the eighteenth century and the descendants want to relocate the remains to the family's burial grounds." A slight lie, but Sam felt it necessary to make a point.

"Phew," Jack exclaimed. "And my job would be?"

"The site is close to a tree stump and we figure the roots might interfere with digging."

Jack rubbed his stubbly chin. "About twenty yards in from the fence, east side?"

Sam nodded.

"Hemlock. I took her down a few years ago. That tree was a beauty before she died; nearly three hundred years old." Jack caressed the side of his glass with his fingers in slow, sensuous circles. "Her roots may be partially decomposed by now, but the root systems of older trees can be thick and several times longer than the tree was tall. To find all the roots, you have to remove soil two feet deep around the stump, then remove the soil around the roots so that you can maneuver a saw to cut them. Ordinarily, we'd use a back hoe, but this is gonna require some tender loving care, isn't it?"

Sam was unperturbed. "You'll do it?"

"Yeah, I'll do it. You're lucky we checked for underground pipes and electrical lines back then. I'll need to talk to the folks at Allens Lane first—since this involves, uh, shall we say..."

"Bones," Sam filled in.

"Uh, yeah, and the coroner's office should be notified."

They let the grating sounds of a stump grinder fill the air. Then Sam spoke with authority. "I'm recently retired from law enforcement; I know how complicated and time-consuming the government can make things. Time is of the essence here; the family needs to do this now." Sam paused a beat before continuing.

"Suppose we get the Lane's permission to dig up a tree stump that is an obstacle and a danger to the kids playing in that field. Suppose when we do this, we just happen to stumble upon a skeleton. But before anyone finds out, the skeleton disappears. Suppose—just to be on the safe side—all of this happens at night."

"Well," Jack said, dragging out the word. "Suppose we do all this, it wouldn't be cheap."

"No problem."

Jack reached in his shirt pocket and pulled out a small notebook with an attached ball point pen. He clicked the pen several times. Narrowing his eyes, he jotted down a number and passed the notebook to Sam.

"No problem," Sam said, handing it back.

"Done. I'll have my secretary write out an itemized estimate and mail it to you."

"Now," Sam said. "I want this job done tonight."

"*Jeez.*" Jack leaned back in his chair with his arms folded across his chest.

"There's a bonus in it for you if you agree. And one more thing."

Jack chuckled. "Yeah?"

Sam's tone never changed. "There must be complete confidentiality in this matter."

"Ha, that's the least of it. See those two guys out there?" Jack lifted his chin toward the two men stacking branches. "My sons. Pat and Jim. Good boys. No problem."

Later in the day, Ed stopped by to tell them of his conversation with the director of the art center.

"And?" Caitlin and Toby asked together.

"Let's just say he wasn't that happy about us digging in his field, but he didn't want to lose my semiyearly contribution either. I said there were plenty of other institutions that would like to have me on their VIP list of patrons."

Things were moving along remarkably well. They eagerly awaited—as Toby described it—the invasion of the body snatchers.

"You better get over here now, Caitlin," Sam said, calling from his cell phone.

"What's wrong? What's that noise?"

"A generator. Come over."

The mantle clock struck one a.m. Caitlin yawned; she must have dozed off while scribbling notes for the brochure. Several hours earlier, they had all walked over to the playing field. Sam let Malindi off her leash and she headed right for the tree stump. Sam insisted that Caitlin go home and get some rest and take Malindi with her.

Caitlin grabbed Malindi's leash and secured the door. She and Malindi crossed the street and ran toward the group in the field. Caitlin sucked in her breath at the ghoulish sight. The area was bathed in a weird yellowish glow from floodlights that cast eerie, elongated shadows across the ground. They stood in a semicircle, some leaned on shovels, all were looking down into a large hole.

Sam reached out his hand and drew Caitlin to him. "Look," he said.

Following his gaze, she looked down, gasped, and shivered at the sight.

"Omigod. Two."

"Two," said Sam. "Facing east. For a reason. I'm well acquainted with Indian burial customs."

Shells, stones, and colorful beads encircled the bones. One arm of the larger skeleton lay across the smaller chest as if to shelter her. Caitlin, overwhelmed at the poignant sight, broke down and cried. "Nessa and Temetet," she sobbed, shaking in Sam's arms. The rest of the group bowed their heads, prayer-like.

"We need to take pictures," she said, after a time.

"Toby and I did that, Caitlin," Ed told her. " We'll need to work quickly if we want to get out of here before dawn; we weren't expecting two bodies." Caitlin climbed into the hole with Ed and helped him remove dirt from the bones with a soft brush.

Jack pulled his sons aside and gave them a few inaudible directions. His boys went to their trucks and returned with thick styrofoam boxes with "Omaha Steaks" labels adhering to the lids.

Ed disassembled the skeletons with great care. Toby, Maggie and Sam secured each bone in foam wrapping paper. They placed them in plastic containers with identifying index cards, then into Omaha boxes filled with styrofoam peanuts. Sam loaded the boxes into Ed's vehicle parked by the curb.

The arborists secured the area with strips of yellow crime-scene tape. It was going to take several hours with back hoe and stump grinder to complete the job. Ed and Toby would leave in a few hours for Washington and promised to call as soon as there was something to report.

❀

Several days later, Sam and Caitlin were on the patio winnowing their way through a pile of neglected magazines and newspapers when Ed called. Sam pushed the speaker button.

"How's it going, Ed?" Sam asked.

"Good. The dimensions are near completion and tomorrow my friend will start molding the heads. We should be home in three or four days. Toby's having a great time watching the work, and we've managed to see some of the Smithsonian." He lowered his voice. "I didn't say anything before, because I wanted the lab's confirmation first. Temetet's skull was cracked from a blow that undoubtedly killed him."

"Omigod," Caitlin gasped.

"Murdered," Sam said.

"Yes, looks like it. I'll call you later as things develop."

After the shock wore off, Caitlin speculated about what might have happened. "Maybe he was trying to protect Nessa. Or the baby."

"But the baby was gone when Nessa died."

"But who killed Temetet and who put him in the grave?"

"I find it hard to believe that the Uchmans would want an Indian buried on their land."

"Right. But how did Nessa die? Could she have died of a broken heart?

"That's possible, Caitlin. Or Nessa might have contracted measles or some other infectious disease that was wiping out the Lenni Lenape at the time. In that case, Caitlin, it was good that the baby was not with her." He pulled Caitlin's head to his chest and stroked her hair. "We may never know."

"We may never know."

Malindi, pummeled and annoyed by falling acorns, ambled off to the apple orchard to take a nap.

✹

Smoke from a wood fire tickled her nose. Maliindi sneezed and opened her eyes. She was in the apple orchard. An odd scene was taking place in there. An unlikely trio—a robin, a fox, and a wolf were engaged in a lively game. The wolf threw a bundle of small sticks on the ground. Each player took a turn at trying to pick up a stick without disturbing the others. Malindi noticed that the wolf and the fox allowed the robin to win every single time. A game of tag followed. The three raced in and out of trees until they fell down panting, making noises of contentment. A short time later, the wolf trotted off into the woods and brought back tidbits of food for his family. Sated, they groomed each other, yawned, curled up together and fell asleep.

Horrified and powerless, Malindi watched the pile of sticks writhe and come to life. Spitting gold coins, the snakelike creatures crept stealthily toward the sleeping robin. They circled the innocent one, swept her up and carried her off into the dark forest.

The fox awoke. Her babe was gone. She howled and pulled out tufts of hair. There was no consoling the poor mother; she dropped to the ground, tucked her tail between her legs and died. The wolf raced through the woods but found no robin. Heartbroken, he returned to the orchard prepared to mourn the loss of his family.

Two wraithlike figures, holding the lifeless body of his beloved fox over their heads, were bearing her away. The wolf snarled, leapt upon the two, tore away chunks of white fabric and flesh. One figure escaped the maddened beast, picked up a rock and struck him on the back of his head, whereupon the wolf sank to his knees and died. The hooded pair kicked and rolled his prone body down the embankment.

When night spread her black veil across the land and the moon was high in the heaven, animals with blackened faces, animals of the water, of the sky, meadow, and forest crept silently over the rise of the hill. The entourage followed the path where the red fox had been taken, the rigid body of the wolf floating above them.

CHAPTER TWENTY-SIX

The Chinese red canoe was secured to the roof of Ed's Cherokee. They were headed for Shawmont: a hilly section of the city between Ridge Avenue and the Schuylkill River. At the bottom of a steep hill, they veered to the right. Ed explained that the next two residential blocks served as a connecting link in the twenty-two mile bike path that ran from center city to Valley Forge. As if to prove his point, they found themselves stuck in the middle of a pack of undulating in-line skaters and bikers dressed in Crayola colored spandex pumping up an incline. At the top of the hill the gaudy group vanished into the woods.

Beyond the train tracks of the Norristown Local, the road dipped down again and the scenery changed into that of a campy resort town.

"I've never been here before," Caitlin said. "I love it."

Ed nodded. "Residents here share a mutual interest—water and boats."

"Like it, Sam?" Caitlin asked.

"I do."

The narrow road stretched for three more miles that took them past trailers, stilted houses, and modest year-round cottages built close to the banks of the Schuylkill.

"There's a richness in this exclusive section of Philadelphia,"

Ed told them. "Although, as you can see, pickup trucks, flatbeds, jeeps, and motorcycles are the vehicle of choice here. Porches and Mercedes belong to those tony manses across the river."

"I prefer it on this side," Caitlin said.

At the road's dead end, Ed pulled into a short driveway. Porcupine grass and a high thicket of bamboo shielded them from a shabby trailer and a yard overrun with plastic yard ornaments and crates of empty beer bottles next door.

"This is lovely," Caitlin remarked, getting out of the car. "I can't believe we're still in Philadelphia."

A serpentine stream ran through the property and emptied into the river. On the bank, beneath shady willow trees, a park bench and Adirondack chairs faced the water.

Toby romped around the yard with Malindi while Ed unlocked the door of his friend's one-room, rustic log cabin. A pleasing scent of wood smoke and spices drifted out to greet them.

"It's not fancy but it's homey," Ed said.

"It's wonderful," Caitlin replied. It reminds me of our cabin in Canyon de Chelly, doesn't it Sam?"

Sam smiled.

"Well, folks," Ed said, stepping back outside. "Let's see if she floats." He and Sam untied the canoe and carried it to the river's edge.

"Wait, we have to christen it first." Caitlin took a bottle of sparkling water out of the cooler and handed it to Toby. "Toby, you're doing the honors."

Toby unscrewed the cap, raised the bottle over the canoe, and said in a ceremonious tone, "I christen thee, 'The Nessa.'" He poured the fizzy contents onto the bow.

"Ladies first," Ed said.

Caitlin held up her hands. "No, no, no. You're the boat builders."

"Well, if you insist," Ed said.

"Maybe she doesn't trust our handiwork," said Toby with a sly smile."

"Hey, I'm sending my three favorite people on a maiden

voyage into uncharted waters. That's trust isn't it? But put those life jackets on will you?"

Ed sat in the stern, Sam in the bow, and Toby in the middle on the floor. Caitlin pushed them off and waved. "Bon voyage."

Malindi paced the shore. She tested the water with her paw.

"*La*, Malindi. No, the current's too strong." Malindi parked herself at Caitlin's feet.

The canoe glided upstream close to shore and around a bend in the river. Caitlin gave Malindi a reassuring pat on the head, but she was relieved too when the canoe came into view again.

"How was it?" she asked, when they were closer.

"Rides smooth as butter," Ed said. "Your turn Caitlin," This time Sam steered.

"Cast off mate," Toby said, in the bow, waving his paddle.

Caitlin dragged her hand in the water and day dreamed. She pictured Temetet in his canoe, Temetet fishing from the shore, Temetet and Nessa with Fiona and their three goats returning from their wedding on the opposite shore. She tried envisioning the New World as it was then, rich in an abundance of natural resources. And felt an ache in her heart for all that had been lost. Particularly for the original inhabitants, the Lenni Lenape. She turned to look at Sam.

"What are you thinking Caitlin?"

"Nothing." She blew him a silent kiss.

All too soon, the ride was over.

"Can I take Caitlin out this time, Granddad?" Toby asked. "Please?"

"Don't worry, Ed. I've had lots of experience in a canoe."

"Of course, Caitlin. No tricks, Toby. Behave yourself."

"Don't jiggle," Toby said from the stern.

"I'm not jiggling. Let's go."

"Cheeky subordinate. The captain says be quiet."

"Aye, aye, Captain."

They zigzagged crazily upstream; Caitlin held her tongue. The return trip was better; Toby brought the canoe to shore without a hitch.

"Good job, Caitlin," Captain Tony said. "Let's eat."

While the men shored the canoe, Caitlin spread a red and white checked tablecloth on the picnic table, distributed plates, cups, bottles of iced tea. When everyone was seated, she handed out sandwiches and condiments from the cooler and chips from a canvas bag.

The river glistened like a field of scattered diamonds. In timely fashion, raucous cicadas heralded the end of summer.

"I can't believe summer's almost over," Ed said. "Toby, you'll be going back to school soon."

Toby hung his head over his paper plate and half-eaten deviled egg. "I know. This has been the best summer of my life. I'll never forget it."

"Me either," Caitlin's eyes grew moist.

Ed raised his eyebrows. "It's not the end of the world, Toby. We'll see these folks often, I hope."

Sam put his arm across Caitlin's shoulders. "We might even settle in Philadelphia, Toby."

"Which reminds me," Caitlin said. "Marny is going to call tonight to confirm their time of arrival."

"But what about the exhibit?" Toby asked. "Where will you live between now and then?"

Caitlin patted him on the arm. "Don't worry, Toby, we won't be homeless. The Hillman's may offer us a guest room or the carriage house."

Toby gestured toward the cabin. "You could stay here. We could go canoeing, have picnics, play games."

"Or you could stay at my house," Ed said.

"See, Toby. No problem," Sam said.

As it turned out, the problem was resolved that very evening.

❀

"But of course you can stay on at Cogslea," Marny told Caitlin over the phone. "We have more room than we need. As a matter of fact..."

"Yes?"

"We'd like to extend our vacation and go to Paris for a few weeks."

"Oh, that's lovely. You should."

Marny lowered her voice. "Lee's in the other room, so I can say this. Before our vacation, we'd been having marital problems. Once we got out of the house, everything was fine."

"That can happen on vacation, Marny."

"Yes, but let me ask you—how are you and Sam getting along since you've been at Cogslea?"

"Uh, all right. Not bad. What do you mean?"

Marny whispered, "Call me crazy, but there's something about that house that seemed to drive a wedge between us. It's hard to explain. Anyway, we're going to put it on the market this winter. Hello? Caitlin?"

"Yes, I'm here. I'm sorry to see the house go, but I'm happy that you and Lee have resolved your differences. Talk to you later."

Caitlin sat back and studied the clean, uninterrupted lines of the house. Cogslea had a history of housing women who desired recognition on their own terms. Women who survived by using their creative talent to get ahead. Including herself. But she had Sam and Sam was a partner, not an adversary.

Was Cogslea hostile as Marny suggested? Did it have a pulse, did it harbor a grudge? It didn't look threatening; it was actually very benign. Maybe, since Nessa's calls for help had been answered, the house could settle into its foundation and forget.

Or maybe she had too vivid an imagination.

Sam and Caitlin spent the remaining days of summer absorbed in the tranquil atmosphere of Cogslea. They read, took walks, visited places of interest. Caitlin worked on her portraits of Nessa, Temetet, and Fiona. Sam puttered in the garden; she tried her hand at recipes from Marny's collection of ethnic cookbooks.

When the exhibit was less than a week away, Gina claimed

that she had finished her statue. Proofed galleys of the journal were ready for printing. Toby and Ed were on vacation in New Hampshire with their family. Malindi moped about like a lovesick teenager pining for Toby. Maggie was down the shore. She was upset that she had made little progress with her genealogical search and had taken her computer down with her.

✾

Labor Day arrived clear and cool, but residents in the City of Brotherly Love were not to be fooled; Indian summer was sure to follow and flapjack them back into sizzling heat once more. Wall Street Journals gathered on driveways as "hillers" extended their vacations in Cape Cod or Northeast Harbor.

Caitlin and Sam watched the news on a small Sony Watchman in the kitchen. A reporter on Channel 10 was talking over footage of families who were staking out space for barbecues on the banks of the Schuylkill. The news switched to a clip of people congregating at the ballpark.

"Be forewarned," Caitlin told Sam. "I may cheer the Fightin' Phils or boo the stinkin' Phillies. It all depends on the team's performance today. Phillies fans can be brutal, but then we've been disappointed so many times."

✾

That evening, sitting on a patio step in the middle of her obligatory phone call to her parents, Caitlin held the receiver out at arm's length, rolled her eyes at Sam and made "yakety yak" motions with her hand.

"Someone's at the door, Mother."

Sam ducked around her, laughing. "I'll get it, Caitlin."

Her mother was bursting with gossip and the usual complaints. At least there was no mention of a wedding, but Caitlin knew she wasn't off the hook yet. She squeezed in a goodbye and pressed the off button.

"Thought you might need this." Sam handed her a tall glass of iced coffee.

Caitlin took several long sips then pressed the cold glass to her cheek. "You have no idea. Who was at the door, Sam?"

"Maggie."

"Maggie? Where is she?" Caitlin made a motion to rise.

"Oddest thing. She dashed in and headed straight for the cartons in the pantry. Her jaws were going a mile a minute and she smelled of tobacco."

"Uh, oh, chewing gum; she's started smoking again. What did she want?"

"Didn't explain. Just ripped open the cartons of samplers, unwrapped each one, said, 'Eureka' and left. I just finished rewrapping them."

"That's not like Maggie to leave a job unfinished. Let me call her, she might be home by now." Caitlin dialed, waited, left a message, and disconnected. "I'll try her cell phone." A minute later, she said, "It's dead. How very, very peculiar."

CHAPTER TWENTY-SEVEN

Hunkered down behind the steering wheel of her old Studebaker, Maggie sped northwest on Germantown Pike, a Mint Ice JuJu stick dangling from her lips.

"Hey, Mike, we're finally getting somewhere," Maggie said hoarsely between clenched teeth. Mike Schmidt, the Phillies bobblehead doll sitting over the dashboard looked excited but did not respond.

Thirty miles from center city, where Germantown Pike and Ridge Pike converge at Perkiomen Creek, Maggie crossed a low, quaint bridge and eased her way through a busy intersection onto Main Street in the small borough of Collegeville. Mere seconds later, she was past the shops, eating places, and the front lawn of the Victorian residential village of Ursinus College. In the equally small borough of Trappe, Pennsylvania, she spotted St. Luke's church, turned right and parked in their small, empty lot.

She got out of the car and read a small sign on the front door of a white colonial building informing her that this was the Historical Society Headquarters and Museum, ca. 1740 and it was open Tuesdays and Thursdays, 9 to 12. "Drat, missed it. Wish I'd known that before." She turned to face what she was looking for — a graveyard.

Beyond the parishioners' cemetery, a sprawling farm, complete with shiny silver silos, brick red buildings, and a pond inhabited by countless Canada geese created a picturesque backdrop.

The cemetery, Maggie figured, was about the size of her elementary school yard. She started checking dates of death on the first row of headstones. If Fiona was born in 1704, kidnapped in 1707, and if she lived to be a hundred, she could have died anywhere up to 1804. All the dates on these stones were post-1900.

She crossed over a few rows where she located the oldest burial site. The earth had a strange, spongy feel under her feet. She shivered. "Creepy." She scrutinized the worn inscriptions: the earliest dates of death did not occur before 1815. She checked every row to the very back. Nope. But not to worry; there were more little red squares on her map and each one represented a cemetery near Perkiomen Creek.

Several blocks farther up Main Street, she spotted the white steeple of Augustus Lutheran Church and parked in a lot designed to accommodate a huge congregational membership. Off to one side of the red brick church and its annexes stood a stuccoed stone building with a plaque over the front door that read: "The Olde Trappe Church. The original church, ca. 1743." Maggie was encouraged. "There's gotta be early eighteenth century burials here," she told Mike.

Behind the church buildings, a narrow brick path took her to a cemetery the size of at least three baseball fields. Undaunted, Maggie traversed row after row seeking older headstones. To no avail. A fraction of the way through, she rested on a bench and looked back at the old stone church. She slapped her forehead. "Yo, dummy. Wouldn't it have been logical to bury their parishioners there, by their church?"

She hurried over and skirted around the marble slabs on the ground that marked the tombs of The Reverend, Dr. Henry Melchoir Muhlenberg, first pastor of the church, his wife, and his son. A few yards away, beneath willow trees and old oaks, several dozen thin, white stones marked the resting places of the "new frontier's" earliest residents.

Her eyes were drawn to a stone encased under glass. A heading engraved on a copper frame said, "Oldest legible stone in cemetery. Here lyeth the body of Hanna Chrack, died 1736."

Maggie nearly jumped for joy. "Alright-tee, Mrs. Chrack!"

The only thing Maggie had to go on was the name Fiona and her last name, Stewart—unless she'd married—and any death date before 1804.

Time and weather had eroded and blackened the carved letters and her key chain penlight was useless in the gathering twilight. Crawling on her hands and knees from one stone to the other, she felt the indentations with the tips of her fingers.

"Holy Mother of God," she cried, falling over backward. A small creature scurried past, squeaked, and disappeared into the bushes. "Why did I come here in the dark? What the heck am I doing way out here in the sticks?"

Maggie was a city girl, born and raised in the tight little community of Manayunk. Where neighbors gossiped on row house porches knit together on steep narrow streets. Where, if you tripped, you could roll right down the hill into the Schuylkill River. Where women never failed to have a supply of casseroles in their freezers ready for the next wake. Maggie had never been camping, never encountered any wild animal larger than a chipmunk. Except for tree rats—the "Yunkers" name for squirrels. Maggie was certain that she was surrounded by all sorts of wild animals ready to pounce on her.

Squatting over a fallen stone, fumbling to find a date, she was suddenly bathed in a beam of Celestial white light. "Mother of God," she gasped, turning into the glare.

A voice floated toward her. "Sorry," it said. The beam lowered, but all Maggie could make out was the outline of a lumpy black figure.

"Officer Duffy here. C.P.D., Collegeville Police Department. I'd like to know what you're doing in the bone yard in the dark, M'am," the officer said in a gruff tone.

As Maggie's eyes adjusted, she could make out a uniformed, middle-aged man of stocky build. She stood and brushed the dirt from her knees. "Now, I know this looks crazy, Officer Duffy, but I need to locate a certain party by tomorrow night."

"Hmm." The policeman rubbed his chin and softened his

voice. "Never heard of an emergency like that." Chuckling, he waved his stubby fingers toward the extended grounds. "I don't think these folks are going anywhere anytime soon. Can't it wait until morning young lady?"

Young lady? He must be half blind. "I guess you're right," Maggie said, feeling flattered and a little silly.

Duffy patted his breast pocket. "Cigarette?"

"No thanks, I've given it up." Maggie was glad the pack did not materialize. Old habits died hard. Regardless.

"Let me walk you to your car." He took her elbow and escorted her down the path with his flashlight. "When I saw your car, I thought a couple college kids might be making out on some poor old deceased Sunday school teacher's grave. You have a great car by the way. A real antique, and I can see you take good care of it." He opened the door and shone his light on the dashboard. "They don't make them like that anymore. Look at that chrome."

"You know," he said when she was seated, "The church office is open from nine a.m. to three p.m., Monday through Friday. Eliza, the office manager, is real nice and might be able to help you find your, uh, ancestor?"

"That's great. I'll come back tomorrow morning. And, it really is an ancestor that I'm trying to find. The family's having a reunion tomorrow and I'd like to report what I found, ya know?" She turned on the ignition and Officer Duffy's eyes glazed over as the engine purred into action. "Officer Duffy, do you happen to know a motel around here that won't cost me an arm and a leg?"

"Huh? Oh, sure. There's a Mom and Pop Motel back on Ridge Pike, about two miles south of the Perkiomen bridge. I'd recommend that."

"Well, goodnight. Sorry if I caused you any trouble."

He tipped his hat, sighed, and lit a cigarette. Exhaling deeply, he watched the beautiful turquoise jewel roll away into the night.

Back at the intersection, Maggie stopped at a McDonald's drive-thru and ordered a quarter pounder with cheese, french fries, and a strawberry shake. Two miles down the pike, she came upon a red white and blue sign, pulled in, registered, and unlocked one of the motel's eight blue doors. She turned on the television, flopped on the bed, and bolted down her dinner. She could not remember how many times she was supposed to chew her food. It wasn't important.

※

In the morning, Maggie ferreted out a Wawa near the college campus and picked up two large sweetened white coffees and half a dozen jelly donuts.

Before driving off, she studied her ADC Montgomery County, Pennsylvania map. A winding purple line representing Perkiomen Creek ran vertically across five whole pages. Dotted here and there, several pale green areas stood for park, forest, recreation, and wildlife areas. She drove to the closest one and parked in a gravel lot facing the creek at the head of a multipurpose trail. She took a long swig of coffee and studied the picturesque creek. The water looked shallower and the current slower than the Wissahickon; there were no stony banks and rocky precipices like the Wissy; these banks were bare of vegetation. But it would have looked quite different three hundred years ago.

After devouring a third donut, Maggie checked the time and headed for Augustus Lutheran. Mothers were coming and going like clockwork dropping off toddlers at the church's day care center.

She checked her image in the rear view mirror. "Yikes, Mike. I look a sight." She ran a finger through her wiry hair, adjusted her jeans, and smoothed her wrinkled "slept-in" T-shirt. Rats, a grape jelly stain. She rubbed the offending purple blotch with a napkin, shrugged and gave up.

"Still time to examine more headstones." The cemetery looked almost cheerful in the light of day, although the sun, still low in the sky, hit her eyes as she tried to read the inscriptions. She chortled. "Nothing jumps out at me today. Hee, hee. No animals, no cops." At nine o'clock she walked around to the front of the church, entered a vestibule with hallways to either side, a double door into the nave straight ahead. Piping voices of children came from the

241

left; she turned right and found her way to the office.

A pleasant woman behind the desk greeted her. "I'm Eliza, may I help you?"

Maggie shuffled through the doorway, trying to cover the grape jelly stain with her hand. She probably looked a bit wild-eyed too. "I'm looking for a certain grave." She gave Eliza as much information as she could to help her locate Fiona's resting place.

"Henry would be happy to guide you through the old graveyard," Eliza said, nodding toward an elderly man stuffing envelopes. "But it might be best to look through the church records and registry first."

"That would be great," Maggie said.

Eliza got up and walked over to the rows of steel files that lined the walls. She removed a heavy loose-leaf book from one of the drawers and invited Maggie to pull up a chair beside her at her desk. "Burials in the cemetery date from 1729. I'll go through the older entries and you see if anything rings a bell."

Fassbinders, Oberholtzers, and Schenks. Putzkummers, Yeager, Spitznamens; none had the first name of Fiona nor the last name of Stewart.

"Are you sure she was buried here?" Eliza asked.

"No, but I am pretty sure she lived around here; I'm guessing that she died here too."

"Hmm, I wonder," Eliza said, tapping her fingers on the closed registry on top of her desk.

"Huh?" said Maggie. "What?"

"I'm thinking the same thing," said Henry, rising from his chair. He ran his fingers along the brown leather spines on the library shelves. "Aha, here it is." He pulled out a large tome. "Volume One of Pastor Muhlenberg's Journals."

"Henry's a docent and knows everything there is to know about the history of this place. I bet he even knows the page we're looking for."

"Not quite," Henry grinned and placed the heavy book on Eliza's desk.

Running her finger down the columns, Eliza searched the

index pages. "Here it is," she said and turned to a page in the middle of the journal.

Maggie, sitting on the edge of her chair, leaned forward.

Eliza skimmed the passage, looked up and smiled. "Just as I thought. Several of our early parishioners were buried in the Lower Mennonite churchyard in Skippack. Pastor Muhlenberg mentions that he performed their confessions and Holy Supper rites, but,because their homes and farms were adjacent to or near that church, they requested burial there. No names though."

Maggie leaped out of her chair, thanked Eliza and Henry for their help. In her haste to get on the road, she scarcely heard directions to the cemetery. She sat in the car and checked her map. "Uh, huh!" She used an orange highlighter to circle a little green rectangle and tiny black cross. Cemetery and church.

"It's about two miles northwest of the bridge," she told Mike Schmidt. Mike bobbed his head. She tapped her finger on red letters on a large gray area—a space as big as the boroughs of Trappe and Collegeville combined. She hunched her shoulders in a mock shiver. "Graterford Prison. We'll want to stay away from that area, won't we, Mike?" Skippack was two inches—or half a mile—from a stretch of lengthy state park green.

Following a narrow country road that wound through softly rolling hills speckled with farms and modest homes, she came to Evansburg State Park Headquarters and veered left. A short distance down the road she spotted the church.

"I have a good feeling about this," Maggie told bobbing Mike. He nodded his head in agreement.

Interchangeable letters affixed to a framed announcement board advertised the topic of Sunday's sermon, the minister's name, plus an invitation for all to attend The Lower Skippack Mennonite Church, founded 1702.

"1702. Much better, hey Mike?" Mike said nothing but looked hopeful; his eyes followed her as she got out of the car. It was a plain church, white stucco over stone with narrow white shuttered windows. No adornments, no steeple A small cemetery next to the church yielded only twentieth century headstones. Maggie cast her eye across the street.

Situated between a memorial softball field and a wooded area, with a hilly open field as a backdrop, a second cemetery, equal in size to the adjacent ball field, beckoned to Maggie. She entered through a plain iron arch centered in white pipe fencing. The grass was sparse and brown. No potted plants, plastic flowers, or American flags. Two low obelisks broke up a pattern of small, modest stones. Strictly no-frills, although some had an abbreviated tulip motif or just one word, "Rest" or "Asleep."

By the process of elimination, Maggie worked her way through the left half of the cemetery, stopping briefly at the grave of a civil war soldier who had died from wounds at the Battle of Cold Harbor, June 3, 1864. He was twenty-seven years old.

"Phew, it's hot." Maggie sat down on a low white stucco wall that surrounded the sides and rear of the grounds. She took a long drink from her water bottle.

An eerie shadow moved across the sun. Shading her eyes, Maggie looked up and saw a monstrous bird with wide wings and a threatening, down-curved beak circling overhead. It drifted lower. "Geez, a pterodactyl. Shoo. Go away, you're scarin' me." Lazily, the bird sailed away on a breeze to the adjacent cornfield.

Maggie looked toward the remaining rows of grave markers. "You better be there or I don't know what I'll do," she said. Her memory stirred. What was it Caitlin told her about spotting animals in Africa? "Look for the unusual, the form or shape that doesn't belong."

Maggie rose and walked purposefully toward the unexplored area, drawn toward a section that contained a few reddish brown, unevenly shaped stones, the largest no bigger than a telephone book. As if crudely scratched with a stone fragment, the fieldstone markers contained very little information: one or two initials and/or date of death.

1760, 1764, 1765, 1775, 1778, 1782. Maggie's heart thumped with excitement. She fell on her knees in front of the smallest marker and crossed herself. "Please, dear God let this be Fiona." "F K d. 1790." F K would have been eighty-six years old when she died.

Below the date, two lines formed a simplistic drawing of a bird: one continuous line for the body and head, another for a wing. "Robin," Maggie whispered.

Family and friends might call her "Hard as nails Mags," but Maggie collapsed over the stone. Pulling out tufts of grass, she wept openly.

Time passed. Maggie sat up, wiped her tearstained face with the hem of her shirt. She gathered herself together and trotted back to the car where she unplugged her cell phone from the cigarette lighter and dialed the number listed on the church sign. While she listened to a looped recorded message listing church services, socials and events, clergy phone numbers, and bible passages, a car drove up. A middle-aged woman dressed in work clothes and sensible shoes got out of the passenger side. The car drove away; the woman unlocked the church door and went inside. Maggie smiled. She recognized a fellow domestic when she saw one.

Maggie gave the woman a grace period before entering the church. Taking a deep breath, she inhaled essence of Murphy's oil soap and burnt vanilla cake. She shifted from one foot to the other. This plain interior was a far cry from her church in Manayunk with its great stained glass windows, ornate pipe organ, and white marble statues of the Virgin Mary.

"Halloo," she called out.

A door squeaked open and out of the shadows a woman appeared with a tea kettle in her hand.

"Yes? "Who is it?"

"I didn't mean to startle you." Maggie introduced herself. "I wonder if you could tell me anything about a person buried in the cemetery across the street. I'm looking for a woman called Fiona, and I saw a headstone that might belong to her."

"Well, sure. I'm Ellie. Come on in the kitchen. I was just having tea. I'd offer you cake but youth fellowship ate it all up last night."

Maggie pulled up a folding chair and sat down at a polished enamel table while her hostess set out two teacups on the stainless steel counter. Maggie had anticipated such an invitation and had brought in the remaining jelly donuts.

"I'm independent now," Maggie said, "but I used to have a small business called, 'Clean Corners.' Had business cards and everything, but it got to be too much of a hassle."

"I like that name. Shows how meticulous you are. Not many people bother to clean into the corners." Ellie poured the tea and rolled her eyes toward the cluttered sink. "These kids are supposed to clean up after their fellowship meetings, but they just don't see cleaning the way I do."

"I know." Maggie put two donuts on Ellie's plate and took one for herself.

"Thanks for the donuts. I do enjoy a pastry with my tea before I start work." Ellie took a bite, wiped her mouth with a napkin. "Now, who is it you're looking for?"

Maggie explained her search and how she had arrived at the conclusion that the small brown tombstone across the street might be Fiona's. Ellie sipped her tea, put down her cup, and leaned back in her chair. Maggie waited with baited breath.

"Well, first of all, our church registry wouldn't have information on non-parishioners." Maggie's face fell. "But don't worry. As a matter of fact, I can put you in touch with one of Fiona's direct descendants right now.

Ellie pushed out her chair, went to the phone set on the far end of the kitchen counter, dialed a number, spoke, and stretched the coiled wire to reach Maggie's quivering hand.

Maggie pressed the receiver close to her ear and listened— astounded at what she was hearing.

CHAPTER TWENTY-EIGHT

S am parked a white rented van in the delivery lot behind the Art
Alliance where they were met by maintenance staff ready to
unload their cargo.

"Are you sure I can't stay and help?" Sam asked Caitlin.

"Thanks, Sam, but it's just a matter of supervising—seeing
that things are hung properly and the labels are correct. I'd hate
to leave Malindi alone all day, especially since we're leaving her
tonight. Pick me up later, so I can go home, take a shower, and dress.
Oh, and try calling Maggie again, will you?"

"I will. Phone me right before you're ready to leave."

Since the men were still bringing in cartons, there wasn't
much that she could do for at least half an hour. Galleries were not
open to the public until ten, although this one would be off limits
to visitors until this evening. Caitlin stopped by to say hello to the
guard posted at the door.

"Hey, Caitlin, long time no see."

"It's good to be back, Charlie. I'm going around the corner
to the Wawa for coffee. Can I get you one?"

"Sure can, Caitlin. Black with sugar, please."

"I know, I remember." She returned shortly with two large
coffees and two corn muffins.

"You look just like you did in your freshman year," Charlie
said. She was dressed in faded jeans, a white T-shirt, and her hair
was pulled back in a thick ponytail.

"Thank you, Charlie. I think."

They laughed and reminisced a while until Anne arrived accompanied by several art students lugging folding tables and boxes of tools.

"They're bringing in Gina's statue," Anne said. Come and see. I thought it best to place it directly in front of the door, so it will be the first thing visitors see when they enter."

"Good idea."

Two burly men in gray work clothes with Bucks Foundry printed across their chests rolled in a large wooden crate on a hand trolley. Gina followed close behind looking like she had just tumbled out of bed. Her hair was a tangled mess; she wore a wrinkled red *muu muu*. She lifted a hand in greeting then watched attentively as the men pried off the crate's slats. "Easy guys," she told them.

The men tilted the uncovered statue, lifted and placed it on the floor, slid the crate to one side. Gina took a chamois cloth from her pocket and rubbed the surface.

"My first lost wax. What do you think, Caitlin?"

Caitlin had visited the studio when Gina first started the piece, but at that time, work hadn't progressed beyond the plaster mold. Seeing the finished statue for the first time, Caitlin was stunned. The realism, the accuracy of size, stature, detail, and expression— especially the expression—moved her to tears. Her heart tugged in her chest when she saw the chubby baby tucked in Nessa's arms sucking her thumb.

"It's beautiful," Caitlin said in a choking voice. She touched Nessa's face, moved her hand along her arm. Her fingers caressed the baby's cheek, her tiny folded hands. She leaned down and kissed the baby's mouth. Discomfited, the workmen looked away. Caitlin wasn't at all embarrassed by her public display even though this was a very private moment between her and Nessa. She stepped back. "But she's not directly in front of the door."

"We have a surprise for you, Caitlin," Anne said.

The foundry men wheeled in a second crate, two feet taller than the first. They opened the crate, pulled away thick foam paper, and placed another statue beside Nessa.

"Temetet." This time Caitlin wept openly.

"I'd like you to meet my mentor, Aurora Renzetti," Gina said. "She volunteered to do Temetet."

A reedy woman with a puff of gray hair presented herself to Caitlin. "I hope you don't mind that I took the initiative to do Temetet."

The woman was an esteemed, well-known sculptor. "Mind?," Caitlin said. "I'm overwhelmed. Thank you so much." Caitlin appraised the statue: a tall, broad shouldered Indian whose expression and stance portrayed great strength and reliability. His facial features, she realized, were very similar to Sam's.

Gina was wound up like a spring. "Gotta go. I have a meeting at Hahn Gallery this afternoon. Aurora and I will see you tonight."

Anne was ready to get to work. "I hope you like the arrangement, Caitlin. As an introduction to the characters, we'll start here with Jonathan Payne's miniature of Nessa, followed by all the other portraits. Continue on the far wall with Nessa's drawings and paintings and Fiona's farm animals. We'll end with Destiny's samplers."

"Sounds good."

Anne motioned to the glass cases on columned pedestals in the center of the room. "The trunk over there, its contents and the journal in the cases." We'll have a table in the lobby with copies of the journal for sale, along with flyers describing Carolyn's future novel." Anne's assistants began unpacking the cartons. "Careful with the contents. Lay them on tables, then sort them out."

Caitlin let Anne oversee the assistants, while she took a moment to check the positioning of the table in the lobby. She wasn't there a moment when a crash, followed by a sharp outcry, came from the gallery. Not what you want to hear in a room full of irreplaceable, fragile objects. Caitlin ran back to the gallery.

"Not to worry," the clumsy and embarrassed student said. "I tripped and fell into the table. Fortunately, there wasn't anything on it."

Caitlin stayed until the exhibit pieces were safely positioned under glass and the wall hangings were in their proper places. Maggie was supposed to check with the chef about the evening's fare, but since she hadn't called, Caitlin felt obliged to do so herself. She followed the warm scent of apples and cinnamon into the kitchen

"Everything is splendid, Caitlin," said Monsieur Gregoire, a Frenchman with forty years of culinary experience behind him. He removed a clipboard from a hook on the wall and said, "Perhaps we go over the menu, yes? For drinks, we have a nonalcoholic spiced cranberry punch and a white wine Syllabub punch. There will be skewered roasted vegetables and shrimp, breaded catfish balls, petite wild turkey croquettes, cranberry cornbread squares, dandelion salad with raspberry and pine nut dressing, cranberry and cheese bites on crackers made from cattail flour." Monsieur Gregoire looked at Caitlin and smiled. "Was not easy to get this ready-made cattail flour, but we find a store in Wisconsin that stocks it." Caitlin nodded appreciatively. "So," he said, returning to the menu. "All dishes will be garnished with concord grapes, parsley, and honey dipped pemmican sticks."

"It all sounds wonderful," Caitlin said, her mouth watering.

Chef offered her a warm cookie from a cooling tray. "Hobnail cookies, plain but delicious. *Je crois* the raisins are meant to be the hobnails. So, we have blueberry slump, Indian pudding, apple tansey topped with cranberry ice, and maple sugar fudge. All foods are consistent with the time," he assured her.

"Lovely, truly lovely, thank you." Toby will definitely go into a sugar high tonight, she thought. "And we're all set for our special guest?"

He winked at her and said out of the side of his mouth, "We set ze plan in motion at precisely four o'clock. Shall we synchronize our watches, *mon Capitan?*"

🍁

A snappy looking uniformed chauffeur wheeled Betty Green into the exhibit, tipped his hat and departed.

"How was the ride in the limo?" Caitlin asked.

"I felt like Queen Elizabeth," Betty said, squeezing Caitlin's hand with her good one. "It was wonderful seeing Philadelphia again, but the cigarettes were the best part. I chained smoked all the way down and intend to do so on the way home. Can't thank you enough for arranging this, Caitlin. I don't like crowds and this is a delightful way to see an exhibit."

"Let's do it then." Together, they roamed the room, conversing softly, sharing a mutual appreciation for the artwork and an affection for Nessa's cherished personal belongings.

Caitlin then pushed Betty's wheelchair up to a small linen covered table in the corner of the room and sat down opposite her. Chef Gregoire wheeled in a cart and placed a china plate of assorted desserts on the table. He served Caitlin a glass of iced coffee. Betty nibbled a cookie and closed her eyes.

"Oh, that blissful sound," she sighed. "I thought I'd never hear it again. The sound of a perfectly shaken martini."

Chef poured, Betty tasted. "Dry enough?" he asked.

"Perfect. You just whispered the word 'vermouth' into it, didn't you?" Chef grinned and left them alone.

"This is the best day of my life," Betty said. She directed her vision toward the samplers on the far wall. "Something about those samplers; I felt it when I was cataloging them. Just can't put my finger on it." She looked back at Caitlin. "You'll let me know if they —shall we say—speak to you?"

"I will, Betty. I definitely will."

❀

"The color matches your eyes," Sam said, evaluating Caitlin's peacock blue sheath dress. "Sexy shoes; I like them." He stood behind her, his arms encircling her waist.

"You look nice too," she told his reflection in the mirror. Sam wore a charcoal gray jacket, white T-shirt, sharply creased jeans. But a few more minutes in his arms would surely destroy her French twist; she turned and slid the antique silver concho on his bolo tie up tighter.

"I like your hair loose," he said, checking her hands at his neck.

"Mmm, I don't think so. I'll be ready in a minute. Now go down and console Malindi; she'll be alone tonight."

�֍

Malindi accepted her fate but sulked until they left. As soon as the door shut, she ran into the living room and jumped up on the couch to dream of Amy, Marny's niece, her new true love who, of late, had been bringing her special treats, playing frisbee with her, and taking her for long, interesting walks.

✖

Malindi was running across the savannas of Ah-free-kah. Many other dogs were with her, her brothers and sisters among them. She glanced to the left and saw her father, a beautiful African wild dog with a white patch on his chest and rump. Beside him, Malindi's mother ran effortlessly, enjoying freedom for the first time in her life. On Malindi's right flank, her beautiful little sister, amydogdada, was grinning with delight. amydogdada turned eyes, full of affection, toward Malindi. samdogbaba and caitlindogmama were in the middle of the pack running side by side. Their mouths turned up at the corners, made sounds: "*heh, heh, heh.*" All the dogs curled their lips and laughed too.

A broad flock of tiny birds swept before them, wings beating in perfect unison. In one fluid motion, they soared upward, then side to side and down again. Malindi jumped to catch one, but her jaws snapped at empty air. Traveling alone, a hyena stopped to laugh at the passing parade of dogs. A pair of jackals, their pointed golden ear tips barely visible above the ochre-colored grass, paused in their hunt to watch the chase. A herd of giraffe, feeding on acacia trees at the edge of the grassland, turned their majestic heads. Gentle eyes scanned the distance until they settled on the movement of the pack. Sitting on the limb of a tree, a sentinel baboon followed the tall animals' gaze. He sprung up and screamed a warning to the troop foraging on the ground below. The baboons climbed to safety in the treetops, all the while chattering encouragement to each other. Zebra watched the chase from afar with dispassion. Their stripes merged into one expansive black and white confusion. They need not run. They were not the victims today. But maybe tomorrow.

Partially submerged in swampy water, a harem of female lechwe heeded their male's abrupt snorting cough and left their reedy refuge to follow the white flag of his tail. The gallant male turned his head and rolled a white-rimmed eye toward the approaching dust cloud. His long, lyre-shaped horns would be of little use against so large and skilled an adversary.

Suddenly, the pack of dogs turned direction. The ground under Malindi's feet felt wet. The dogs splashed through swampy water, sinking lilies, scattering web-footed jacondas. The herd of seven lechwe leapt through the water, their adaptive, elongated hooves gaining traction in the soft, mucky bottom. But in their panic to escape, the antelope split the herd, and the pack of running dogs singled out their prey. *"Heh, heh, heh."*

CHAPTER TWENTY-NINE

Sam managed to find a parking space in a pricey garage on the top level of a high-rise apartment building on Rittenhouse Square. They walked to the Art Alliance where visitors were filling the reception hall and gallery. Anne, standing in the reception line, waved to Caitlin and Sam.

"The mayor is here," she said to Caitlin." He'd like to meet you."

"Come on Sam." Caitlin tugged on Sam's sleeve.

"I don't think the mayor is interested in me, Caitlin."

"Nonsense."

There was no mistaking the beefy figure of Philadelphia's charismatic mayor. "You've done a fantastic job here, Caitlin," the mayor said in his raspy voice. "Nice to meet you Sam," he added, pumping Sam's hand.

"Nice to meet you too, Sir. Please excuse me." Sam was swallowed up by a group of jabbering women who thought he was Temetet. They pushed him toward the statue, blotting out the demure figure of the artist, Aurora Renzetti. No matter how much Sam protested that he was not Temetet, they refused to believe him.

"What an interesting story, Caitlin," the mayor continued. Philadelphia will need a boost in tourism next summer. Something different. Would you consider holding this exhibit at the Atwater Kent or the Visitor's Center?"

"Actually, Mr. Mayor, I haven't decided the future home for

all this," she said, sweeping her hand outward. "Besides, decisions will have to come from the committee.

The mayor nudged her with his shoulder and winked. "I've heard rumors about how you came to discover this stuff. You must tell me all about it sometime. The Irish will believe almost anything, you know." His blue eyes twinkled as he waved off her protest. "Dunna wurry, Caitlin. I can keep a secret. Lovely house, that Cogslea. Might just buy it meself."

Caitlin spotted Toby and beckoned to him. "Here's a committee member now. Toby, come meet the mayor."

"Pleased to meet you, sir." Toby's hair was trimmed; he was dressed in tie, khaki pants, and a navy jacket emblazoned with his school emblem. He looked grown up, mature. He exchanged a few ideas on education with the mayor until a tottering dowager, bowed under a ten-string genuine pearl necklace, stole the mayor's attention.

"Here comes Granddad," Toby said, as Ed herded his family toward Caitlin.

"I'd like you to meet my son, Angus, and his wife, Jeannie," Ed said.

The resemblance between Ed and his son was remarkable, Caitlin thought. While the group made small talk, an attractive girl inched up to Toby.

"This is my friend, Ashley," Toby said, his face glowing.

Caitlin silently appraised the girl. Poised and self-confident. Very Nice.

"And this is my sister, Wendy." Toby put his hand on the shoulder of a charming little blonde clinging to his side. Suddenly, his eye twitched. "Sorry, I'm not used to contacts."

"That's it. You're not wearing glasses," Caitlin said. His lips parted in a wide grin. "And no braces."

Caitlin leaned in and whispered in Toby's ear. "Ashley's very cute, Toby." He blushed, but not as deeply as he would have a few months ago.

"Caitlin, have you heard from Maggie?" Ed asked her.

"No, and it's odd. Her sister called and said she was away on very important business."

Just then, Gina made her grand entrance. She was dressed in a filmy orange tunic and pink harem pants, with a lime green scarf tied in a band across her jet black hair. She looked like Scheherazad from *The Arabian Nights*. "What a turnout," Gina said briefly before swishing away to stand by her statue of Nessa.

Carolyn arrived looking radiant. Caitlin shot her a questioning look.

"Jess and I didn't work out," Carolyn said. "But, you know that publisher Ed put me in touch with?" Caitlin nodded. "There he is. Caitlin, this is serious. And I do mean serious."

Moving forward, the publisher put his arm around Carolyn's waist and introduced himself. Caitlin wanted to shout. He's perfect. Tall, good-looking, great smile, right age. As they turned away, Caitlin gave Carolyn a thumbs-up.

Sam finally broke away from his admirers and came to stand beside Caitlin in the reception line. He shifted on his feet as visitors filed by. "I hate these things," he said, during a lull. "How do you do it?"

Caitlin gritted her teeth behind a forced smile. "Has to be done."

An elderly couple, elegantly dressed for a late night black-tie event at the Academy of Music, fawned over Caitlin. The noise level rose; people began to gather around high bar tables in the lobby to partake of the evening's fare.

"I can mingle now," Caitlin said. She and Sam slotted themselves into a space in the gallery. An amateur photographer pounced on Sam and cajoled him into posing by Temetet's statue. Sam threw Caitlin an uneasy glance, but she could only shrug in apology. She was approached by a reporter from the *Inquirer* who wanted to interview her for the Sunday Arts and Living section. She was giving the reporter a quick run-down of her awards when she noticed that all conversation had stopped and bodies were turning toward the door.

Advancing full force, arms flailing, Maggie cut through the crowd shouting "Where's Caitlin?"

"What the...?" Caitlin was puzzled by Maggie's explosive entrance, her disheveled appearance, and the wild look in her eye. "Maggie, where have you been?"

"Let me tell you," Maggie said, and steered Caitlin toward the samplers on the wall. Like a school of fish changing direction, people turned in unison and went with her. "Where's my committee?" she asked. "I want my committee to hear this." A path cleared for The Cogslea Ten (minus two) to forge their way to the front.

Maggie had the attention of the entire room. She cleared her throat. "For the past weeks, I've been trying to find Nessa's descendants. I went to the Bureau of Records at City Hall, the main library, genealogical internet sites—blah, blah, blah—to no avail. The Maritime Museum did show me an original passenger list from 1703 stating that a Douglas Stewart and his daughter were on the the the vessel, *Belfast Lass*, out of Belfast, Ireland and that her father died at sea." Maggie reached in the pocket of her jeans for a piece of gum, but changed her mind.

"When I was down the shore, I spent hours exploring the internet for clues. I was reading about the Lenni Lenape and their language when all of a sudden, it hit me." Maggie turned toward the collection of samplers on the wall. She shook her head. "This is all wrong by the way. They're not in order, so bear with me." The crowd leaned in closer.

"In Destiny Wickham's samplers, along the borders or within the text, she always added one larger symbol. These symbols were not random placements, but were well planned. Each one represents a place. If each symbol were drawn on a separate piece of tracing paper in the exact position that it appears on the sampler, and then if all the papers were laid on top of each other, uh, super—what's the word?"

"Superimposed," Toby piped up.

"Right, superimposed. You would see a pattern—a pattern of towns on a map." Maggie lifted her hand. "If I just had a piece of paper I could demonstrate." Anne motioned to her assistant. The young man ran to the storage closet on the first floor and returned with an easel, chart pad, and black marker.

Maggie drew a large horizontal rectangle on the paper. "Think of this as a regional map of the very tip of southeastern Pennsylvania. Now, we shall find towns to put on the map. She pointed to a sampler.

"Destiny did three samplers with this same verse on it. Let me read it to you.

"See me in the leaves above. Feel me in the summer breeze. Hear me in the robin's song. Remember me."

"Now—see these two bears eating berries in the center of the top border of this sampler? There's a small town outside of Allentown that the Lenape called *Macungie*; meaning 'the feeding place of bears.' This will establish north on the map." She marked an X in the center of the top of the rectangle.

She moved to an alphabet sampler and pointed to a head of a Lenape Indian chief centered in the bottom border. She marked a corresponding X on her paper. "This is the town of Lenape, near West Chester. This is the southernmost part of our map."

Maggie pointed to a sampler of the Twenty-third Psalm. At the end of the line, *"I will fear no evil,"* there were two parallel blue lines stitched into the border. "The Lenape called this place, *Neshaminy*; their word for a double creek." She put an X in the middle of the right hand side of her map. "East."

"Hear the instruction of thy father, and forsake not the law of thy mother." Maggie snorted. "I bet Destiny's parents made her do this one. But, see, in the left hand border, Destiny added a bunch of snakes with snowflakes falling on them. The Lenape called this little town in Lancaster County, *Cocolico,* which means in their language, 'where snakes den in winter.' It's thirty miles northwest of Philly. West." Maggie marked her map accordingly and turned to face her audience, listening with rapt attention.

"We have established the boundaries of north, south, east, and west on our map. Now, let's find Philadelphia."

Toby moved forward. "May I put the X's on the map?"

"Sure, Toby." Maggie handed him the magic marker. "This sampler of the Lord's Prayer, with the border of pineapples, locates Philadelphia. In the lower right corner, there's a blue line with a boat

258

on it which meets up with a narrower blue line. It's the Schuylkill River emptying into the the Delaware." Toby marked an X on the rectangle in the appropriate place.

"I think this sampler is really sweet," Maggie said. "This is a scene of Cloverhill Farm where Destiny lived. And over here, the blue line with a whiskered catfish on it is the Wissahickon Creek. The Lenape called the creek, *Wissahickon* or 'water of catfish.'" Toby marked an X above and a little to the left of downtown Philadelphia.

On another sampler, a spot motif of a green valley between a river and a line of weeping willow trees corresponded to the township of *Conshohocken*. "Or 'pleasant valley,'" Maggie told them. "It's a few miles above Cloverhill Farm." Toby marked the spot.

Maggie stood back. The onlookers waited. "Okay. So what's missing here?" she asked, tapping the map.

"Places in the middle," Toby answered, along with a few others.

"Right you are, Watson." Maggie pointed to one of the remaining samplers. "Here's an alphabet sampler with thistles in the border and in the dividing lines. A little to the right of center, we have a wavy blue line hanging over two slanted brown lines with footprints on them. This is where two original Indian trails—Ridge Pike and Germantown Pike—meet at the Perkiomen River Bridge." Toby marked the map and Maggie moved on to the next sampler.

"This Remember sampler has honeysuckle blossoms and vines around the borders. Honeysuckle stands for enduring faith; something Nessa had, without a doubt." The audience murmured in agreement. "The spot motif here is a tree growing out of water: *Skippack*, the Lenape word for 'wet land.'" Toby made a mark close to the previous one.

Maggie turned to Caitlin and said, "Would you take down the last sampler, please, Caitlin?" Caitlin's hands trembled as she removed the white on white sampler with a Remember verse. She handed it to Maggie.

Toby had the next and last X in place before Maggie began her explanation. "The exact center of this sampler shows a place on the river above the Perkiomen Bridge: a place the Lenape referred to as, 'the land where there are cranberries.'"

Maggie held the sampler up for the audience to see. It was a scene of a meandering stream with thickets of berried vines lining the banks. The only threads of color used were for a perching robin with a single red berry in its beak. Those who knew that Temetet and Nessa had called Fiona, "Little Robin," caught their breath.

"This is where the kidnappers took Fiona," Maggie said, triumphantly. She reddened at the unexpected applause.

Caitlin hugged her. "Good job, Maggie."

People crowded around Maggie to offer words of praise before dispersing, leaving Maggie with her Committee of Ten, minus two."

"What happened next, Sherlock?" Toby asked, the exuberant adolescent again.

"Well," said Maggie, placing the sampler back on the wall. "I hotfooted it up to Perkiomen to check out the old burial grounds and cemeteries to see if I could find Fiona's grave." Maggie eyeballed Toby.

He couldn't resist. "Whooooooo. Cemeteries at night." Ashley and Wendy giggled.

Maggie rolled her eyes. "As I was saying..." She gave an accounting of her detective work. The importance of her report was not lost on anyone, and they eagerly awaited the conclusion of the story.

❀

"So," Maggie said, clasping her hands together. "Ellie, the lady I met in the Skippack church, has a friend who recently did a genealogical search of her family, and she got as far back as..."

Toby interjected, "Holy Toledo." Maggie didn't bat an eye. "Yes, as far back as Fiona Krause. Krause was her husband's surname. The dots are connecting, yes?" Heads nodded. "It gets better. Ellie is godmother to her friend's daughter, Vanessa."

"Vanessa?" Toby's voice cracked.

"Go on, Maggie, please," Caitlin urged.

"Vanessa lives in a house on the banks of the Perkiomen Creek just above Collegeville. She has a two month old daughter named Fiona."

A subtle force rose up in Caitlin like a bird fluttering its wings. She felt a presence behind her taking shape and turned slowly around. A pretty woman with auburn hair and green eyes stood in a pool of light, holding a pink bundle in her arms.

Caitlin's body lurched sideways. In that instant, everyone else in the room shifted into transparent, muted figures. The walls around her split and fell away; she drifted upward through the open roof. Floating over the city, she looked down on the Art Alliance, the Parkway, City Hall, the Art Museum, the Delaware River, traffic on the Schuylkill Expressway, the tightness of row houses, the press and bustle of urban life.

Materializing out of a clear blue sky, a rainbow stretched between horizons and released droplets of color onto a giant canvas that covered the city. The result was a painting of Philadelphia as it would have looked in the early eighteenth century.

William Penn's fair greene countrie towne was comprised of a cluster of colonial houses and government buildings. Sailing ships rested in the harbor, merchants barkied their wares on Market Street. She saw Indians, prostitutes, statesmen, fine horse drawn carriages on cobbled streets, children romping in square parks under the watchful eyes of ladies sheltering from the sun under silk parasols. A few small settlements and farms were visible in the distance, but beyond the boundaries of Philadelphia, there was nothing but vast forest: a peaceable kingdom, a place that existed before the earth's resources were ripped, spoiled, or shot into extinction.

A flock of noisy birds clattered by, sweeping her into their midst by sheer momentum and pumping wings. Heading north, they sailed above a serpentine river on an air current. They veered abruptly to the right and followed a silver thread of water, barely visible through the lush tree tops. Caitlin, enjoying this sight-seeing expedition, was disappointed when her escorts deposited her on the dry bank of a small stream before continuing on their mission.

She heard a rustling sound behind her, spun around and saw a bear lumber out of the woods. Downstream, a wolf stood in the cool water to take a drink. She was aware of other animals in the brush watching her, unafraid.

She turned her attention back to a charming, domestic scene on her side of the creek. Nestled in a clearing, behind a white picket fence, there was a small, rustic log cabin with a vegetable garden in front. An old mare, a cow, and three goats grazed in the adjoining meadow. Chickens scratched near the tree line. Songbirds flitted among berry bushes, butterflies among the wildflowers.

A heady fragrance of roses enveloped her. Gurgling sounds rose up from the creek; a sound so intense that she felt she was holding it in her arms. She pulled her arms to her chest and looked down into the smiling face of a cooing infant. The baby's liquid brown eyes locked on hers, its mouth curled into a cupid's smile. Caitlin stroked the glossy black hair.

"Caitlin." Someone called her name. She turned, looked across the creek. Temetet emerged from the woods and glided toward her, arms outstretched, smiling. Surrounded by his love, she welcomed his kisses. But then he sighed and faded into the atmosphere.

"Caitlin. Caitlin," Sam whispered softly in her ear.

Wrenched back to reality, Caitlin leaned into him and sobbed.

"Let it go, Caitlin," Sam said.

Yes. She would let it go. She lifted her face to the pretty woman who was speaking to her. For a split second Caitlin thought the words were in Lallans.

"I'm Vanessa and this is my baby, Fiona," the young woman said. "We are so grateful to you, Caitlin, for honoring the dying wishes of my ancestor, Nessa Stewart."

Vanessa stepped forward and Caitlin took the baby in her arms. Fiona reached out a plump arm and wrapped her dimpled hand around Caitlin's finger—a gesture that made Caitlin want to weep again. Sam slipped his arm across Caitlin's shoulders and breathed warmth into her hair.

Caitlin felt that she had crossed through a portal and she would never be the same again. Later, she would tell Sam that, God willing, this time next year, they would be holding their own dear baby in their arms.

Caitlin's eyes traveled across the room to the portrait of Nessa Stewart. You are not forgotten, dear Nessa. Dear sister.

Three centuries ago, a young woman had been dreadfully wronged. Now she looked back at Caitlin and lifted the corners of her mouth in a smile of love and gratitude.

4525078

Made in the USA
Charleston, SC
04 February 2010